The Marriage of Anna Maye Potts

The Marriage of Anna Maye Potts

A NOVEL

DeWitt Henry

THE UNIVERSITY OF TENNESSEE PRESS
KNOXVILLE

TENNESSEE PETER TAYLOR
BOOK AWARD PRIZE FOR THE NOVEL

Co-sponsored by the Knoxville Writers' Guild and the University of
Tennessee Press, the Peter Taylor Prize for the Novel is named for
one of the South's most celebrated writers—the author of acclaimed
short stories, plays, and the novels *A Summons to Memphis* and *In the
Tennessee Country*. The prize is designed to bring to light works of
high literary quality, thereby honoring Peter Taylor's own practice of
assisting other writers who cared about the craft of fine fiction.

Copyright © 2001 by The University of Tennessee Press / Knoxville.
All Rights Reserved. Manufactured in the United States of America.
First Edition.

The paper used in this book meets the minimum requirements of
ANSI/NISO Z39.48-1992 (R 1997) (Permanence of Paper). The
binding materials have been chosen for strength and durability.

Library of Congress Cataloging-in-Publication Data

Henry, DeWitt.
    The marriage of Anna Maye Potts : a novel / DeWitt Henry.—1st ed.
    p. cm.
ISBN 1-57233-139-9 (cl.: alk. paper)
1. Working class women—Fiction. 2. Middle aged women—Fiction.
3. Single women—Fiction. 4. Alcoholics—Fiction. 5. Widowers—Fiction.
I. Title.

PS3608.E57 M3 2001
813'.54—dc21   2001000822

To

Connie

and to the memory

of my parents

and

Richard Yates

The Factory Day

Every Monday through Friday, she quietly left her house at 6:00, walked down the block to the edge of the park, and waited for the bus that came at seven after. Mrs. Brickey, a middle-aged lady, cook at a restaurant in the city, would be the only other person up for such an early bus; they would share the bench in the shelter, under an all-night light that was thick with bugs. The early hour, streetlight shadows, darkened windows had made them intimate these past two years—she would listen; Mrs. Brickey would confide. And she would listen patiently—no matter how unkempt or irritable Mrs. Brickey might be, or rough her language—feeling much better since there was someone between home and work to say good morning to.

When the bus came, with lights on inside and three or four passengers, Mrs. Brickey would sit at an open window, holding her great straw purse in her lap, while she herself would take the aisle seat. Their conversation would continue. She liked to hear about Mr. Brickey and the five children, although Mrs. Brickey only complained about them, and about the job, the bursitis, the troubles with the neighbors, the garden out back (one morning Mrs. Brickey had brought tomatoes for her in a paper bag), and sometimes it wasn't only that she liked to hear, but that she really needed to. She would be uneasy if Mrs. Brickey ever missed the bus.

Stenton and Germantown, fifteen minutes later, was her stop; she and Mrs. Brickey would wish each other a good day, and she would hurry to get off. She would walk slowly two blocks up Stenton Avenue to John P. Manville Co., Confectioners, where she had worked for nineteen years, ever since her high school graduation.

No one else would be here yet, at least not in this part of the building; there would be no light, no sound. She would let herself in through the front door with her own key; stand for a moment in the dark office vestibule, smiling—because there were familiar differences in temperature and atmosphere and smells that meant the factory to her, and because at once she felt confirmed, secure. And would feel even more so, after she had gone ahead through the "Employees Only" door, down an empty passageway—dark except for the single light at the turning—and had pushed open a heavy, insulated door with a whoosh! and been buffeted by a sudden draft of cold, dry air, and smells of chocolate, ammonia, cardboard and glue, and the sense of space. And the door would close behind her: whump!

She would turn on the lights, whose sudden brightness startled her, and there would be her whole department: conveyor belts, tables and scales, and the new packaging and cellophane-wrap machines that meant now she could run five different items at once, and the boards stacked up precariously on dollies, and the machinery gleaming from the bare overhead bulbs, and all of it so quiet and still she could hear the refrigeration blowing. She especially loved her room this time of day; she liked to associate the beginning of her day with the beginning of the factory's.

Everyone remarked what a loyal, hard worker she was, and said that she was married to her job. That pleased her; she was more than glad to make personal sacrifices, to give up her own time, her energy, her whole heart for the company. And not for the money, either, but to earn her right to belong here, where she mattered—where she had a place with these complicated, expensive machines and this big concrete building and the other employees, nearly a hundred and fifty, including Mr. Manville himself. And everything was united by a single purpose; Mr. Manville said that they must produce more and better candies at less cost. There must be profits; everything must pay. He explained about the company making or losing money and how it all depended on each and every one of them.

That meant, in her department she must get as much work as she could from her girls, see that they wasted no materials or made any mistakes (an eight-ounce window-box of mints must weigh eight ounces) and that they never got behind. She must never have to tell them at the enrobers next door to slow down the conveyer belts which brought her coated candies through the wall, but only speed them up. The warehouse boy must never have to wait to take out the next skid of finished cartons (and he must never leave any of her doors open, wasting refrigeration). The girls must be clean, must wash every morning and during lunch breaks; their uniforms must be fresh (a laundry service was provided); hair must be worn up in nets; their language must be clean (filthy language went with careless attitudes). They must keep candy off the floor. Whenever work stopped, they must tidy up the room.

Then sometimes she herself would be to blame for things gone wrong, which would bring her very near tears. She dreaded Mr. Manville's "Don't let that happen again" or "Next time schedule and organize your girls more carefully ahead of time"; but she dreaded even more the uncertainty of when he never seemed to notice, or when he seemed annoyed with her and she couldn't find out why. If he should ever praise her, she might feel a queer shiver. Perhaps her girls had suddenly made an operation speed along and the other departments had had to keep up with hers. A few moments like those could outweigh more usual worries and cares; moreover, all of it—both the troubles and joys—was part of the larger happiness of being involved in her job, and part of the happiness of feeling alive with the life of the company, which was steadfast, and bigger than any personal, human life.

Just inside the icebox door, her office was to the right. Because of metal walls and glass windows around three sides, the girls called it her toll booth, but it was really called the sample room. That was another task: she must prepare the sample cases for the sales department, varnishing all the items of candy and arranging them in special boxes. Overhead, the long fluorescent light came on—showing the desk bank and shelves inside, and the adding machine and porcelain dishes (full of hairpins and combs), the scales, the punches, the matching planter with bright red geraniums in it, a spare umbrella, two old sweaters, another white cap hanging beside the mirror on the back wall, and there, the large green cushion on her swivel chair. These things and others had been together so long that what was hers seemed to be the company's and what was the company's, hers.

She would have to make sure of her appearance next, unpinning her cap, straightening her hair, adjusting her clothes (which might be a little clingy before the refrigeration dried them out). And then she would throw a sweater around her shoulders, and, leaving her office only for a moment, go around into the lunchroom—an area that was partitioned off this end of the larger, busy room, and where she had a sink, a stove, benches, tables, lockers for her girls. She would put the coffee on. Bill O'Neill, head of maintenance, and Louie, who must get the chocolate mixing and set up his machines, and Dave Case, getting his moguls ready for the day's run, and Ralph Sheets, the head shipper—they would all have to come to work even earlier than this. She expected them for coffee at seven o'clock. They would feel special together, joking and teasing over their coffee, with their important responsibilities in common and the building deserted. And all were department heads now—had never worked anywhere else (except Dave Case, who had come here two years ago from Windsor Chocolates, to take Otto's place). Ralph Sheets and Louie had been with Manville's longest; they had started just before the Depression (the company had been built up by Mr. John Manville a whole generation before that). They would tell about John Manville running things there, in the other building, and then, after several years, making the difficult move to this one, setting up and outfitting here; and about Mr. Curtis Manville coming in with his father, and the difficulties during the war. She could remember those difficulties too because that was when she had first started out as general helper and sample girl under Nora Ransom. She had hardly ever seen Mr. John Manville before he passed away; she couldn't remember him. But Louie would tell the stories about him.

Sometimes Louie stopped in earlier than the others to talk with her; if he did, he would find her back in her office, busy scheduling her operation.

He was a stocky man; his uniforms were soiled with chocolate and grease, and he had a small bit of a black mustache. His rough, crude manners, his personal conceit, the way he would sneer at Mr. Manville (or anybody or anything else people respected): these things annoyed her just as they did everyone else, but she also knew that Louie was a loyal, valuable employee who took his job seriously and was very efficient, and was as anxious to please Mr. Manville as she was herself. Once she had told him: "Louie, if you're going to tell bad things about people; I'd rather not hear." Later she had guessed that he might be afraid of people hurting him. He had certainly been raised in a bad environment (South Philadelphia, a neighborhood of toughs), and was to be admired for working all his life to better his surroundings and to give his four children the environment and education he had never had. Hadn't he just moved them out of the city to a nice development in New Jersey? He was proud of them and their accomplishments; just recently his first grandson had been born. What she understood most, however, and what brought her closer to him than all the years they had been working together, were his personal misfortunes: for one, his youngest daughter, Josephine, aged twelve, was mentally retarded; for another, his wife (his second wife, after an early divorce) was sick with cancer. She knew how people needed to talk out things like that.

When the others came in, with glistening faces and stained work shirts, they would talk about the news—whatever was developing on the radio this morning or in the paper last night—or about some new idea the management was trying, or troubles in their separate departments, or about projects at home—a boat, a car, trips they were planning, wives, children. Or they had jokes to tell—Dave Case was the best one for that; he had such a funny way of telling and so many stories from the Windsor place, and he could always compare his experiences to theirs (which made Louie angry).

They would break up by 7:30, when Dave's and Louie's men were due; then she would clean up after them and return to finish up her scheduling.

More people would be in the building now, more sounds. The moguls would be running. Center batches, fondant, caramel would be mixing and cooking in the steaming rows of big bronze kettles upstairs. Perhaps Mary Lloyd would be in by now, ready to start the upstairs finishing operations.

Down here, the girls would wave or call good morning as they passed her office on their way to the lunch area. Some of them were young, just seventeen, others older than she was herself: Negro, Italian, Polish, Irish, Hungarian—twenty-five in all, in blue uniforms with white collars and caps. At the last minute, she would get her boxes and cartons from Ralph Sheets; then the bell would ring. The girls would take their places around the machines she had assigned them to, the machines would start, and soon the room would come alive: the girls at the conveyer belts talking, the machines clicking, the candy shaken into boxes, and the boxes, wrapped in cellophane, packed in carton after carton. She would be delighted to see the quickness of hands sorting, performing their tasks, and the intent faces of the girls. They did create problems concerning discipline, however. She could not be, like Louie, "a little Mussolini." (He was proud that Mr. Manville called him that). But on the other hand, she mustn't get "too personal with personnel." She was told that she'd better learn to face up to the trouble-makers. But even after five years of being forelady, she still felt terribly guilty if she had to report any-one; and if she had to raise her voice, it trembled.

At lunchtime she would buy hot broth and a small milk from the vending machines out in the hall; the rest of her lunch, the sandwich and the cake, she would bring with her in her purse. Only rarely would she consent to go out; it was disagreeable enough having to leave her refrigeration to go up the stairs to Mary Lloyd's, and changing temperatures like that too often, you were asking for a cold. Mary Lloyd's daughter, Betty, who was switchboard girl in the office, sometimes joined them, but usually not. Mary Lloyd had only been with the company for ten years, but had been promoted two full years before herself, and now had charge of thirty-five girls, and did all the cupping and polybags (and wasn't modest either about the polybag machine, and Mr. Manville's bringing people in to see it). Of course Mary Lloyd was eleven years older, and more clever, and had been the favorite of Margarite Bell, and so when that lady left to be married, had been recommended for the job. She was thin and angular with curly gray hair (dyed an ugly shade of brown or sometimes even red) and could never keep her uniforms looking fresh and smart. She did organize her department well. But she could also be too free with her advice when no one asked her for it and very common with her gossip and her stories. Sometimes they had spiteful, bitter fallings out.

Mr. Manville himself would come through her room on his day-to-day inspection stroll, later in the afternoon. He was a large man, nearly bald, but very well groomed, about sixty years old; he would wear tan overalls to protect his clothes when he walked around the plant. His face and the top of his head were ruddy—the hair on the back and sides startling white in contrast. That was because of his golf: for Christmas and his birthday (April twelfth), she and Mary Lloyd would buy him golf novelties, and the other department heads would contribute. He never failed to have some particular thing to say to her. And he was so attentive to details, so thorough, noticing the slightest thing that wasn't right: the temperature and humidity, the way the box flaps were tucked in, or if one of the girls wasn't busy, or perhaps one had her hair net off or was wearing nail polish. Nothing in the factory was insignificant to him; he would tell her that there wasn't one nut or bolt, or one person in this building, that he could afford to neglect. He was always taking mental notes. "How many skids did you finish yesterday?" She would, of course, remember to ask him about his children too, all of whom she had met over the years. When they were younger, he had brought them to the factory, and she had given them paper sacks to fill off the conveyer belts and trays; when they grew older, each of the boys had worked at least one summer for his father. The oldest, Jack, had been a mechanic (and had been in an awful accident here that cost him the end of his finger); then Ted had worked in the office with the bookkeeper; and the youngest, Charles, for Ralph Sheets in shipping. They were all grown now. The girl, Janice, was married and had three children. Jack was in the construction business out west. Ted was a doctor, just married; Charles was in New York and worked for Time Magazine. She kept track of them all, excited by their lives, genuinely concerned. Mr. Manville said he was proud of them all setting out on their own; he put it just that way. And she would ask, how was Mrs. Manville?

Her afternoons passed quickly. The day seemed to end before enough was done; she would be surprised when she glanced up at the clock, saw how late it was. They had to shut down at 4:30, to put things in order for the night. The girls would chatter loudly and shout and slam locker doors; she would stay until the last of them had left, and the room was empty again and still; would stay as late as 5:30, making sure of things. Louie and Mary Lloyd would say goodnight to her before they left. Then finally she would leave, but only with reluctance, concerned that she had overlooked some necessity, or with the knowledge that some important part of the work was unfinished and had to be postponed until tomorrow morning. Also she was reluctant to face the unpleasant weather outside, and the hot, crowded ride back home.

Louie at Large

Four o'clock now, he couldn't leave until he made sure that Frank and Tommy, the enrober operators downstairs and up, would shut off all the belts and motors, heat up the kettles and enrobers, and clean out the revolving pans in the pan department. He'd found Frank all right, who would see to things downstairs. Now he was riding up the freight elevator in search of Tommy. Creeping upwards slowly, he met the idle, vacant and slightly mocking gaze of one of the warehouse kids, who was lounging on the handle of his empty truck. The platform jerked to a halt; he threw up its wooden cage front.

"What's the matter, can't you find no empty drums?" he asked the kid.

The kid smirked, rattled the truck past him onto the elevator and pulled down the gate.

"Wait a second!" he commanded, through the wooden bars. "Look, you don't waste your time riding up and down that thing with an empty fork, got it? Next time you're up here you take some of them drums!" The kid shrugged.

"Ain't my job. Mr. Sheets says bring Mary Lloyd her cartons. I don't know nothing about no drums."

The lift shuddered and began sinking slowly.

"Listen, wise guy, I see you up here with an empty fork again, I'll give you Mr. Sheets! There's drums up here, you take them!" He dismissed him with a wave, turned, and stalked into the candy kitchen, where Leo watched, grinning.

"Wise little punk," Leo offered.

He gave him a sour look and surveyed the area. Big droning exhaust fans beat in the high bank of windows, where the afternoon sun shone against whitened panes. He took off his hat, wiped his brow on his sleeve.

"Here today, gone tomorrow, punks like that. Seen Tommy anywheres?"

"Here a minute ago."

He put his hat back on. "He's supposed to be with his machines." Mixers were grinding and steam fittings hissing as he walked past the rows of cooking kettles with their smells of marshmallow, caramel and mint, stepped carefully over the wet floor that two of Leo's men were washing down, then out the door of the windowed partition to enrober Number Two. The women barely noticed him, busy at the far end of the feed belt lining up centers; Mendez, at the other end, was crouched down fussing with the bottomer and looked up gratefully as he approached: "Hey, Mr. Louie, I think I got some trouble here."

He crouched down beside him: "What kind of trouble?"

"There's some blooming on the bottoms."

"Check your timing on the belts?"

"Just like we set them earlier."

"What about blowers, any variation there?"

"Not that I can see, Mr. Louie. Must be this thing here, I figure, this cooling belt here. Running too thick just after lunch, so Mr. Tommy, he adjusted it. Must be too warm now."

"Don't you fool with it. Let me see the candy first." He stood up and selected a piece from the belt, just before it went under the enrober. The chocolate on the bottom was soft and sticky, not even set up.

"So where the hell is Tommy now?" He crushed the candy in his fingers and tossed it into the scrap box.

Mendez stood up, and shrugged: "He go talk to Mary Lloyd. Ten, fifteen minutes maybe."

He clenched his jaw. "Wait a minute." He walked down to the other end and asked the women: "They just bring these centers over?" They had. He reached up and took one off the tall stack of boards, which the oldest woman, Mrs. Dawson, was shaking into the feeder. The center was soft; he tossed it aside.

He went over to the mogul department, got hold of Dave Case, bawled out the kid who pulled this fresh dolly of boards out of the holding room, got a dolly of hardened centers to replace them and sent the others back; then went into the refrigerated packaging department on the trail of Tommy. Headaches.

He looked around—no Tommy—as he marched up the aisle along the conveyer where a score of women were operating the weighing, boxing and wrapping equipment, followed by others who packed the boxes into cartons and the cartons onto skids. Mary Lloyd was at her desk.

"Tommy was in here, last fifteen minutes or so?"

She was busy with a sheaf of invoices: "Tommy? No. Couple hours ago, maybe. Why, what's he up to now?"

"Didn't come in and speak to you about nothing?"

"No, I haven't seen Tommy! I see him, I'll tell him you were looking. Now let me finish this stuff, will you, please?"

One of her women came over; "Mary Lloyd?"

"Ahh!" He crossed the room and started down the opposite aisle, where a second row of women were sorting and packaging. Then he noticed: that little high school stuff, new here, cute little ass: he didn't see her on the line.

Down by the door that led to the freight elevator was an alcove full of discarded equipment; stacks of boards and finished skids of cartons hid it from view. He went over and stood there watching for a second: "Tommy!" The women at the end of the line turned to look. "C'mere. C'mon out here. I want to talk to you."

The two of them jumped up, crushed out their cigarettes; the girl straightened her skirt, looking embarrassed; Tommy looked smart and belligerent.

He beckoned angrily, wheeled and pushed open the insulated door: out into the glow, heat, noise and smells of his own department. "Look you," he said to Tommy, who came out after him, "how about you taking care of that stuff on your own time? I catch you fooling around like that again, I don't care you're union boss, what the hell you are, you're going to get the sack. Goddamit, you get paid to stay with them machines; and goddamit, you stay!" He bulged his eyes, poking his forefinger at Tommy's chest. "You're in there feeling up that little twat, you got blooming out here on Number Two and Mendez don't know nothing."

"Aw, get off my ass." Tommy walked away.

He stepped after him and turned him by the shoulder.

"Now, watch it, Louie. Don't try pushing me around. I do my job and you know it. Now, you want to report me, go ahead. But I got a couple of stories of my own."

Tommy was young and wiry, with a narrow, hard face and a reputation with a knife—besides being shop steward.

"Way I see it," Tommy said, with cold, sly eyes and a sneering expression, "I'm entitled to a little break. Mendez needed me, I told him where I was. Now there's some blooming over there, okay, I'm going to take care of it. But you're not riding me, Louie."

Little stars of rage burst in his veins, but he controlled himself, opening and closing his fists, working his jaw. Any kind of union stink, he'd have Manville to answer to. Besides, Tommy was his best operator: he couldn't risk a showdown over nothing dumb like this. Just then the freight elevator came to a halt: they had to make way for the truck boy, who pulled his skid of cartons past.

"Okay, okay, so you can take a break," he said flatly. "But look: I catch you pulling that stuff again and you're in trouble. Anything goes wrong on them machines and you're the one responsible. So let's just leave it at that, huh? Now see you shut down and heat up tonight, regular time, and no more slip-ups. I'm starting home."

He turned away with that, stepped back onto the elevator, slammed down the gate and jerked the cable. Tommy held his eyes for a minute, then hiked his belt and headed off towards the machines. Sinking from sight, he took his hat off, ran his hand over his face. Overhead the white sky glared down through iron girders and slats. Shakily, he lit a cigarette.

Downstairs in the supervisors' head, he was shaving. Work day done, he put its headaches out of mind, already thinking of the night ahead. They'd have some drinks in Nick's maybe, then go dancing. He'd suggest they go back to her place. He smiled and chuckled, holding the razor. Then sighed, and finished up, with careful strokes around his mustache.

"Well, looky here," Ralph Sheets said, closing the door on factory noises. "Look at him all shaved and prettied up."

He paid no mind, wiping his face with a towel and rummaging in his locker for the clean undershirt, which he pulled on over his head. Sheets slammed the stall door and called out, as he was pissing, "Got a little action tonight, huh?" The toilet flushed and he came out, fixing his fly. "Where the hell you keep running into it, anyhow? You got a special place you go?" He came to the sink to wash his hands, leering shrewdly through his glasses. "I mean, I could use a little fun on the side myself, y'know."

Buttoning up his sport shirt, tucking it in, he looked up at the guy: "You? C'mon now, you're supposed to be watching your health. You're in no kind of shape to go pulling that stuff, and you know it." He motioned him aside and leaned in front of the mirror, combed his hair. "Besides, your old lady'd kill you."

Ralph winced and squirmed, drawing himself up: "That ain't fair, goddamit." He took his glasses off, scowling. "That's my lookout, ain't it? Well, I can handle that all right—as good as you." He wiped his glasses on his shirt, defensive and brooding, then hooked them back over his ears. "Look, Louie," he tried again, narrowing his eyes and edging closer: "How about this bar down here, Germantown and Chelton? How about, you know, maybe one night next week, we could—"

"Can't help you, Ralph."

"Well, shit, you want to be that way about it. I ain't asking any favors. You don't have to get all uppity, just cause you got yourself some hot deal out there."

"No offense. Just forget it, willya? It's for your own good."

The door swung open and Dave Case came in, "Hey, Louie! What's this big beef you got with Tommy all about? Man, you oughta hear him up there; he's cussing you out right and left."

"Ahh, him. You know him. He's got trouble up there on Number Two and I catch him in Mary Lloyd's fooling round some little twat. So I chewed him out, that's all. He'll get over it."

Dave raised his eyebrows and nodded, snorting: "You hope. Didn't sound that way to me." Then he noticed the clothes and shook his wrist, impressed. "Look out!"—he winked at Ralph—"Gramps is on the loose again!"

"Sure, he's a big shot, all his broads."

"Must be takin' them vitamins, huh? How about it, Lou? What's your secret?"

He stashed the shaving kit away, along with his toothbrush and toothpaste, slammed his locker, twirled the combination dial, grabbed his hat down from above, and, pushing by Dave, went out the door with a disgusted wave: "See you Monday!" He heard their laughter from the hall, as he put his hat on, and smiled. Sorry for Sheets, of course, but the guy was dumb. He checked his watch. Next stop, across the hall, was Anna Maye's. He found her in the sample room.

"Well, you're certainly all dressed up!" she exclaimed; the woman gluing samples with her glanced up too, then back down, pretending not to listen. Putting her work aside, wiping her hands on her apron, Anna Maye came closer: "Leaving early or something?"

"Yeah, yeah. I can't talk. Got to hurry. Planning something special for the wife tonight. What I was wondering, you got a box of the assorted chocolates? You know, something special."

She regarded him evenly for a moment: "Well, that's very thoughtful, Louie. She'll like that."

"Yeah, well, I want to surprise her," he said, trying to sound casual, but feeling sheepish and annoyed.

She smiled and turned, and reaching up to a shelf, lifted down a box. "I can't just let you have this for free, you know." She placed it on the counter. "No,"—she held up her hand and shook her head, friendly, but firm—"no arguments. You're entitled to a 30 percent discount, just like everybody else."

He looked into her round, soft face with its broad nose and heavy brows and those sad, but kindly eyes that kept insisting on the best in you; and, grudgingly, he paid her—three dollars.

"Can't nobody argue with you."

"Wait. You want it wrapped, don't you?" She opened a drawer in the counter and pulled out some gift paper. Then she was concentrating, trying to remember: "It's not your anniversary, is it?"

"Naw. Like I said. A surprise."

"You didn't mention it this morning."

"Just thought of it, you know?" He glanced out the door at the women working, then at his watch. She folded the ends of the paper close to the box, taped them, turned the box over, took some ribbon from the drawer, wound it around, crossed it over; had him hold his finger on it, while she tied a fancy bow.

"Well, it's nice. You should think of things like that more often. I mean flowers and magazines, things like that. Surprises can mean a great deal, especially when you're feeling low."

"Sure, sure, I know."

She brightened up: "Well, there you are." And handed him the package. "Tell me Monday how she liked it."

Just outside Maple Shade, an hour later, he turned off Route 73 into the East Gate Shopping Mall. The sun was lower, but still hot, glinting off of acres of parked cars. He made his way down to the Acme Market, at the far end, hoping to find her waiting out front, but felt more bitterly assured than surprised as he drove past and found that she wasn't. She got off at six and it was 6:20 now; she probably got fed up and took a bus home. He found a space, anyway, parked. He rolled his window up, put the candy out of the sun, under the dash, shoved across the seat and got out the other side; rolled that window up too and locked the door. He'd have a look at least. Stiffly, he crossed the baking asphalt, twisting his shoulders to loosen the shirt from his back, dodged between cars starting from the pick-up lane, brushed past people coming, going, on through the electric doors and into the market, instantly relieved, gratified, by the cooler, drier air, and distracted by the activity, displays, colors and size of the place. Everyone was crowded, rushing or waiting; a battery of cash registers dinged and chattered. He searched around, half-dazed for a minute, before he finally spotted her. She was sitting in a line of chairs along the big plate-glass window, flirting with some young jerk who looked like he worked here—crew cut, pimples, wore a gray coat had a name badge on it. Aside from the stab of impatience he felt at this—the two of them familiar and involved, and the kid acting smart like he thought he was making time—the sight of her moved him. She'd waited; it'd be all right. "'Scuse me," he said, blocking the path of an old woman struggling with a shopping cart. Irma leaned back and recrossed her plump legs, tweaking her cigarette in an upright ashtray and idly waggling her foot. She glanced his way, but didn't see him; laughed at something the kid was saying.

He came nearer.

"—pullin' crazy stunts like that all the time, these guys. They're a crazy bunch. Another time, we had this party. We went down to the shore, see, down Atlantic City; we got us two motel rooms, then we hear about this dance, so we go there and pick up a couple girls, bring 'em back to the room, and we've got this case of scotch, so we start boozin' it up and dancin' and all that; we're gonna keep it up all night, y'know? Well, pretty soon we're plastered; one of the girls is sick and the other's whinin' about goin' home, when all of a sudden Auggie gets this notion he's just gotta ride a roller coaster, no matter if it's all shut down or not. It's like two or three in the morning, see? Well, then the chicks decide they really wanta try that too, so we all go down there where they got these rides—"

"Hope I'm not breaking in on nothing." He tilted his hat back and folded his arms.

Irma turned around surprised; then mocking: "Well, look who's finally here!" The kid gave him a once over. She explained: "Danny, this is Louie. Louie, Danny. Danny's been a peach, sitting here with me, keeping me from getting bored. What held you up, anyhow? I've been waiting here for half an hour!" She stubbed her cigarette out.

"Aw, I had trouble at the plant, and then the traffic. But I ain't all that late either. I said six."

"You're lucky I waited."

"Yeah, lucky I decided to come on in here for a looksee, too, isn't it? You were gonna wait outside, remember? How was I supposed to know you'd be in here?"

Danny Boy stood up (his name badge said "Curley"): "Look, Irma, I'll tell you the rest of it some other time, okay? I mean, I better be takin' off, myself. I got a heavy date and there's still some stuff I gotta do round here. So—you have yourself a good time, huh?"

"Oh, I'm not worried about that," she said, and grinned, glancing from Danny back to him.

"Yeah. Well, I'll see ya then."

"Um-hm. So long, now." She smiled.

He sauntered off, snapping his fingers and tossing his head.

"What's he? A bag boy?"

"He happens to be a stock clerk. And he's a darn nice kid too, so don't start making any cracks."

"Looks like a jerk to me."

She glared: "He's a friend of mine, Louie. And he's got a considerable amount on the ball, too, if you'd like to know. He's just got out of the Marines, and now he plans to finish up night school and maybe even go to college. So maybe he's a more worthwhile person than you'd think."

She stood up and straightened her skirt, and slung her handbag over her shoulder:

"That's what burns me up. I like people, all kinds of people, but you just think they're trash. You don't have a good word for anybody, Louie. Like my girlfriend, Barbara, for instance. She's a 'jerk' too, isn't she? So who cares if you hurt her feelings?"

"Now, wait. Who injected her into the conversation?"

"I did."

"Well, come off it, willya?" He glanced behind him as another kid pushed by a train of carts and slammed them, clattering, into a row of empties. "Are we going to sit here talking about Barbara all night, or are we going to get out of here? . . . Well, c'mon!" He took her arm, but she held back and shook his hand off, then started for the door herself. He caught up; they walked in silence together out the electric doors. Then she stopped.

"Well, where's the car?"

She gazed around, fingering her neck.

"Over there."

Down the curb, between cars, they started across the lot, her handbag bumping between them and her high heels clacking, scraping.

"Hey, look. Come on, now, cut this stuff out, willya? What the hell's eating you, anyhow?"

"I don't care to talk about it, Louie." She kept walking straight ahead, without looking at him. "I've just been doing some thinking, that's all."

He blinked and grimaced, scowling.

They came to his car; he unlocked the passenger's door.

"Phew! It's like an oven in there!" she complained.

He left her rolling down the window and went around to the driver's door, which wasn't locked, got in, slammed it, and rolled down the window. "C'mon, it won't be that bad once we get moving." He held his hands on the wheel, already sweating. She pushed her bag across, stepped in, plumped down heavily, and slammed the door. Then as she squirmed around, getting settled, saw the package.

"Hey! What's that?"

"Something I got you."

"Well!" She cocked her head and considered him uncertainly, then broke into a grin.

"Okay," he said wearily. He bent down and handed her the box.

"I just can't understand you sometimes."

"Well, go ahead and open it."

"Okay. I am." She gave him a look, and started scrabbling at the ribbon, prying it off the corners, tearing the wrapping away, until the golden script of "Manville's Assorted Chocolates" was exposed on the glossy pink lid. She glanced up, with bright, eager eyes.

"That's our best. Five bucks a box."

She chuckled softly and bit her lip, raising the lid. "Um, will you look at these!" Tentatively, she selected a chocolate from its paper cup, bit into it, chewed and swallowed, and turned to him with a look of smug delight. "Maple cream!" she said, finishing off the remainder, then licking her fingers. She put the box up on the dash and scrunched over beside him, smacking her lips, reaching her arms around his neck and offering her mouth. He bent his head back and kissed her roughly, almost vengefully, groping for her thighs with his pinned right arm and reaching around and pulling her closer with his left. She held back at first, but then her lips were moving eagerly under his, tasting of lipstick and chocolate, and her arms were tightening around his neck. The sense of well-being spread through him, soothing all the rawness. "Hey . . . hey . . . come on, now. Enough." She pushed herself free and glanced around. "We're in a parking lot, remember?" She shoved back across the seat and straightened her skirt. But her face was flushed, her eyes still feverish and soft, as she turned to look at him again.

He looked back; then leaned forward and started the car, smiling a slow, expansive smile. She didn't speak; just took the candy off the dash and held it in her lap, frowning to herself and staring out the window.

He hadn't been mixed up in anything like this, not since the bad times, years back. Out all night, home drunk, screwing up at work; he'd almost lost everything. Paula'd moved out with the kids and gone to see a lawyer. The shock of that had wised him up. He had a choice to make. He loved his family; they were his and all that mattered. The women didn't matter. He woke up beside this one one day, heard her kids screaming in the next room, and felt plain lost and scared. He had to get home and make it up. His family was his life;

and had to cut out all the craziness, just like a rotten arm. And he did, he was left scarred-like, and a little crippled even, but living, healthy. He and Paula made it up. Life got better for a while. He got promoted. His boys grew up and left, and quit siding against him (especially Frank). Paula'd softened towards him too. They'd found a special day school for Josie. Paula was working again, and between that and not having the boys to support, it looked like they could get a house. So the idea of a house—someplace nice for Josie, someplace out of the city—the more they talked and dreamed, and searched the papers, and went out driving weekends: it brought a kind of youthfulness back in their marriage, a sense of pride and common purpose, like they were starting over fresh.

But no sooner had they found a place, sold the old, and packed up and moved, than Paula started getting sick. He'd thought it was just the strain of the move and if she took it easy, it'd clear up. But it was more than that. He hadn't wanted to take her to the doctor's, but after one bad bout of throwing up and stomach pains, he panicked and called the hospital. And, grimly, he'd prepared himself—operations, bills, convalescence, medicines—but what they told him caught him worse than unawares. Cancer, stomach cancer. Operated on her, twice; then said the operations did no good; and even them, the doctors, they were helpless. She'd have nine months more, maybe—like that— towards the early fall, they said, like they were taking about her being pregnant or something. And there was nothing anyone could do, except to keep her comfortable, of course, and in a minimum of pain. And maybe try to carry on with life, as normal as they could.

Four months now, they'd lived like that: knowing, not knowing, and only having the doctors' word. And if she'd really been sick—in bed, in pain—maybe that'd make some sense. But here she was puttering around the house, cleaning and gardening and looking after Josie. Sure, she'd lost some weight; she was weaker, paler than usual, maybe; but she wasn't sick in bed. The medicines were working fine; she needed rest, that's all. But then he'd curse himself: who was he kidding? Time was slipping past, and life, and him unequal to it somehow, like he should hold it back or make it count some special way— and yet he couldn't. He found himself resenting her: choked and dragged down by her, personally. He had to shut himself against her pains, her needs. He blamed her that she couldn't make it easier. For always he'd relied on her. She was the strong one. And when he'd hit the bottom, she was there, forgiving, demanding, helping him through it. But now her spirit was as broken and despairing as his own, and he had no one, nothing else to turn to.

They'd told the kids, of course; she did. Dom and Victor each made special visits; Frank and Nancy stopped down when they could. But they weren't any help. They kept after him, accusingly: weren't there better doctors? shouldn't she have a nurse? what about radiology or something? wasn't there something they could do? And how could he tell them: pay the doctors, pray, cut your arm off, love till your heart bursts—none of it did any good? They weren't listening, not to him. Blaming him was their excuse. There were trembling red-faced blow-ups, but these just put him further in the wrong. So he sank back, watched them take over, watched them relax and calm her. And grudged them. What did they know? Hadn't they gone off and got their own lives now? Hadn't they deserted her? What were they coming back for now, except her blessing that they were free to go? He and Josie were the ones that needed her, not them; and when each of them left, and after the glow of their visits faded, Paula seemed even more defeated and despondent.

He couldn't take it anymore. He couldn't bear to be around her. Work was a relief, and afterwards he'd stop off for a drink, or go down to the old neighborhood and maybe try to find a game: anything to keep his mind off things. Sometimes he called home; sometimes not. He wouldn't be accounted for. But she didn't fight him either, like she used to; she didn't stand up to him and bawl him out. All she'd do is put on these tired, hurt silences, yearning at him, pleading, following him around, bumping against him, filling him with strangling hopeless rage that only drove him out again: to play with Josie, go on errands, work the yard, paint the house, anything to get away.

But now that he'd found Irma, he felt confident again, and shrewd. Irma changed the tone of everything—even her memory hovering before him, memory of her silkiness and youth, the eagerness of her desire. For wasn't he sufficient afterall, wasn't he resourceful and determined—a vigorous, hard-working, seasoned older man, who knew the angles, who deserved respect? And didn't it take something special to make it with a piece like her? That she had done those things with him, and that she'd trusted him and understood and shared his need to break away and find release: it promised him another life—a different life—like he was thirty again, and everything was possible and just within his grasp. At home, surrounded by his usual life, speaking, spoken to, watching TV, lying open-eyed in bed at night: he felt triumphantly immune; elated by this newfound ease, this gift of comfort where there should be pain. He could listen to, watch, or touch Paula even, without the helplessness returning. He was like a visitor suddenly, like his sons, free to sympathize and act concerned, but not confined or burdened by it anymore. Because she was the one dying, not him; and he had plenty left ahead of him: times like he'd had with Irma, things he'd been missing out on now for years because of her, because he'd been afraid of losing her.

They were eating at the Shang Gree La, in downtown Camden. She'd been acting funny all evening, not just playing smart like she'd been on the phone that first time—she'd gotten over that, even though it took him several calls and she'd kept putting him off until he got good and worked up—but really moody and disdainful; and the friendlier he tried to be, the more good natured, the more she clammed up on him, thinking her own thoughts.

"Louie, just tell me something, will you?"

"Sure," he said, shoveling in a forkful of chow mein, "anything you want to know."

She leaned forward, breasts stretching her blouse, chin on her palm, one eyebrow raised: "What's your wife think of all this?"

He swallowed his mouthful and held her eyes.

"My wife?"

"You're not divorced."

"What are you talking about?" He cleaned his gums.

"There's no use being cute about it, Louie. I don't like liars."

"Aw, c'mon off it, willya? Here, have some more of this egg stuff."

"Don't try to change the subject." She sat back squarely, cold-eyed and severe.

He put his fork down. "What do you want? I told you. I been married twice. I got four kids, and my wife remarried, and she's living down in South Philly someplace, and I don't even speak to her no more."

"Sure, and you're living with your sister and your mother now, aren't you? And they get all upset if you aren't in by midnight, huh?"

"Yeah, that's right. So what" He was getting pissed: their food was going to waste—special, expensive food—and their evening too, if she didn't cut it out. What did she want to go pull this kind of shit for, anyhow?

"So you're in the Moorestown phone book, that's what." She looked at him firmly. "And I called your house last night—"

"You what?"

"—and the woman who answered said she was Mrs. Miscello, and when I asked her could I speak to her son, please? she said, which one? and I said Louie, and you know what she said then?"

He stared, trying to make sense of it: how she could sit there so positive and calm, with her solemn little smirk, like someone safely sealed behind a wall of glass. He concentrated hard, then shut his eyes and bowed his head, clamp-jawed, gripping the edge of his seat, fighting back surges of disbelief and rage, and feeling dull and empty too, his whole life swerving—slowly, hugely—out of his control. Paula knew; okay, he'd face that later. What mattered now was Irma. She had to quit accusing him; he wasn't just some low-down chiseling bum. She had to understand: he needed her. He meant no harm to her or anyone. He'd been stuck, that's all; she'd given him the chance to be himself again. He had to make her understand: the cost was his, not hers, and she was worth it to him—she had to be. She had to quit this crap and show concern, and be as warm and sensitive and generous as she'd been before.

He looked up fully, pleading: "Okay, sure. But listen to me. . . ."

"I'm listening, Louie."

"My wife and me, we aren't divorced—okay. But that's not the point. . . ." He faltered, groping, realizing suddenly he couldn't tell the truth, not all of it. "We're separated, understand? Well, not exactly separated, either; what I mean, we're still living together, but I'm out looking for another place, and soon as I find it I'm getting out. So what's the difference? Her and me, we're finished; that's all . . . it's nothing. But, see, you—you and me—this—that's what matters, right? I mean, we got something special. We can talk, we understand each other. I never met someone like you before, and now I have, I tell you, it's a whole new world. I know what I'm doing, I know what I like; and all that other shit—and you know what I mean, cause you've been through it too—that's something . . . that's not me, that's some other guy. I'm me, Louie Miscello. I got my life to lead, same as you. No ties, no claims, doing what I want do, living any way I wanta live. Cause I've earned it. No one's telling me different. Half my life I played their games, and what did I get out of it? I got nothing. Nothing, understand? Fifty-six, my kids looking down on me. My wife blaming me: I'm selfish. Everything I ever done is nothing in their eyes. I'm nothing. Well, screw 'em. I don't have to take that kind of crap. You made me realize that. Life don't gotta be a prison. We got good times; do anything we want to do. Cause I'm being good to me from now on, and I got no more time to waste. I want to be with you, I'll be with you; I want to party, have my kicks: that's what I'll do—and I don't care she knows or not, see? She's got nothing to do with it."

She kept staring at her plate, shaking her head: "It's no good, Louie."

"What do you mean, 'no good'?" He grabbed the table and thrust his face forward. "Wait a minute. Don't you see? I'm saying. . . ."

"I know what you're saying. Will you listen to me for a minute please? I don't want to get involved—it's as simple as that. Now don't get excited, just listen. I've thought this out. I don't care you're married, or divorced, or getting divorced, or whatever it is: all I know is, I'm not getting mixed up in it. I don't need that kind of trouble. I like you, sure. We had our fun a couple weeks ago. But don't try to make that into something it isn't. Like I told you before,

I'm perfectly happy with my life as is. I don't want to worry; I don't want to hurt anybody. I've got no time for lies and games. I'm a very simple, straightforward person, and what I'm telling you, I'm telling you for your own good. I'm not your answer. Whatever it is you need, I don't know, but you're just going to have to look for it some-place else."

"Hold it, will you? Who said anything about getting involved?" Something was narrowing and tightening in him. He saw the pic-ture now, leading him on, waiting until the middle of the meal. She wasn't gonna get away with it. He felt vivid and alert. Let her talk, let her go ahead and pull her stuff.

"Listen, I'm no fool. I'm just not gonna be the other woman, okay? I don't want you thinking about me that way. I don't want you calling me up every time you feel lonely. It's not my part to take her place or help you live with it, or anything like that. I've been through all of this before, and I'm not getting forced into it again. I'm not your special party-girl. You don't have rights over me. I mean, I know you have your troubles, and I'm sorry, but there's nothing I can do. I just don't want to be bothered with you."

"Who says I'm gonna bother you? You're talking to me—I'm Louie, remember? I'm not one of these half-ass jerks out here. I'm not some green kid. I don't want to force you into nothing. All I'm say-ing, we can have some fun. You're worried about my wife; forget it, I'll take care of that. You need an older guy like me to understand you. You been messing around with the wrong kind of folks, is all. These jerks out here can't do nothing; sitting in that apartment's not doing any good. So why don't you . . . look, I ain't gonna mess you up. I want to take you places, do things for you. I was even thinking, y'know, like one of these weekends we could go to New York or something. You know, do it up—big hotel, nightclubs, see a show or something like that. I'm no cheapskate. You got nothing to worry about with me. I mean, c'mon now, we got good times ahead of us. No reason to get all head up. Give it a chance, willya?"

She wasn't buying any. She just sat there, squirming, looking down, shaking her head, like this was all some bad mistake. She'd never come out here, never done those things with him before, never led him on. Stubbornly avoiding his stare, she scowled off across the room. Those clamped lips, set features, that stylish hairdo, the motion of her hand as she rubbed her throat: all of her was hateful to him suddenly. He had to make her feel him—be aware. Overturn the table, smash things, grab her. Waken fear in that smug little, cheap indifference. Make her realize.

"Well, c'mon!" he pressed, more dangerously. "Will you?"

She busied herself lighting a cigarette. Around them people ate and murmured. Then, exhaling thoughtfully, she met his eyes with a determined, steady flatness: "There's no point arguing about it. You're obviously not the kind of person I thought you were, and I'm not what you're looking for either. So let's just drop it."

He looked at her for a long moment, blood pounding. "That's the way you want it."

Vaguely, he was heading for New York, past Mount Holly, Bordentown and Trenton, past Fort Dix. Black, flat farmland stretched out all around him, and heat lightening flickered, lighting up the clouds. The motor hummed evenly, and the wind whipped at him hot and pungent. He wasn't pushing now, just driving, keeping under sixty, hardly interested in it even, keeping to the truck lane, so cars and clusters of cars came steadily to overtake him, drawing past or snapping past.

The fear was past, defeat was past, the rage, disgust: everything connected with it, as if that all had happened long ago and now lay far behind him. Not just Irma: everything—his wife, job, daughter, sons, his home—all of that was ruined, finished. He was finished. Nothing left to do but keep on driving, keep moving, as if the motion could suspend him like the holding of a breath, and he was through with caring, feeling, making any effort now but this.

He reached down for the pint beside him, and steering with one hand, took one deep swig and then another. Nothing, then the warmth was spreading, and in its thickening, velvet lull, he thought of Paula, sure and warm, and how her trust had calmed him, how her life lay open, in his hands, all of it there and up to him to tender and protect, and how this opened him up too, and how he'd be the man his old man hadn't been; he'd give his family things he'd never had, a place in life, a house, good education. As sure as he was anything, as natural as his strength, they'd keep on making steady progress, each step forward, more to build on, more to gain, and never any losses, nothing that could break them, nothing that could spoil.

He gave it up. He couldn't drive. He had to piss; he needed gas. The speed, the traffic, headlights, taillights: the pressure of it stifled him. He wanted to pull over and get off. Let the rest of them go on, those faceless drivers, numberless, perpetual. All he wanted now was stillness, some deserted pocket in the blackness of this night, away from cars and lights and houses, somewhere he could drink in peace.

A sign for food and fuel flashed by. He saw the glow, the arc-lit grounds, and slowing down he took the turn-off, surprised to find the parking lot was full, the traffic massed together here and scattered out in double rows, people eating, sleeping, smoking, people coming, people going, groups of guys, girls, couples, families, license plates from everywhere. It wasn't what he wanted, so he turned out of the lot and cruised on past the restaurant, past the lines for gas, pulled around in back, where the tractor trailers and the semis rested darkly in the shadows. Threading his way farther back than them even, he parked along the fence, cut his motor, lights. For a moment, he went blank. Then roused himself: unlatched the door, climbed out; head hung, feet scraping, went around the car and pissed, came back, slumped, grabbed the bottle, sucked and gulped at it until he gasped for breath.

But even here, each swallow numbing him against all memory, need or care, and set loose drifting down a cloudy darkness where he knew no shape or name, even here some stray thought would betray him. Suddenly he'd come alive to everything: Irma, doing that to him! She wasn't gonna get away with that. And then he'd writhe and shift: don't think. And drink again. And Paula, no. And then the aching bitterness would come—that he was lost and no one cared—and then he'd turn against himself: why should they? He was rotten; all he'd ever done was cause them harm. Except he knew he wasn't rotten. Something in him still deserved. Forget it. He finished off the bottle, tossed it, heard it smash. But just as he was nodding, slipping, letting all things go, and as the welcome grip of sleep took hold and drew him downwards with its sure enclosing, like something glimpsed, or dreamed, he saw his daughter standing straight and whole, as lovely as a bride, and she was calling, reaching out; her words were tender, beautiful, and there was comprehending pity in her eyes.

The Family House

She came in through the porch, closed the screen door gently behind her, heard the children's TV show up loud, and Howard shouting over it:

"Honey, I can't hear you! What did you say?"

Her sister shouted from the kitchen:

"Forget it! Never mind!"

"But I didn't hear you!"

"Any sign of Anna yet?"

"Here I am; I just came in!" she called out. As she stepped into the living room, the breeze of an electric fan blew at her, passed by. She glanced at Howard to her left, slouched in his chair with the newspaper and a beer, under an orange cast of light. He wore no shirt; his nakedness startled her. The breeze swept by her once more. Across the room the girls were sprawled; beyond them, the flickering, bluish light and violent sounds. "Hello, Anna," Howard said; then shouted from his chair: "Mary, she's here!" The children looked around. Just then Mary came through the lighted doorway from the kitchen— rollers in her hair, shirttail over orange Bermudas, slippers flopping.

"Did you get my dress? Well, where is it? Didn't you stop?"

This startled her, caused her to frown and close her eyes: "Oh, no! I forgot!"

"Forgot? You said you'd pick it up! We're going out tonight!"

"Mary, I'm sorry. But there's nothing I can do now." The fan swept slowly past; she looked up at her sister, reached out to put her purse down on the hall table.

"Honey, don't get all excited," Howard cautioned, sipping his beer.

"What the hell am I supposed to do? I can't go like this!" There was a surge of music from the television. "Susan, turn that down right now! Susan!" She stepped and slapped her on the back of her leg; abruptly turned off the TV. The room darkened, grew larger. Ruthie, the three year old, cried out: "Mommy—!" "Go on upstairs and wash! Go on, both of you! It's time for supper anyhow."

The children rushed around her, up the stairs.

She asked Mary: Didn't she have anything else she could wear? The white and pink stripe?

"That's just the point. Nothing clean!"

Well, of course there were other dresses, whatever they were going to. And now she was too tired—her own clothes were clinging; she longed for the privacy of her room, to change from her uniform to a house dress. "I'm sorry about this, Mary," she said again. "But you'll have to excuse me. I'm going up to change." They were silent as she climbed the stairs. When she reached the landing, she heard the children in the bathroom, and from below:

"For godssake, I ask her for a little favor. She tells me she's going to do something!"

She turned down the hall to her open door, paused; plumbing shuddered; she heard the children:

"Ruthie, wait! . . . No! No! . . . Ruthie, let me wash your hands, now here's the soap."

She went into her room and closed the door. She walked around her bed, drew curtains, turned on the corner lamp, sank into the chair to take off her shoes. Her feet were throbbing, her ankles swollen; she strained to reach down and work off each shoe. After a while, she rose and carried the shoes to the closet. She chose a summer house dress from its hanger and lay it on the bed. Unzipped, unbuttoned, she struggled out of her uniform, and after that, there was the slip, the stockings to unfasten and draw off, and finally the girdle itself. She was a large, soft woman, flabby and loose-fleshed; but free of her clothes she felt lighter, even giddy. She put on her slip again, glanced in the mirror and straightened her hair. Opened the door. Gathered her things and went around to the bathroom. TV sounds came from below.

Before long, the doorknob rattled, startling her.

"Aunt Anna! Aunt Anna!"

"I'll be through in a minute!" she said, sharply. The doorknob kept rattling. "All right! I'm coming!" Still in her slip, she held a towel in front of her as she unlocked the door. "What is it, Ruthie? You have to pee?"

Ruthie shook her head and peered into the lighted bathroom. "What do you want then?" Ruthie wouldn't answer. She had chubby little legs and arms and beautiful skin, smooth and pale; her hair was fine, light-brown, her face delicately formed, with small, wide-open green eyes. Her head was crowded by her shoulders, her eyes by her cheeks, her thumb and knuckle hiding a corner of her mouth. She giggled.

"You!" she said, dropping the towel and stooping to gather her. She kissed the back of her neck, while Ruthie squealed and wriggled.

"Anna!" Mary called. "Supper's ready!"

"Be a couple more minutes! Don't wait for me!" She leaned back. "You go on. That's supper time." And spanked her fondly; picked the towel up, stood. "Go on." Then turned to powder arms, her shoulders, between her breasts, while Ruthie watched. "Go on, Ruthie." Flushed, turned off lights. "Out!"

She slammed the icebox door, which never shut first time and swung open behind her; she had to press her hip against it. "Howard!"

He was coming in from the living room, wiping his hand across his face.

"Dinner's getting cold. We're going to eat."

She had to pass in front of him to get to the table, carrying the pitcher of tea, the head of lettuce. She put them down; he'd come up behind her; reached arms around her waist, nuzzled her neck.

"Come on. I mean it." She turned in his arms, against his body. "Get your shirt on, and call her. Will you, please?"

"Why don't you just relax, about the dress and all, huh? It's no big deal."

She pushed herself free. "Look, it's hot. It's been a lousy day. I want to get out of this house and have a little fun, okay?" She went back to the stove, where pots were simmering.

He pulled a chair out, sat down heavily. "But why keep picking on her?"

She didn't turn to look; she had the pot of vegetables and was draining them. Steam rose in her face. "Just call her. Please! All right." She carried the pot back to the table and set it before him.

"Hey—"

But she went directly out into the darker, cooler living room, leaned on the phone table as she looked up, and called: "Anna, will you please come! It's getting cold!"

She bowed her head, waiting. "Anna!" she called louder, looking down, examining her fingers on the table top. The television filled in behind her.

"Go on, Ruthie," she heard.

"Ruthie? Are you up there? You come down here, will you: now!"

Ruthie appeared suddenly. "We're coming," Anna said, holding Ruthie's hand.

She folded her arms and watched them starting down, step by step. She turned away. "Susan," she said, "turn that off. It's supper time."

She made them wait while she dished vegetables and mashed potatoes and the raisin sauce into bowls. She took the ham from the oven; the odor of it filled the room and then she carefully carved slices and put them on a serving plate. The girls were squirming for attention, fussing about some TV show. Anna was fixing the salad; Howard, seated at the end of the table, was buttoning his shirt.

"Aunt Anna," Susan asked, "you're going to sit with us tonight, aren't you?"

"I guess so," Anna said.

"There, I told you," Susan sneered at Ruthie. "Well, 'The Wizard of Oz' is gonna be on. It doesn't start until 8:30, but you'll let us stay up, won't you?"

"You don't mind, do you, Anna?" he put in.

"Aunt Anna? Won't you?"

"Yes, Susan. If it's all right with your parents, it's fine with me— of course, I don't mind. I'm here. I'm happy to do it."

"Can we stay up, then, Daddy?"

"Oh, for godssake, Susan. Yes," she said, bringing the hot bowls to the table; returning for the meat. Ruthie clapped her hands; Susan grinned and slouched back down into her chair.

"I just don't want you feeling put out or anything. I mean it's any trouble, well, just say so, okay? I mean, we both appreciate it, really."

She brought them the meat. "There," she said, sitting down at last, "that's everything, isn't it?" He tightened his jaw and reached towards her with his fork, taking two large pieces of ham. Anna poured herself tea; then asked her where they were going.

"Bowling," she said. "We're meeting friends—Give me your plate, Ruthie. Carefully, now; that's the way. Thank you, Susan.— That's if we ever get out of here. Can I have the salad?" She dished out portions of fruit and salad on the girls' plates. "Potatoes?" Exchanged the salad for the potato bowl and tapped out helpings with the metal spoon; next was the meat: she cut that with scraping sounds.

"I want ice-tea!" burst out Ruthie, hitting the table.

"Say 'please,'" she said.

The words were muffled because his mouth was full: "Just cut the nonsense!" Everyone went silent. Anna reached across for Ruthie's glass, put sugar in, poured tea.

"What do you say to Aunt Anna, Ruthie?"

"Thank you!" Ruthie took the glass in both hands.

"Can I have some too, Mom?"

"Tea, please, Anna, and the sauce too. Thank you." She filled Susan's glass. "How was your day?

"Fine."

She watched Anna lift a fork full of potatoes to her mouth; her own hands met and pressed in her lap. "Well, mine wasn't," she said.

"This heat has been murder. The kids have been all over the place. Mrs. Bocosky came over. I vacuumed, cleaned the bedrooms and bathroom . . . ," she began. But the girls were stirring their tea, knocking their spoons against the sides of their glasses, faster and faster.

"You're gonna break the glasses, you keep that up! You kids hear me?" He raised his voice, but they kept rattling the spoons against the glasses, trying to outstir each other. He slapped Ruthie's hand. She knocked her glass over.

He stood up, brushing off his shirt and trousers. "Aw, shit! Chrissake! I told you kids, didn't I? I told you quit messing around!" He grabbed Ruthie by the shoulder, and she fought against him: "No!" Anna stood up while Ruthie was still howling and ran to the sink for towels. "Let her go. Here, here, let's get this cleaned up," Anna said, back right away, handing him towels, mopping the table. Ruthie struggled down from her chair and pushed her way between Susan's chair and the wall, but when she tried to burrow in her lap, she held her away. "She wet her pants too! I knew it. Is there any on the chair?—Ruthie, I told you. You wouldn't do your pee, would you?" She turned her around and hit her bottom sharp, hard slaps. "Now go on upstairs. Go up to your room!"

Ruthie staggered back; wheeled and ran howling into the living room. She got up and followed her, to make sure she started up the stairs: "Do what I say!"

As she sat back down, "All right, what's your problem, Susan? You want your supper or not?"

They finished cleaning up the mess; Anna took the used towels to the trash. When they were all settled down again, she said: "Well, why don't you say it? You don't approve of the way we raise our children, do you?"

Anna stared at her. "I'm not going to fight with you, Mary." And looked away.

"They're our children and this is our house, and I don't care what you think."

Anna refused to look up; Howard sat back in his chair; Susan was pushing potatoes with her fork.

Their father, William Potts, had died three months ago, leaving them the house and furniture to share. It was their family house, and though Mary had gotten out, she, Anna, had never left. When her mother had died, she had taken over the responsibility of keeping it together and alive, seeing Mary through school, preparing regular meals, putting things in order, and helping to provide for the three of them by working at the factory.

Mary had been his favorite, and it was Mary he praised and spoke gently to, though Mary who knew him or cared for him least of all. Mary had finished school finally and come to work at the factory too for a while, but underneath she was restless and wanting to leave home—and she did, when she was twenty-one. She claimed to be in love with Howard Muller, but the Army called him, so she began to carry on with other girls like herself, taking trips to places where they could meet boys from the city; and when she quit at the factory and left home, it was to go live with those girls and to take a job as waitress in a center city bar.

"You made your sister leave. You drove her away from here with your jealousy."

He'd sit at the table after dinner—the two of them alone, their empty plates before them—and he would slouch back until his chair creaked. His hands were thick and heavy; his whole body was big. He weighed more than two hundred and fifty. He had a large, round head, eyes slightly bulging, nostrils flared, lips fleshy, teeth badly stained. His face could be red with anger, or with laughter, thrown back, bunched and creased with the mouth open wide. His hair was thinning, yellowed white.

But she would never listen. She understood; she knew he meant to hurt her and hurting her was his way of showing how he loved her. After her mother had died, he'd come and asked her what she could do for him, and her life had been her answer to that.

She kept his house, laundered his clothes, fixed his meals, listened to his talk about his day. She woke him before dawn, still in her bathrobe and went down to fix his breakfast, and while he was upstairs shaving, she put his coffee on and set his place and squeezed his orange juice or cut his melon. She cooked his oatmeal or his hot-cakes, or his eggs and bacon and toast. She called to him and waited to hear him on the stairs or the sound of his clearing his throat. She packed his lunch box, and filled the thermos. She sat with him while he ate, watched him spill things and chew with his mouth open, slurping and grumbling and talking no matter if his mouth was full.

After her day at work, she hurried home and found him in the living room, in his sagging chair, watching the five o'clock movie or the news. She hurried to change her clothes and come back down to start their supper. She had no time to shop, or even for housecleaning really, except on weekends. One evening she must spend washing, another ironing, another sewing. Some evenings he'd sit and watch television, others he'd spend working at his bench in the cellar. His hobby was woodworking, and she loved to watch him, or at least to hear the sound of his electric saw, or his hammer; he had refinished nearly everything in the house once or twice, and made several things, and sold others. He also helped when there were important household chores: the plumbing to fix, steps to repair, furniture to move, screens to put up and take down and paint in the winter, the cellar to clean. Every Friday he took the trash and garbage cans out to the sidewalk, and every Saturday he brought them back in again.

Mary never visited, never came home for a vacation or even a meal. Several times she did telephone about things she'd left behind—clothes, records, furniture—and once she stopped by with friends in a car to pick them up. But she'd never come home. Not until Howard was back and she came with him to announce they were engaged. He'd been back for two months. He had money and a car; he was partners with his father in the butcher business. He and Mary hoped to be married right away. No need for any excitement or bother, Mary said. But Father had insisted: if there was to be a wedding, it would be a real wedding, in church, with family guests and friends, with a wedding cake and dress and flowers and gifts. He would give her away; he'd wear a tuxedo. There would be rings.

Listening to all this, she'd felt confused and hurt. And after they had gone, she'd shut herself in her room and she'd begun to choke and cry, quietly, so her father couldn't hear.

Mary found new reasons to visit after the marriage. She demanded reassurances and praise from everyone, and maybe Howard had some influence too, wishing for closer ties.

Before much longer, Mary was pregnant. During the visits, which were on Sundays, she would gossip about herself, their apartment and neighbors, about her clothes, her doctor, and her sickness, her weight, the vitamins she was taking, the exercises she was supposed to try; or she would poke fun at Howard, telling them how sloppy he was, how the woman down the hall flirted with him, how he grouched in the morning, how he was constipated or had a headache.

Then Father fell very ill. Other times he'd only been sick with flu or a bad cold; he'd been able to care for himself during the day, when she was at work. But this time his yell woke her in the middle of the night; she'd run out into the hall in her nightgown, groping for the light-switch. He yelled again—her name—as she stumbled to his door and in. She found the light. He gasped for her to help; he was staring, his face pale and wet, and he was doubled up and clutching his stomach. She was sure it was his heart. "What is it? Where's the pain?" He trembled, groaned, tossed and gripped her hands. She wrapped him in blankets, wiped his face, hurried down to telephone. Called the doctor and ambulance.

They came and took him to hospital, struggling with him on the stretcher down the stairs. The doctor told her it was his gall bladder.

But Mary had refused to come.

"What can I do to help, anyway? Howard will drive you over if you really have to go—won't you, honey? He says, of course, he'll get dressed right now. But calm down, Anna! He's in good hands."

Mary never did go to see him in the hospital, nor did she help out during the convalescence at home, when she, Anna, was forced to stay with him at the risk of her job. But finally she did come to visit and Father was pleased. She talked about how healthy her doctor said she was; and she talked about the baby things she and

Howard had discovered today when they were searching the cellar—
a dismantled crib, a bassinet, a carriage—it was all right to take them
home with them, wasn't it?

As soon as her father was on his feet again, Susan was born.
Could Anna come stay with her now, Mary wanted to know, and
help with things for a few days? Some bad feeling arose when she said
no. But she and Father contributed to the salary of a temporary maid.

Mary came to boast: "You ever see such beautiful skin? And
she's so strong! Look at her trying to sit up. See, she recognizes her
Daddy." Mary pointed out how much Susan and her grandfather
enjoyed each other. "Anna, come on and see. You can't miss this."
Susan would squeal and sit on his bouncing knee. He would give her
her bottle. The baby seemed to please him as nothing else ever had.
But why then couldn't she love it too? She ought to, but she couldn't
help feeling indifferent, and even disgusted. She felt to love the baby
in front of them would humiliate her. Mary would point: "Look at
Anna with Susan!"

Ruthie was born two years later. Once more they had to hire a
maid. But this time no one seemed proud or excited. Mary complained about all the hardships of motherhood—Ruthie was colicky,
crying all the time, ill-tempered, sickly—and of course there were
other troubles: Howard's father wasn't well; their apartment was
crowded with the new baby; they were short of money. As a result,
she, Anna, came to touch and handle Ruthie the way her father had
Susan; had the opportunity to love her, apart from the others, without anyone really noticing or caring.

Their father had been sixty-two years old when he died. He had
just shaved; had been in the act of dressing. She'd been waiting for
him downstairs with breakfast.

In those first weeks after his death, when she'd been left alone in
the house, she'd been lost; nothing was fixed, no direction. She couldn't
sleep, but lay with open eyes, or sat in her chair. When Howard, Mary,
the minister or Mrs. Bocosky came, she only felt their cruelty. But
gradually her body roused her; she ate, she slept, she began to know the
house again, the shaping patterns of things around her: the toilet
thumping in its peculiar way; neighborhood sounds; the corner of

linoleum catching her shoe; the icebox door that wouldn't close. She went into his room and looked through his clothes. She saw pictures, his chair, his bed, pairs of shoes, ties, belts; in the bathroom she found his razor, shaving cream and lotions, his pajamas hanging on the back of the door, a towel with paint stains on it. She went through all the house and felt the will of things—all the way to the cellar, to her washing machine, a basket of dirty clothes, his workbench, the sawdust, the shaded lamp and sagging shelves and all the family clutter.

That was when she'd cried. And later was when the questions took form: how could she live now? What could she do? What did she matter? Where was there to turn? Three cards came in the mail, one from her aunt in Pittsburgh and two from the factory. Mr. Manville's card had a silver front that said "With Deepest Sympathy" and on the inside said "Our heartfelt thoughts are with you in this time of sorrow," under which Mr. Manville had signed his name and added the postscript, "Take two weeks vacation." Mary Lloyd, she was sure, had chosen the lovely card signed by all the department heads; it had a cool green picture of little bell-like flowers, fragile and gentle, and inside, the poem:

> May you find comfort in the thought
> Your loss is shared today
> By those who care and sympathize
> Far more than words can say.

She called the factory and told them she'd be back tomorrow. And next day she woke early, went down to make herself breakfast; and went to work; returned in the evening. But she knew that working wasn't enough. She needed to be part of other lives. And since she had no single friends, no one close, since she would never marry, she felt grateful and relieved to hear of Howard's and Mary's plan—that Father had left them half title to the house, and half to herself, that they were subletting their apartment, and wanted to move in as soon as possible.

The shower had ruined everything; her hair would never turn out. She should have thought of that first, but she'd been hot and rushed, and there hadn't been time for a bath, so she'd gone ahead, and even though she'd had a cap on, the steam had taken out the curl. And here it was, stringy and clotted, hanging on either side of her round, tired face. She brushed and brushed and finally just gave up and slipped a ribbon on. Her hair, face, her dress. She glared into her own glittering eyes and for a moment there was such a dropping in her, she clenched herself tighter and tighter, but then let go.

She got to her feet and kicked the stool out of the way. She crossed the room, then came back more slowly, shaking her head and scowling at the floor.

She could imagine him down there. Could see him trying to smooth over everything, sympathizing and consoling, and telling her, "Aw, don't you worry now—."

She sat down on the bed, to do her shoes. Sat hunched, leaning heavily on her arms, listless, hot and sticky. Reached down and picked up a shoe and stared at it, its little buckles, and grasped it hard.

Nothing was her fault.

And then:

The hell with it. She wanted to get out of here. She wanted a drink, some fun. As for Ruthie, let Anna Maye take of her.

She heard his step and closed her eyes. They never quit. She put on her shoes.

When he came in the door, he gave her a startled, guilty look, frowning. "About ready?" he asked.

She stared at him blankly.

He frowned, looked her up and down and gathered himself. Then turned and sat down in his chair. She glanced at the clock and jumped up.

Ignored him. Concentrated on the simple business of buttoning her front. Zipped up her side, pulled her dress into place; rearranged the ribbon, fluffed her hair (bitterly, grimly resigned), hastily combed down her bangs.

Picked up her open purse, threw some things in, snapped it shut, turned and walked right past him out the door.

"Ruthie," she called softly, feeling for the light switch.

Lights came on; things leapt at her. Ruthie never made a sound, all twisted in the sheet, eyes glaring, knees drawn up, hands in fists under her chin, the round, pink button of her pacifier hiding her mouth. Her face was puffy, and strands of tangled hair were matted to her temples. She was still in the clothes she'd wet at dinner.

"Oh, Ruthie." She hitched her skirt and stooped. Ruthie stared at her with what looked so much like hatred, she caught her breath. She reached out, and just very gently touched, and parted her hair back, and smiled. Then she tugged the sheet to free her, and reaching under the hot shoulders, lifted her up close and held her tightly.

She turned off their light and left them—telling them sternly to be quiet now and go to sleep: Go to sleep now. Then she picked up in the bathroom.

"No, Aunt Anna, I don't want. . . ." Susan called.

And Ruthie's cries: "Mom-haha-my! My Mom-Mom. . . ."

Ignoring this, she went to her own room, turned, started downstairs, slowly, heavily, so they could hear. Stopped half-way down: "That's enough! Be quiet now!"

Downstairs, picked up in the living room (her heart still beating rapidly, nerves taut). Put away Susan's papers and crayons, straightened pillows on the couch, removed the pillows, dug out a pencil, a gritty piece of candy and a penny from the seams, remarked new stains and splits. Her eyes were smarting, as she yawned and stretched. She turned on the TV. She took up Howard's shirt from the sewing basket and held the collar she'd been turning closer under light. Her harshness had been necessary. They were tired and hot, demanding, cranky children tonight—even Ruthie, who was worn out to begin with—neither of them heeding her, denying their own heavy eyes and spent, clumsy bodies. She must deal with them like sick people or people in pain, for their own good: force them to bed; carry Ruthie, wailing, upstairs, threaten Susan. ("You're tired. . . . You don't know what you want. But get a good night's sleep now, and you'll wake up tomorrow feeling much better. Your Mommy and Daddy will be here.") They left her with a winded, empty feeling. She'd wanted to make things happier and help them to forget the angriness at dinner. Yet now she worried: Had she wanted this too much?

She folded Howard's shirt, lay it on top of the basket, rose, turned off the TV, collected dishes and glasses and went out to the kitchen where she put them in the sink. Running water and the chinking of glasses were the only sounds, as she added these to the dishes already standing in the rack. Then she was opening, closing cupboards, putting them away: where did Mary want these saucers? where did this pan go? Her hands fumbled with Mary's serving dish, but held it.

She cleaned the stove-top, work counter, icebox door; swept; carried the plastic trash basket out to the back stoop, emptied it into a can. Lights shone from back porches opposite; shouting voices reached her, music, TV sounds, and distant traffic sounds. The night seemed weirdly limitless, and she shrank from it, dully, bringing in the empty basket; hooked the screen, shut and locked the door.

She went to the ice box and fixed some salad and a glass of milk, took her place at the table, and ate greedily, alone. As she listened to the house, the icebox motor started up.

Down in the cellar, she fingered tools that cluttered her father's workbench; some winter coats and crib mats had been carelessly tossed on top of them, and she cleared these away now. Then lifted up his drill-gun in both hands—unwieldy, strange and brutal, the metal cold. (She'd seen it buck in his hands, with a shrill whine, as he forced it into wood or metal—or with the sanding attachment, his grim face hunched over it and wood dust everywhere. She'd seen the fury of his work: His red face sweating, looking up afterwards, as from another world.) Her hands clutched tighter, tighter, the bulky weight and sharp ridges, and she frowned, turning her face aside, blinking. She laid it down, pulled the cord from the socket, stood opening and closing her hands. Mary had wanted to throw out everything when they'd gone through his closets and drawers: who would want this now? Or these, his chisels, files, hammers, his power saw; any of his tools? Would Howard want them? Should they go to Louie, or to Bill O'Neill? Her eyes burned, and shaking, she wept. She pressed forward with her weight, needing to feel hardness, strength. She found relief in tears, and in the ache and sharper pain as her clenched hands crushed against the litter scattered on the bench.

Something was in her room.

She sat up and turned on the light, heart thudding, breathing hard, blinking: unprotected. A large, heavy moth was fluttering in the far corner of the ceiling. She pulled herself together and after a moment got up, harried it out of the corner with a rolled-up magazine, then trapped it on the curtain with a glass. She held her hand over the mouth of the glass, the moth's wings wildly scrabbling across her palm and making a ringing sound against the glass. She carried it out through the dark and silent hall into the bathroom, managing the light, and shook it into the toilet, which she immediately flushed.

She washed her hands, wiped neck, breast and face. Her face was splotchy, harshly shadowed, with dilated pores and lines and sagging jowls; a broad, upturned nose; mouth drawn and set; eyes somber, reddened, staring blankly from under gathered brows. She avoided their gaze.

Ruthie lay in an awkward sprawl; Susan's arm dangled down. They seemed dumped in their beds, all in a heap, sheets kicked back, mouths gaping, eyes sealed tight. She listened to their shallow, measured breathing, gasp and sigh, smelled the scent of their sleeping bodies. Streetlight flickered on the wall, on the dresser, on her then, as she moved closer, cautiously. She stood beside their bunk bed, poised and alert. Susan drew her arm back suddenly, wiped her face, and turned over on her back with a cranky murmur and a jouncing of springs. Ruthie slept on; her right knee was raised, left bent out, right arm lying on her stomach, left stretched out to the side, fingers

clutching the sheet; her face was turned towards her. She wanted to
promise them something, but couldn't find words. Stooping down
stealthily, softly, she reached across and drew up Ruthie's sheet with a
slow, agonized deliberateness, and when Ruthie stirred, she leaned
over and kissed her hair with a kiss she'd never know about.

Back in her room, the clock said 12:20.

She couldn't sleep.

The way Mary stalked out, she thought. She was staring across
at the dark corner where the photographs hung: Father, Mother,
Mary-and-herself (she thirteen and Mary five). She really didn't
need to see the photographs to know them, or any details of this
room. The wallpaper, faded bar on bar of twining roses, she'd chosen
at age eighteen (Mother died just after that). The chair, the dresser
had stood there nearly all her life, as had this bed, with scrolls and
posts beyond her feet.

She gave them most of her money. She tried to please them; she
kept out of their way.

A car door slammed; footsteps, voices. She sat up. The screen door
yawned. She got up, hurried to close her door. On her way back, the
front door squealed. She turned off her light, quietly lowered herself
and rolled onto the bed, squirmed, lay still. Footsteps scuffled downstairs. Beneath her door, a glow appeared. Her heart was thumping
and her head throbbed; she blinked up at her darkened room.

"She might have left a light on," Mary said.

"Shh!"

Closet door closed. Just then something went thud and scattered on the floor: "Damn it!" Saw Mary's bag and Mary squatting;
there were sounds of picking up little things and tossing them back
in. "I can do it!"

"Look, pipe down!"

"Don't you shush me because of her!" Clilup, clilip, Mary's footsteps went into the kitchen. Bang! a cupboard slammed.

"Aw, Mary. What the hell. . . . Come on, now," he urged, passing into the kitchen where his voice grew muffled, "I thought we settled this."

She strained to hear.

"We settled what?" came Mary's voice. "I can't move. I can't make a noise around here without you jumping down my throat!"

"Will you shut up?"

"I don't care if she hears. I hope she does hear! What does she mean to you anyway? Why do you keep protecting her?"

"You're not even making sense." His voice went on, too low for her to catch the words, insistently reasoning, rebuking. Then he paused, and in a friendly, final tone, "C'mon," he said (he must be near the doorway), "let's call it quits. Let's go to bed."

"If you don't want her here, why don't you do something?"

"What can I do?"

"You can quit acting like you're afraid of her! She's got you wrapped around her finger. Oh, sure, make a face. Listen to me. I want this house; I want my family to myself! Do you understand? What've I got to do? . . . Five years I've been married, and what do I get from my husband? Do I get a decent living? Do I get friends? No! No, I don't! I get kids, and a stupid, stinking little apartment and a fat stupid husband wallowing around on his fat ass all the time, and scared of his own father and too damned lily-livered and lazy to get out and accomplish anything! And finally, when we have a house left to us, what then? You don't want to see my sister hurt. You'd rather have her here hanging on our necks, when all you have to do is simply tell her, 'Look, we need the house. We want you to move out.'"

"I'm stupid, lazy, and what? Hold it! Wait a minute! I'm afraid? Jesus. I'm trying to be fair! Maybe that's something you can't understand, but you better learn. And don't give me this crap, I'm letting you down. I give you a steady living. I do my best. You could damn well show some gratitude. And as for Anna Maye, how you can stand there, drunk or sober, and talk about just throwing her out, when she's got no place else to turn; your father hasn't been gone for three months, even. What's wrong with you?"

"Oh, shut up!"

"You think you just step over people?"

"Shut up! Don't you dare criticize me! I'm talking about us, and the interests of this family. I'm telling you I can't stand her. I can't go on living with her. Now don't you turn around and tell me, 'Be kind. Be fair.'"

"All right, Mary; calm down. Will you calm down a minute and listen to me? Whose idea was it, moving in here in the first place?— Wait a minute!"

"Keep away from me !"

She had nothing to do with this. Nothing.

She still heard Howard: "She's not hurting anyone! You can't get along with her, that's more your fault. . . ."

They were in the living room. Her head turned and she rubbed her face, raked her hair, while her leg bent and pushed against the sheet and darkness pulsed with living, swarming things that crawled and crept and flew against her with their poisons.

". . . forcing herself on us! . . . interfering . . . intruding on our privacy! And you like it, don't you? Don't you?"

She groped for the lamp, the socket, pushed the switch: light blinded her, plunged her into molten orange. Eyes clenched, she twisted away and sat up, blinking.

"You think you can push me to the wall . . . ," continued Mary, tearful.

He should slap her; slap her down—now. Her own hands itched to.

But he wouldn't slap her, couldn't, no more than Father ever had. Her eyes circled the room. He'd let her go on and on, sneering and jeering and shouting filthy sickness from the bottom of her sick little heart. Her eyes fastened on the dresser, then the mirror, where a yellowed block of ceiling met the wall. She gripped her knees. She couldn't leave: didn't Mary realize that?

Her steps came tramping upstairs, nearer, nearer. She slammed the bedroom door. Below was silence.

Clumsy, bumping sounds came from the bedroom, a cry of hangers, scuffling sounds, then silence. The door opened, the switch clicked; Mary strode barefoot past her door and into the bathroom, shut that door.

She turned off her light and slid down in bed. Heard sharp, violent noises: water wrenched open and strangled off; fitful fumbling in the medicine cabinet. Something small and metal fell and rattled in the basin.

She raised her hand to hold the throbbing in her throat. She'd done everything for Mary she knew how. She'd forgiven her. This was just her drunken anger talking.

The toilet flushed, and still no sound of Howard. Hall light seeped beneath her door and at the edges. She lay still, scarcely drawing breath, choked and parched, exhausted.

Later Mary turned restlessly in bed, separated from her by only inches through the wall. They both heard Howard coming up.

"Don't speak. Don't say a word!" snarled Mary, shifting away.

He took his shoes off. Dropped his coins on the dresser. Came out, went creaking past her door. She heard his stream in the bowl. He turned off the lights on his way back and shut their door.

She lay staring at her window, where a strip of blue, lighter than darkness, defined the night.

They lay like two bodies, raw with sores. They kept shifting their weight around, stiffly, gingerly, as if some new positions could reduce the strain. The sheets were hot, abrasive; the air was sticky. Outside were distant sounds of traffic passing. They lay so close, yet rigid, each one clenched and shunning the other. They stared up into the darkness and listened to each other breathe and swallow, grind their teeth. She felt their minds churn backward over the details of their quarrel; she felt the fitful, nagging doubts, the accusations, the cramped, raw twitchings of their nerves. Howard cleared his throat and yawned. They were aware of her. She felt their wills press through to her like rays. Their curses thickened, gathered, swelled. Her own mind reeled. She cringed away, far, far, deep within herself, shrank away, doubled up and hiding, afraid to move, afraid to stir, and fighting all her body's processes.

Until, finally, came a rustling and a throaty groan. They turned together, wordlessly. They grappled, squirmed, and gasped, and grunted, heedless of their noise.

Louie at Home

The sky was lightening. He drove with concentrated effort, but couldn't stop his mind from drifting, and then the car would weave and he'd struggle to control it. Now and then a car came at him down the highway, headlights shining, then burst past with a fresh, dawn whoosh. The streets were empty; street lights shining. Traffic lights blinked. He turned through the darker, tree-lined residential blocks. Lawns were empty, except for bicycles and toys left out; doors closed; blinds down; cars parked on the street or in driveways, and misted over with dew. Then, turning the last corner into a newer neighborhood that wasn't quite so classy or expensive, but still was nice, he pulled into his own driveway. He cut the motor off, pushed in the lights, rolled up his window and climbed out.

He started towards the back porch, halted, then veered away, ducking under the clothesline where his and Josie's swimming suits hung, and sat down at the picnic table. Birds were twittering in the trees, darting across the lightened sky. He held his head in his hands, facing the small, two bedroom bungalow that they'd worked for all these years, but now they had it, so what? The paint job that he hadn't finished—flaking beige or his own pea green, what difference did it make? His ladder stood by Josie's window, as far as he'd gotten on this side; the paint and brushes under the tarp from two, three weeks ago. He'd built this picnic table, the barbecue; he'd bought the swings and pool for Josie, fixed the fence, dug the garden, reshingled the roof—but for what? It might as well belong to someone else. All it meant now was the life they could have had, but never would, impossible even as they moved within it, denied them even in the granting, hurtful if they dared to care.

Except he had to care. It wasn't what they might have had that mattered, but what they did. He knew now: caring was the answer; caring made the difference. His greatest shame was that he'd held it back and turned away, and even now sat lingering, reluctant to go in.

The first rays of sun came slanting through the trees, across the roof, rose up the chimney with its wrought-iron "M." A breeze stirred, fragrant with a clammy freshness. A strange dog came trotting around the garage, saw him, froze, lowered its head and sniffed, then trotted off, stopped, pissed on a bush, and disappeared around the house. A robin fluttered to a swaying perch. He had to go in. Simple as that. His head was pounding, eyes gritty, joints stiff, mouth pasty, stomach queasy and delicate.

At the back door, he opened the screen, which squawked on its spring, and stopped, and peered inside, shading the window with his hand. Then pulled out keys, right one, slid it slowly in the lock and turned, and slowly swung the door; inside, then, pocketed his keys, and just as slowly, silently, closed the door, locked it, listening. Wiped his feet. Kitchen was empty, surfaces dully gleaming in half-light. His footsteps squeaked on the linoleum; the floor creaked. He felt a gathering, crawly apprehension, steeled himself, as he moved into the hall—footsteps cushioned now, and darkness, and the spill of twilight from the open bedroom doors. No sound. No movement. Only the closeness, as he slipped inside the bathroom, the shower curtain glowing pink, and shut the door behind him, relieved. And went to piss, unbuckled, dropped his pants and sat down to be quiet, steady. Farted softly. Bent down and took off his shoes. Sighed, got up, pulling up his shorts, bent down again to strip off socks and pants when his keys fell out, and he froze, and clutched them tightly in his hand; then shook out pants and draped them on the hamper, and shakily undid his shirt and wriggled out and tossed it too. Over to the sink, he ran water, cupped it in his hands and rubbed his face, back of neck, up through hair and over his bald pate; then leaned down close to quench his thirst, again, again. And soaping hands, forearms, face, neck, shoulders, reached out for the soft, clean towel neatly folded on the rack. And combed his hair, and quickly brushed his teeth, and turned to leave, intent on slipping in beside her, stretching out in cool sheets, settling into his hollow, finding sure excuse in sleep, as if he'd never been away.

The bed was empty, covers thrown back, pillows gone. He looked in Josie's room, and Josie was there, cuddled in sleep with her dolls. Then guessed, or knew, and turned back down the hall and saw a light come on, and as he turned the corner, there Paula was, squirming upright on the couch, putting on glasses, clutching at her robe.

"What time is it?"

He shrugged. Nothing but to shuffle forward, vulnerable in his underwear, collapse in his chair across from her.

She twisted around and squinted at the wall clock.

"Card game," he muttered. "Want to call the guys? Want their names? Vince, Curt, Larry, okay?" He rubbed his eyes, the bridge of his nose. Not now, not like this. The sight of her unnerved him: fleshy, sallow, hollow-eyed, her faded pink robe, her roller cap. On the floor beside her, a cup and saucer and an ashtray full of butts. Something in him tightened and grew mean.

"It's six o'clock in the morning!"

She had to let it go, forget it. He couldn't take this now. Couldn't she see? What did she want to go and start this for? They had too much at stake. She had to realize, give him credit. He'd come back, self-despising, self-accused. She didn't need to rub it in.

"Look" he answered roughly, "what do you want? I'm here, aren't I?"

"You're here," she sneered. "Six o'clock in the morning!" She sat up, bare feet planted on the floor, somehow too alive, too shocking.

"Don't you think I know? I know where you've been. I know all about that little whore of yours! So don't tell me 'card game.' She called here! She called two days ago. I talked to her, Louie. I know! And I've been waiting, I've been up all night. You don't call, you're off whoring around, boozing, having a big time, aren't you? And I'm sitting here half out of my mind. I don't know you're in a car wreck, or if you're ever coming back, or if you're with that little whore, or where you are. And I'm through, I've had it! I told you years ago, you ever pull this stuff on me again, we're done. I won't live through all that again. I can't!" She lunged forward, stood up, fists clenched, red-faced, wild-eyed.

"Aw, c'mon. Quit your crazy talk! I'm not chasing any broad. I was in a game, I told you. Go ahead, call them, you don't believe me! But don't start giving me this crap about some goddamn broad."

She came closer: "Liar!"

"Shut up! I'm not gonna—"

"Liar!" she shouted. "You haven't changed! You're still the same lousy, good-for-nothing you always were. You don't have a scrap of decency. You don't even wait until I'm gone! You take and take, and when there's nothing left to take, you quit! Go on, get out! Go rot in a gutter, go on with the other bums!"

"Cut it. Cut it out!" He got up, clenched and glaring, but she charged at him, crazy, arm raised, trying to slap, to hit, except he blocked her arm and caught her wrists, and breathing sharply, fought and shoved her—harder than he meant to—and she stumbled back and fell and looked up from the couch aghast. His heart leapt to apologize, but then tightened in defiance. "Get off my back!" he threatened. "I'm not going to listen. I'm not going to answer talk like that!"

She looked at him, slowly panting, all her strength crumpled and gone, but her haggard face and her stark, dazed eyes were more dreadful to him than her shouting or her blows. "You don't care if I'm alive or dead," she said, tonelessly.

"Don't give me that. I'm here, ain't I? Now leave me alone!"

"Come back!" she cried after him.

He stalked down the hall—fuck it! And Josie was howling. He slammed the bedroom door. Fuck that too. He heard Paula bumping down the hall behind him. "Josie—sh! It's all right. I'm coming!"

He stared at the twilit room, grabbed a heart-shaped dish of hairpins off her bureau, threw it, smash! And sat down on the bed, trembling. Desperate for a drink, but scared of going out to face her while he got it. He twisted and rolled over, stretched out, teeth clamped, wide-eyed. His house. His bed. This was what he got. No pillow, he lay on his side, head on his arm, sweating. "Shh, baby, it's all right. Mommy's here." Josie kept howling, with that blank, crazed moan that set his teeth on edge: "Uhhhhhh!" He put his hand over his ear, and snorted, tightly closed his eyes. That was his fault too, wasn't it? Come home, try to make up; this was what he got. She wasn't telling him get out! She better shut that kid up too! He turned over on his back, fists clenched, but then the cries grew shorter, weaker, stopped; all he heard was Paula's voice and water running, so he turned over on his stomach, shut them out, concerned now with his weariness, the aching tension in his flesh, adjusting, welcoming the bed, the heavy darkness, silence seeping, like the promise of his strength's return and peace of mind and life brought back to normal somehow. Nothing else meant anything but that.

He woke from fitful sleep to cooking smells. The room was bright. Chainsaw rasping. He turned back over, stifling a hard on. His bladder ached. The noises of the day, clattering dishes, Josie's squeals, the radio, now and then a word from Paula: awarenesses collected, blocking off his hope for sleep. He was hot, sweating; sheets tangled, mouth stale, pangs in his gut. He propped himself up, groggy, blinking. Pulled his knees up, swung his legs over and sat up, when suddenly his memory cleared, and as he sniffed and hawked and rubbed his face, he realized the mess he'd gotten into, what he'd done, and what she'd said, and swore; he stood up, looked around, and started towards the window, needing air, but felt a biting pain and jumped back, clutching at his foot, and sat back on the bed, squeezing, cursing—fucking dish!— until the pain relented. He stood up, and wary of the pieces, went to the window, raised the shade and shrank back from the blaze of noon, but took it, squinting, lifted the sash. The sawing noise came louder, but fresh air came in too, kids yelling, birds, and he felt heartened somehow, even as he turned, and like the shambles of his life, stood blinking at this light-blanched, unmade room: the bed, the closet, open dresser drawers, her robe and nightgown draped across the chair.

He took his time. Showered, shaved. With a towel around his waist, he carried his shoes and pants from last night back to the bedroom. He scraped up pieces of her dish and hairpins, and dumped them in the basket. Taking out a starched work shirt, underwear, socks, and a clean pair of khakis, he dressed; he straightened the bed; and feeling better, steadier, he walked down the hall and turned into the kitchen.

"Daddy!" Josie's wide, excited, nearly toothless smile. On the counter, the radio blared, up loud, the way she liked it, and he winced from the noise, while Paula turned and gave him a hard glance and then went back to washing dishes.

"Daddy!"

"Hi, sweety! How you doing?"

She broke into a grin that closed her eyes, and lolled her tongue and banged the table with her spoon.

"Eating soup!"

"Lunch, huh? Looks pretty good."

"It's . . . good!" she crowed.

"And what else you got? Sandwiches?"

"Sandwiches!"

He stepped closer, hugged her to him, running his fingers through her curly hair, and she buried her face in his stomach and flung her arms around, and held him fast.

"Hey, careful now. C'mon." The strength and blindness of her clinging troubled him, as always, but also made him proud. "I got to get my breakfast." He spoke to Paula: "How about it?" Swaying with her.

Paula kept on washing, like she hadn't heard.

He leaned back from Josie, tilted her face up—"You love me, don't you, sweety? You're my girl. How about a big kiss?" She dropped her head back, mouth wide, gurgling laughter, and he bent down, smacked her cheek. "Go on, now"—loosening her arms and stepping away—"eat your soup." She swayed and watched him, kicking the rungs of her chair, pumping her arms. "No, go on. Eat your soup. Show me how you do it."

Paula turned abruptly: "Josie, quit playing. Eat your lunch!"

Josie gaped at her. "Huh?"

"Leave Daddy alone. Just eat." Paula stood there, watching, until scowling with concentration, Josie bent down, slowly scooped a spoonful to her mouth, and slurped; then looked up, grinning, the spoon still in her mouth. "That's it. Good! Now go on, do another. That's the way."

She pulled off her rubber gloves, tore a paper towel off, wiped her hands. Her face looked worse than last night even: creased and ashen, mouth fixed, sockets dark as bruises. Adjusting her glasses, rubbing her eye, she sighed and frowned at the floor.

"You been up all night?" he asked softly.

"What do you think?"

"Look . . . I. . . ." He cleared his throat.

She brushed past, swung the icebox door, took out eggs and bacon, slammed it. "Look, leave me alone! You want your breakfast, okay, sit down. But just don't bother me. Stay out of my way."

He swallowed, and as she went back to clatter the pans on the stove, he scraped his chair out, sat down, sagging. Then leaned forward, elbows on the table. Cattycorner from him, Josie stuffed a sandwich in her mouth, grinned and leered, as if they shared a private joke, except he hardly paid her mind, troubled with his cramping stomach, the fluttery weakness in his hands, each spiteful, jerky bang and clatter Paula made. He needed coffee. He couldn't take that stupid radio.

"Hey, turn that thing off, willya?"

"It's for Josie."

"Well, turn it down then. Jesus, I get sick of that junk." He started jiggling his knee, drumming the table with his thumb. "Can't you get nothing with a little beat in it? Wanh . . . wooo . . . sounds like sick cats or something."

"Wah . . . Yaaa!" Josie shouted, spitting fragments and waving her arms.

"Josie. Cut it, calm down!" He glowered at her.

Paula clicked off the radio. "Can't you even keep her quiet?"

"It's okay. . . . C'mon, sweety, just calm down, eat your lunch. I'm talking to Mommy." She lolled her tongue, swayed, stuffed her mouth again. But then he wouldn't look, so she started babbling, and next thing stretched her arms out on the table, laid her head down, watching, making noises with her mouth.

Paula brought his coffee, curtly. "Josie, get up."

"Naw, she's okay. Leave her."

He sipped his coffee, but the silence made things worse. No words, just footsteps, bacon snapping, its smell, and Josie's sounds, and then that dangerous, bitter silence, tightening his scalp, making him unsteady, like an emptiness beneath his feet. He watched her at the stove, spatula in hand, her hair in tight curls, gray, the droopy round-ness of her back, the familiar house dress, baggy from her loss of weight, the backs of her knees, lumpy and blue-veined. And despite his anger, he was moved with pity, longing, and need that if she turned now and saw it, then she would have to understand, forgive him, like she had always before. But she wouldn't turn, and didn't, and even if she had, some darker feeling gripped him, shameful, and he put down the cup, clenched his eyes, and rolled his forehead on his wrist. When he looked again, she was draining the bacon. She broke two eggs, dropped shells in the sink, took out glasses and a plate, put bread in the toaster, and just as he managed a weak smile for Josie, who was squirming, she turned and started for the icebox, where she poured him juice and milk.

"I don't want juice, thanks," he muttered.

She put the cartons back.

"Daddy!" Josie whined. She put her hand to her forehead, look-ing anxious.

Wearily, he played along: "Okay, let me feel." He reached over and felt her forehead, which was damp, but cool. "You're okay. No problem."

"Daddy!" She put her hand up again.

But he wouldn't this time: he shook his head and took a sip of coffee, staring at the table; kept on staring, fixedly, even when she grew more shrill and restless, twisting her body, crooning nonsense.

At last the toaster popped, eggs were done: Paula set the plate before him, the juice and milk, fork, paper napkin.

"Well, you've had enough, I guess," she said to Josie. She cleared her plates away and sponged the oilcloth, catching refuse in her palm. She cleaned off Josie's face and hands with a cloth, while Josie squirmed and fought and gave a chuckling yell.

"Shh!" Took her bib off, pulled her chair out, took her hand: "Come with me." Josie craned around, grinning at him, as they left.

He sucked a forkful of egg and bacon, chewed, swallowed, staring at the empty kitchen. Sipped his coffee, put his cup down. He couldn't let himself believe it. No matter what he'd done, there was still something else, something deeper, the thing that brought him home last night. And yet he knew no way of showing her, and having to was crueler, almost, than his fear of what would happen if he couldn't.

He heard them coming back: Josie stumbled in, careened around, and threw herself across his lap.

"Just watch her for me, huh? I'm going to lie down."

He looked up, blinking, noncommittal. "Sure. Go on. We're okay." After she left, he felt relieved, fondling Josie's hair, the hard round of her skull. She needed sleep, that's all, and time. She'd made him breakfast, hadn't she? And yet the heaviness remained, the sense that all was long since lost or horribly twisted, turned to uselessness and ruin in his hands.

They first found out about Josie when she was three and a half. She had brain damage and needed to be put away was what the doctors told them.

They'd had other setbacks, sure, but this was different, sudden. It was like his old man deserting them and him the only son, sixteen; like his mother dying later; like his first wife cheating on him; like the colored moving in; like old man Manville retiring and Curtis taking over, threatening to fire him; like disrespect from his sons; like Frank in the war; like his own needs betraying him: like all those things, but worse, and all at once. He wished she hadn't been born; he couldn't stand to hear or see, or have her in the room. But then he'd go and pick her up and hold her, raging: she was his.

When she was four, they'd sent her away. But six months later, they got her back. The doctors at Belmont said she wasn't retarded, just "emotionally disturbed," which meant she could grow out of it. "Something mental" they could work with, overcome. At first she was quieter, no tantrums, ate well, gained weight; but then she started slipping back, and the promise of those first few weeks just made it harder than before. She was banging her head, bed wetting, tipping over furniture, running away, refusing to obey. He couldn't touch her, but Paula did, frantic sometimes, spanking, hitting; he'd have to tell Paula, calm down; then other times, he'd just lamely let it go. One day he came home, and Paula had told him in tears that she'd tied Josie in a chair, but Josie had wriggled free, now wasn't that proof how clever she was? A few months later Paula called up Belmont, but the bed they'd held was gone, and when she looked for some place else, some nursery school or something, she found nothing.

That had been his own worst time: smashed fenders, absent on the job, blackouts, bitches, nights away from home, money thrown away. Victor was gone, drafted, in Kansas, but Frank was home with a scholarship to St. Joe's, and Dom was a senior in high school, both of them working, bringing money home; they had turned on him, finally, and told Paula she should leave him, tell him get out. He was the one wrecking the family; he was making Josie sick. But still Paula had stuck by him; one year, two, kept fighting with him, pleading, until he'd forced her to a choice. If he refused to help himself, then she had to quit him for their sake.

He had nothing else.

She had to take him back. He'd do anything, face anything. Despite the boys, somehow she had taken him back. From then on Josie was his chance to prove himself. They'd never put her away again, not now. He had to find out more, ask questions, go back to that center, join a parents' group. They had to fix her teeth; if one dentist refused, then he had to find another. He studied over articles, listened to the doctor, went to meetings, lectures. He spent his free time with Josie, playing, going for walks, focusing on what things she could do: learn a new word, or say or understand more complicated sentences, obey commands, brush teeth, dress herself. They both kept working with her. In time, Paula grew to trust him again, and to depend on him, and Josie was his way of feeling safe with her. It was just the three of them alone: Frank was out of college, married, working for the FBI; Dom's asthma got him out of the National Guard and he had a good job and an apartment of his own; Victor they didn't hear from—he was bumming somewhere around Las Vegas, then LA. The last five years had been like that: Paula, him and Josie.

"Hey, let's go outside, huh? Let's go for a walk."

He found her shoes in the kitchen, and helped her to tie them.

Outside the day was hot and bright: grass bright, trees, gables of houses, sun high, clouds bunched, drifting, white on blue. She held tight to his hand, and in her other hand she gripped the scrap of paper he had found her. To the left, next door, Leavitt was hammering; to the right they heard barking, saw kids on bikes weaving down the street. He was curious about Leavitt, but Josie tugged him towards the street, full of purpose: "Walk! Go walk! Hee-ah!"

"Okay, wait a second." He stopped at the car. "Gotta get my hat."

"Hee-ah!" she insisted, tugging.

He opened the door—musty and sour inside—reached, got it off the back seat, put it on. "There we go. Okay."

The same kids came riding back: a girl, three boys, the dog chasing with them; they swept on past, without a special look or notice. Except the biggest boy wheeled around at the corner and came coasting back, pulled up beside them. "Hiya, Josie!"

"Hey, Jimmy!" The boy waved the other kids off; they waited half way down the next block.

Josie grinned and waved her paper at him. "Huh-oh!"

"How are you?"

"My Daa-ee."

He was thirteen, fourteen, one of the Phelps kids from around the corner. "My name's Jimmy, remember?"

"Jim-my!" she repeated, with glowing relish. "You name's Jim-my!"

"I was talking to Mrs. Miscello, uh, a couple days ago," he explained. "She told me some of the kids were wising off, but I fixed them. So you just tell her Jimmy says it's all okay. Those kids won't bother her no more. But if they do, you let me know, cause I'll take care of them."

Something in him tightened: what kids? what wising off? But he held it back: "Yeah, I'll tell her. Thanks." Then he softened, grimaced, wanting to keep friendly; "You're the key man on the block, huh?" Meanwhile he pulled Josie back, to keep her from fawning on the kid or fooling with the bike.

"Well, I'm older. I understand better than they do."

"Yeah, well, thanks. You're a good kid—Josie, shush!—Appreciate it."

"That's okay. Tell Mrs. Miscello I say hi. Bye, Josie. What you got there? Paper?"

She held it out.

"Yeah, she feels better when she's got something like that with her when she walks."

Jimmy gave an understanding, solemn nod. "Well, I gotta go. Nice talking with you. So long, Josie! See you later."

He waved and wheeled away, standing up and pumping hard.

"Bye!"

"C'mon." He frowned and sighed, bothered. They walked down to the corner, turned left. Some neighbors were out, nameless to him but familiar. One guy had his hood up, motor idling, working on his car. Someone practiced a trumpet. A woman was hanging wash, another sweeping the sidewalk. Some of the people were okay, saying hi, or nodding, smiling; others gave them saddened or offended looks. The guy in that brick house across the street had come up to him once, red faced: "Why don't you keep that kid indoors?"

"It's a free street, ain't it?" he'd let him know.

But mostly people just ignored them, let them pass.

Farther down, some kids were playing stickball in the street. As he and Josie got closer, then walked past, Josie stared and strained towards them. "Hey, shush!" he told her. "C'mon." The kids, who where eight or nine, kept playing, doubly serious, intent, more scared of him than of her. Up the next street, which was quieter; back on their street, then, home stretch. Past the Maleks, Baltzlys, DeCannios, Mrs. Carzo watering her lawn, Hanson's. He walked slowly, jealously admiring Leavitt's new Pontiac, which was parked out front. He heard the hammering and stopped at Leavitt's driveway, with Josie cringing close and wincing from the hammer blows.

Leavitt was a Camden cop, in his forties, gray haired, skinny, tall. They'd talked about Frank a couple times. His kid was on the local j.v. teams. A six-foot stockade fence—Leavitt's—separated their yards. He was building some kind of platform, it looked like, up on sawhorses, shirt off, oblivious.

"Hey, Leavitt!" he called.

Leavitt looked up, nodded, finished driving in his nail; put the hammer down and wiped his arm across his face. "Miscello."

They came on in. "Stinking hot, huh?"

"Yeah." He bent down, picked up a beer and took a swig.

"What you building?"

"This? Backboard for the kid. Got him a basket for his birthday—over there. Supposed to help me with it, but he's off caddying, y'know?"

"Jesus, this heat?"

"Yeah, he's a workhorse, that kid." He took another swig.

"Where are you putting it?" He glanced around the neatly kept yard, cut grass, trimmed bushes, brand new fixtures on the house.

"Garage, over the door there."

"Pretty good." Inwardly he cursed the thought of shouts, a basketball thwacking right outside his bedroom windows. "Hey, Josie, watch it! That's sharp!" She'd picked up a two-penny nail. He squatted down: "C'mon, give it to me. Here, don't you want your paper?" He got the nail away, tossed it, then pulled her close and kissed her hair.

"How's she doing?"

"We just been walking, haven't we, sweety? Just had a big walk?"

"Weah walk-ing!" she told Leavitt, who nodded stiffly with a twisted grin.

"How's the wife?"

"Okay." He held her closer.

"Yeah, well, I guess I gotta finish this," Leavitt said, putting down his beer.

He stood up, filling his chest, and took her hand. "We better be getting back too, huh, Josie?"

"Good seeing you," Leavitt said.

"Yeah, see you."

On their way out, the hammering began again. Around the fence, into their yard: he saw that their bedroom windows and shades were down. "Hey, sweety," he said on sudden impulse as they turned the back corner, "How about a swim? Want to go swimming?"

"Swim!" She brightened up. "I like swim!"

"Sure. And you can help me fill the pool. But let's go get our bathing suits first and then go change, okay?"

The pool was blue, inflated plastic ribs with a yellow bottom, six feet in diameter, two feet deep. It had cost him forty bucks. She hunkered down beside it, drank from her coke, paddled one hand in the water, tentative, watching him and chortling, while he put their towels and his beer down on the picnic table and stripped off his shirt. "Okay, now, stand back. Wait a minute." He stepped in and picked up the floating toys, handing each one to her. "We're gonna change the water, huh? It's all dirty, isn't it? Okay, stand back." He stepped out and lifted up the sagging bulk, spilling. "Hyeee-ha-ahah!" she shrieked, jumping around. "Watch out, now!" He didn't want to drown his grass, so he dragged it off, sloshing, into the dirt by the fence. As he struggled with it and poured out the rest, she was there and getting muddy, shoes wet—what the hell. He dragged it back and flopped it on a new spot. "Okay, go get the hose," he said. He watched her leaning, straining, drawing the hose towards him from under the kitchen window. "Watch the snags!" He went to help, pulling and shaking it behind her, while she went on, determined, to the pool. "Hey, good!" Taking it from her, he twisted and shook it to free the loops. "Okay, now go turn it on—but easy now, like I tell you now!"

She ran back and crouched by the spigot, watching for approval. "That's it. Turn the handle. Gentle!" The hose bucked, spurted, and shot a stream that splattered the pool, his legs and feet, then lifted to a pluming arc across the yard. He threw it down, dodging the spray as it hissed, tossed, and twisted in the grass, and ran towards her: "Turn it off! No, turn it off!"

But she was grinning, stubborn. "Here!" He pushed her back, heart pounding, one twist, two, three. Can't do nothing. Instantly regretted: no! "Uhh!" And then: "Uh, uh. . . ." Her face was contorted, her body clenched: "Uhhhhhhh!"

"It's okay! I didn't . . . shh!"

She hit his hand away, gasping for air: "Uhhhhhhh!"

He gripped his fists, glanced at the door, the street, tingling with its rawness. Then he caught himself; took it, let it happen—even Paula if she came. "It's okay, okay, sweety."

He turned the spigot gently, gritted his teeth; stood up. "Shh, okay. Let's go fill the pool. C'mon." He took her hand, despite her struggling; led her—leaning back and bawling still, but not so loudly now or ferocious—lifted her up, sat her down on the wet grass, took her shoes off, tossed them . "Let's wash you off now." He reached for the hose, ran it up and down her legs, over her feet, rubbing the mud off, so the howls subsided into sobs and snuffles. "Here, now you do me. Do me." He offered her the hose, helped her to hold it and to run it over his shins, his feet. "Hey! Feels good!" She frowned and pouted, grudgingly involved. "Feels good, doesn't it? Okay, let's go."

He lifted her up—heavy, clumsy—into the pool, and gave her the hose, which she held running in her lap. "Where're the toys? Here go!" He gathered them up, stepped in, dropped them, sat down across from her, arms on his knees, legs spread. The plastic was hot, so he wet it down. Then slowly the pool began to fill, water creeping underneath. "Hey, look at the water!" He splashed in it, rubbed it on his arms, neck, chest. She splashed too, hunched over. "That's it, wet your shoulders!"

"Hyuh!"

"It's filling up, huh? It's gonna get all the way up to here." He glanced at the house—still no sign of Paula; everything would be okay. Josie wriggled forward and started wetting and rubbing his ankle, prying at his foot, his toes, which he raised and wiggled for her. "C'mere," he said, moving his legs, reaching and pulling her closer; heaved, so she settled alongside him; hugged her wetly. "You're my sweety," he said, and gave her a kiss.

The toys began to stir; the hose went under, silent. "Hey, how about the ball?" While they played, the water grew less shallow, rose—to her waist, her stomach—and she swung her arms, jumped up and splashed.

"Okay, show me how you kick." He got out, dripping, and went around to hold her by the armpits to the rim, while stretching out, she began her plunging kick. "Good! Go on! Boy, you got a kick!"

Then the pool was full. He pulled out the hose. "Wait a second, I'll go shut this off." He did, came back, stopped for his beer, which was warm. Went over and stepped in. They played some more: excited, strenuous play at first, then calmer; they talked—he quizzed her on the days of the week, the months, the holidays. Soon she was happy to play by herself, pushing the boat and babbling. Later she got out and strayed off to the sandbox, keeping close, brought back a bucket and doll; went off again, brought back a ball, climbed in, floated things around him, poured water, played with his feet, his hand.

He felt deeply calm, and lulled, his arms hooked over the yielding rim, slouched down, knees bent and turned to give her room, water lapping to his chest, hot sun beating down. He stared off at clouds and at nodding branches, with dappled, shifting greens. He was free to think, even as he listened to her, and farther off, to Leavitt's hammering, which had started again, and to the neighborhood's sounds around them: what did Paula want? What did she need? He knew, and let his knowing come.

Josie was in bed. They'd finished dinner.

"Hey, wait." He cleared his throat. "I want to talk to you, okay?"

"I'm going to the bathroom."

He got up and turned off the TV, feeling weak and fluttery, wiped his neck, sat down, waited. A car passed outside. The toilet flushed, door opened; she didn't come, and then she did. He turned to look, followed with his eyes as she passed. She hesitated, finally turned and sat down on the couch. They waited: him watching her, her scowling down, then off in space, blinking, hands limp in her lap.

"I called Frank," she said, glancing at him. "They're coming over tomorrow." She shook her head, and gripped her cheek, breathing into her palm; then dropped her hand. "I don't know, I don't." She shook with little spasms, eyes clenched; then grunted, sighed, and took her glasses off, and wiped the tears.

"Why drag them in?" he asked plaintively.

"Because they're all I have."

He said nothing, head bowed.

"Oh, sure, you're sorry aren't you? You're always sorry. But you couldn't be and do this to me. It's the same as it's always been: when things get tough, you quit. You don't have the stomach for us anymore. Don't you think I see? It doesn't take some trash calling; or staying out all night, or slapping me around. You walked out months ago. You've just been sleeping here and eating, putting in your time. And I'm supposed to keep on like nothing's wrong. Don't bother you. Take care of everything myself. Well, it so happens I can't. I'm sick. I need you and you only hate me for it. Thirty years of sticking with you, swallowing my pride, always giving you another chance, hoping you still loved us and you wanted to make good. But you just throw it in my face. There's nothing left. I don't have the strength, or time, and you're not worth it. I've got enough, without you too!"

Her voice cracked, ending in a sob. He kept watching, speechless and abashed, while she sat hunched and rigid, turned away, squeezing her face in her hand, and the silence grew more terrible, and the sadness, which he'd thought he'd known, more strange and overwhelming. He didn't know how to answer, but he couldn't let it go on.

"What are you going to do?" he asked softly, gravely.

"I can't stay with you."

He frowned. "Well, what about Josie? What about you? I know you got every right to want nothing more to do with me. But what if I got out? How are you going to make out alone? Or you're going to leave, then where're you going to go? Frank and Nancy don't have room; Josie's got to go to school."

"You should have thought of that before."

"Will you listen? Please? Sure, I should have." Now his voice shook, his eyes stung and watered. "But I couldn't. Want to know why? Because there's nothing I can do. It's sitting here and knowing. And seeing Josie. It isn't I don't love you. It's just I can't stand this is happening. I want to hit at something, fight, except there's nothing there. It just keeps building up until I don't know what I'm doing, I got to get away. Because it's like we never counted, never even had a chance." He paused. "I been wrong, I know that. But see. I mean, look, last night: I was miles away. I was up the turnpike, parked behind a Howard Johnson's with a pint. Woke up filthy, stinking, don't know where I am. I realize, okay? This is crazy. I got my home, my family. I'm throwing everything away—me, see, I'm the one doing this. I can't stand I'm losing you, so I'm going to throw it all away. And that's what's crazy. That's what's no good. See what I'm saying? I got to be with you, work things out. Because it's us, it's loving you and Josie. We're what counts, and nothing's going to break us, if we don't let it. We got to think what's best, and talk it over, say how we feel; and that's what I come back here for. Cause you're my life."

But she kept staring down, hopeless, silent, slumped over her folded arms, as if she hadn't been listening, or couldn't believe him, or it made no difference anyhow. Again he felt no anger, only hurt and pity for both of them.

"Do you see what I'm saying? No sense talking about leaving. There's no reason. That's quitting too. I mean, I cracked, sure, but that's all over now. I'll be okay. I want to be there, helping, taking care of you, seeing Josie's going to be okay. I want you so you can rest, and have it like you want it. Can't you believe me? What else is there?"

"I don't know."

He got up and paced and turned in front of her, fists clenched, struggling for more words, as if for air. But then he stopped and looked. He was lost and she was lost. There wasn't anymore.

He sat down beside her. Waited. "Please," he pleaded. She turned to him, hollow-eyed, like a stranger in her grief. He reached up and put his arm around her shoulders, drew her closer, though she stiffened and turned her face, still refusing as she yielded. And he held her, pressing her head, her hair, against his jaw, squeezing the softness of her shoulder, numbly swaying.

"You don't want me leaving. Nothing's changed. We'll work something out. I promised you, didn't I? I said I'd never let you down, and I'm not. And if it'd do you any good, I'd go, but you know that's no good. You need me here, like I need you, and Josie needs me, and we got to be together. You've given everything. And now it's me. I know I hurt you, but you got to trust me, I'm going to keep on because I got to, because I love you and I always loved you. I love Josie and the boys. They're my life. It's more than promises."

His voice trailed off, and he held her, silent; and when it almost got to be too much, she gradually relented. Her weight shifted and settled against him, and her hand was on his arm, and their breathing rose and fell; and then she turned and took his shoulder, laid her head against his chest, holding him as he held her, the moment fathomless, impersonal; he stroked her hair, and they had nothing certain but each other, and what was gone was irreclaimable and what was wrong past making up, but they were closer now than lovers in their deep embrace. They stayed like that, until finally she stirred and pushed away, sat up, looked at him, and simply said: "I'm tired. I want to go to bed."

"Want me to come?"

"No, I'm going to take a bath, and it's early. I'm tired, that's all. You stay here."

"Okay," he said gently, careful not to tax her. "I'll close up and be in later."

He sat thinking after she'd gone.

Then down the hall, and later, in bed, with her breathing harsh and regular beside him, he sat wide-eyed, upright, shoulders on the back board, head against the wall. His mind kept churning, searching, taking stock. Frank would come tomorrow and they'd talk. Maybe Nancy and the baby could stop by more often. He'd call Dom too, and maybe Victor would come back and they could patch it up. They'd hire a nurse. And him, he had to find out more the little things, come right home, do the shopping for them, clean up, cook a meal, look after Josie, take it off her shoulders. He had to show her he was willing, and it wasn't just for duty, but he meant it and it cost his life. He swallowed, turned and watched her sleeping, and while his heart distended with its vows, trusting, doubting, as brave in tenderness as crushed and lost, and while his loneliness too seemed like a proof and strength: he turned away; his eyes filled. Soundlessly, he wept.

Ball Game

"Look, Anna Maye," Mary Lloyd offered suddenly, "why don't you come with us this weekend? Are you doing anything?"

Confused and alert, she replied no, nothing. Mary Lloyd said they had tickets to the ball game, a twilight doubleheader. She and her husband, Tom, and Tom's brother, Ralph (who was coming in from out of town): they could all go together and have a swell time.

Immediately doubts raced through her mind. She hurriedly straightened the samples she'd been shellacking, glanced out at the girls waving goodbye as they passed her booth. Howard and Mary, what would they think? What about having a man pushed at her like this—also the humiliation of it, coming from Mary Lloyd? But Mary Lloyd knew her too well, and waved aside all indecision: "Oh, come on," she insisted in a gentle, friendly way, "what's the problem? This Ralph is a regular guy."

Before, when there had been these chances, she had always been afraid of the trouble her father would make: Where are you going? Where have you been? What about Mary? What about me? People depend on you. You got no business fooling around. You don't know nothing about life. Get the romance out of your head. You're not going out to no bars and no movies and back seats of cars. Sneaking around. How did you meet this jerk? Your place is here. You don't see me running around, do you? No! I work. I bring money to this house. I respect your mother's memory. Now you stay here where you belong and get these ideas out of your head. Meanwhile Mary, teenaged and attractive, would jeer at her, for Mary was the one he let go out, do anything she pleased.

Also men had hurt her. The boys at school were cruel.

She knew that she was bland and overweight and dull; that what was beautiful in her was locked away like a tiny maiden, far, far away in a tower, too difficult to find or reach. No one but herself could know about the maiden or her worth, and even if they did, no one could ever hope to reach her. She must face her lot, grateful for her family and her work. Life was rich within these bounds, and other longings dangerous.

She accepted Mary Lloyd's invitation.

Tom was a quiet, patient, gray-haired man, but balding, a plumber by trade. He and Mary Lloyd had three children (Betty, the oldest, was home babysitting for them). She picked up her purse and started out as soon as their station wagon appeared. Mary Lloyd waved. Tom honked, and a short, husky man, younger than Tom, opened the back door and came around to greet her at the walk. "I'm Ralph. You're Anna Maye," he announced. "Been hearing all about you. C'mon. We're late. Some day, huh? We're having a time. We got some chicken; you eat yet?"

"Yes. Mary Lloyd said—"

Removing the cigar from his mouth, he stepped closer and took her elbow with his free hand. "C'mon." His hair, receding high on a sloping forehead, was crew-cut and gray; his face was coarse and round, with a short, thick neck and double chin. He wore a sport shirt with palm trees on it, open at the neck.

"Hello, there," she said to Tom. Ralph held the rear door open for her to climb in, went around and got in the other side. Mary Lloyd was wearing slacks and a faded pink blouse. Sunlight glared off the hood and in the windows. Tom wore a felt hat tipped back, one arm crooked out the window and the other resting heavily along the top of the seat; he turned and smiled back at her. He looked tired.

"Well, we thought we'd never get here," said Mary Lloyd. "We got lost and we got a ticket."

"Some dumb cop," said Tom.

"Some dumb driver," Ralph corrected him, blowing out a puff from his cigar. "You should see this guy."

"You know what you can do."

"Running stop signs."

"Don't mind them," said Mary Lloyd. "That dress is sweet. You look so fresh; I like your hair like that too."

Ralph reached over the front seat and held up a chicken leg. "She already ate." He sat back, stuffed his cigar in the ashtray, and began to eat.

"We better get started," said Tom.

"Well, nobody's stopping us."

"Ralph tends bar," Mary Lloyd explained as they pulled away.

"Oh, really?"

"Yeah, I like it. It's this club, actually. Ever been to Scranton? Called The Empire. Got entertainment and bands." He waved his chicken leg. "We get a crowd: miners, farmers, businessmen, all kinds. Mafia, you name it. What I like, everybody's friendly, you know. And it's different. I worked lots of places before, you know, been all over, tried lots of things. But I like this. Like the people and the action, and talking to the people. Course some people don't think tending bar is much of anything, no matter what kind of place. Tom there, you know, he keeps asking me, when you gonna settle down and get a decent job? Know what I tell 'em? Same thing I tell my Mom. I say look, bartending's a profession. That's right. You need a talent for it, you need experience and sensitivity. It's not just pouring drinks and mopping up. Those people come in to be happy, to talk, meet folks, and they all got some kind of problems. So what you got to do, you got to keep it friendly, help them to relax, cheer them up, or trouble-makers, calm them down. But it's that personal touch, see—that's what makes the difference."

"He means it. He's very serious about his job," Mary Lloyd commented. Tom said nothing, intent on driving.

"That's right. That's my work. I think I do it pretty well too; least that's what the boss says. I run the main bar now. What I'm looking for, someday he'll make me manager." Ralph took up his cigar again, dropped the chicken leg, and scratched his neck.

"I don't go in bars," she said.

He looked at her closely: "Well, no. I didn't think you did. Why should you? You look like the home type to me—am I right?"

"I work," she replied, clutching her purse in her lap.

"That's what I heard. You and Mary Lloyd run everything? She's the upstairs, you're the downstairs, right?" Before she could answer, he jumped forward, crowding against her, and snapped the brim of Tom's hat with his forefinger. "Hey, turn that up! I like that." Tom stiffened. Ralph bounced back and started bellowing over the radio tune: "Hit the road, Phils, and don't you come back no more, no more. . . ." Tom reached over and poked the dial. "Hey! What's the matter?"

Mary Lloyd glared at both of them. "Excuse us, Anna Maye. These two have been guzzling like fish. Quiet, Ralph."

"Quiet, Ralph," Ralph mimicked. And then to Tom: "Listen, buddio, those Phillies ain't got a chance. We're going to get them out, one, two, three."

"Well, they got Devlin and Radinsky; they'll shut your trap!"

"Here they go," said Mary Lloyd, apologetically. Tom shifted down and stopped for a light, then turned around:

"You want to put your money where your mouth is?"

"You want to put your mouth where my money is?"

"See this is an important game," Mary Lloyd explained. "The Finches are in second place and they need to win, so they can get the Tigers out. But the Phillies have a four game streak going, and if they beat the Finches, that's all for Dayton, because they'll never catch the Tigers then. It's pretty complicated."

"I see," said Anna Maye.

"So you root with me, see?" Ralph urged, nudging her. "Nobody in their right mind cares about no goddamn Phillies, or no goddamn

Devlin or Radinsky. They got nothing at stake. Why, they don't even rate the gate from this game."

"Three brothers," said Tom loudly. "This one never grew up." Ralph thumbed his nose at the mirror.

"What time is it?" Tom asked Mary Lloyd, ignoring him.

"Aghh!" Ralph waved his hand and looked disgusted, rolling his eyes and nodding in their direction. He shook his head. "So what about this candy place?" he began again. "You been doing this kind of thing very long?" He glanced up front, as if to show he could care less.

"Oh, yes. I've been with Manville's, why, for almost twenty years," she answered, blushing.

"What? C'mon."

"I have. I started just after school."

"She's an old-timer," Mary Lloyd put in.

"Really like it, huh? Well, that's interesting now. I mean, take me, for instance. I could never stick to anything. Factories, clerking, farm work, the Army: I tried everything. Drove a cab, laid bricks. Worked gas stations. I even tried selling. I had itchy feet, you might say. Never stayed more than a year a two at anything, except the service. Had nine years of that, traveled all over. But you get tired, know what I mean? You sow your wild oats; then you come home."

"Oh, then you're from Scranton?"

"That's right. Grew up there. Buddies still there. There's my folks—my Mom and Dad—there's my other brother—Danny's—wife and kids—he got killed—plus all kinds of cousins and all. A man needs responsibility. I'm thirty-eight years old. I tried living other places, but it just didn't work. I didn't belong. I like to be where people know me, know my people, I know them. You come back to your roots, I guess. That's my story, mostly." He was thoughtful for a moment: "Course it's different for a woman."

"Okay. We're here," Tom announced, swinging into a space.

Ralph looked around: "What do you mean, here? What's this? What are you stopping for?"

"We're taking the trolley."

"Trolley? Now what the hell. Ain't we got a car?"

"We got a car; we also got a place to park. I'm not bucking any traffic in there looking for spaces. We take the trolley—pfft!—goes right in. Nothing to it."

"There'll be spaces."

"Come on, Ralph," said Mary Lloyd, hurriedly gathering up some things from the front seat and getting out. Tom got out too and locked his door, then opened the back door for her. "C'mon," he said again. "We've done it this way before. Saves time and trouble. Goes right in."

She glanced at Ralph beside her, then started to get out.

"Okay, buddy," said Ralph. "It's your show. I just follow orders."

"Take this then," said Mary Lloyd, as he got out.

"You got my glasses?" Tom asked, locking up.

"In my purse."

"Radio?"

"Ralph has it."

The sun was bright and hot, scorching concrete, brick and tar, and flashing off of passing traffic. They waited on benches in the shelter. A car came down the line from the wrong direction, stopped and let off two women, then a boy with a bathing suit. Tom paced beside the tracks, fists clenched. Ralph fiddled with the radio: "What do you think of this crowd, Shelley?" an excited voice demanded, with the murmur of a large crowd in the background.

"Hey, listen here! They got the goddamn pre-game commentary on already, for chrissake."

He nagged Tom to drive on in, the hell with parking: their tickets were general admission, right? They wanted any kind of seats, they better get there fast. Meanwhile the radio clamored on about Chandler, who would be a threat today, and Radinsky, the starting pitcher: best on the club, nine wins this year, control good, fast ball. Mary Lloyd was tapping her foot, glaring at them:

"We certainly have had a time of it," she complained. "The kids first, then these two. Ralph came down late last night, so we stayed up all hours drinking beer and talking Finches this, and Phillies that. And you know what my day was yesterday, what with that breakdown on the polybag machine and Mr. Manville bawling me out when it was Bill O'Neill's fault if it was anybody's. I was mad enough to spit! Did Bill O'Neill say anything to you? Well, never mind. That's just a lot of bother anyway." She reached over and pressed her hand, looking purposeful and smiling: "Listen, I want you to just relax now and enjoy yourself. Don't let these two make you nervous. We'll get in there all right and a few minutes one way or another isn't going to make a bit of difference. You'll be glad you came. You'll see."

At last their trolley came: one car, half-full. They took straw seats beside the door and sat preoccupied and silent, staring at the passing street. There were stops and starts and more and more people getting on, and then they were getting off. and there was a mob— everyone in twos and threes, bunches—overflowing the sidewalks and crowding the streets, bustling towards various gates of the huge walled stadium. So many people, intent and hurrying, excited her. The men bulled forward together, while she and Mary Lloyd hurried after.

"C'mon. This way!" Tom called.

He knew just what to do and where to go. Everywhere around them the crowd murmured, vendors shouted, children tooted. Great dark walls of the stadium towered overhead, vaulted like a night-mare. Some people crowded into lines, still hoping to buy tickets, but the booths were closed: sold out. She felt a thrill of privilege as they shouldered through the ticket line and inside the special gate, into the shadowy girded and fenced area, where everyone was clumped and milling together, confused, asking the way of park attendants. She struggled to keep up. Then they were climbing endless concrete stairs up into the stands, and there was the great cheer and roar of the crowd outside. "Hurry up! They started!" When they came out into daylight, it was as if she'd never seen a crowd before, or a sta-dium, or the vivid green of a ball field: she simply wondered, breath-less, blinking at the sight.

They worked their way up through a mass of people almost to the top of the bleachers, in the direct afternoon sunlight. The men went together, while Mary Lloyd kept turning to see if she was com-ing and reaching out impatiently for her hand: "C'mon. C'mon! You with us?" There was so much commotion, the roar and murmur, shouts and razzing horns and blaring radios. And all these people watching her. She felt self-conscious, on display. She was relieved when they finally found some seats. But even then Tom wasn't satisfied; he wanted to move a whole section further over to where they could get seats with arm and back rests instead of just a hard bench. But Ralph said, "Naw, we can't get nothing over there," and Mary Lloyd agreed, so they sat down finally and she felt secure.

"Any score yet?" Tom asked people behind them.

"Devlin just drove in a run!"

"One, nothing!" Tom informed them as they got settled, Ralph to her right, then Mary Lloyd, then Tom, with people crowded close in front, behind and to her left. Devlin was on second; Schatz at bat. She saw the players: outfielders near them and farther in the distance, dwindling in perspective, the infield and the batter, who swung: a foul tip popped up high into the net behind home plate, rolled slowly down as the crowd went: "Whoooo-up!"

"We should have brought a beach umbrella," said Mary Lloyd. "It's baking out here!"

"Watch this guy!" urged Tom. A hit! The crowd rose, cheering; the ball was rising towards them, closer, closer—a home run, maybe— but it dropped out of sight below them; the crowd groaned; the announcer said the fielder had caught it. She saw it shoot back towards the infield, and players started running everywhere, changing places. Ralph relaxed.

"Ralph," she said, touching his arm, "now which ones are the Finches, and which are the Phillies?"

"Huh? Oh." He took out a fresh cigar and prepared to light it. "The Phils were just at bat, see, with the red? And the Finches— they're the ones with blue, okay? They're up now."

Grown men were sitting everywhere without their shirts on: Ralph began unbuttoning his. Mary Lloyd teased: "Oh, lord, look at Tarzan. What about you, Tom?" Tom said nothing. Ralph squirmed out of his shirt; he was flabby, blemished, and hairier, even, than Howard, with tufts of brown hair on his back and shoulders. "Hairy means you're gonna be rich," he confided, puffing his cigar, "but I'm still waiting, you know? Hey, you bring the oil?" he asked Mary Lloyd, who searched in her bag, pulled a little bottle out, and called across to her as she handed it to him: "You better use that too. I'm serious. On your face and arms and neck, you'll be sorry otherwise!"

The sun was burning, dazzling, a forceful pressure beating down, making her head light and her clothes hot; she squinted up into it, perspiring, trickles down her back and front and itching in her hair.

"Okay. Here we go." They were playing ball. "That's Myers up now. C'mon baby! C'mon, c'mon, you can do better'n that. At's it!" Ralph shouted, as he rubbed the oil—which had a pleasant, tangy smell—on his arms and shoulders. He put the bottle into her hands: "Hey, rub some on my back, will ya?—Yeah, frozen rope! C'mon!" He was on his feet, conspicuous in this section of the stands, and drawing angry stares. He sat back down, offered her his back again—calling something tauntingly at Tom. She looked at the bottle, then poured some oil into her palm and tentatively reached up and touched him, then began to rub, slowly, shyly, then more and more in earnest.

"Good," he said. "Good. Thanks." She did her own face then and neck, and the creases of her arms, and handed it across to Mary Lloyd.

She smiled to herself, feeling dazed and lulled, basking. She didn't mind that the stands were filthy, with papers and ice-cream, chewing gum, coke containers, cigarette and cigar butts and their ground-in remains. She didn't mind the heat, the sweat, nor the closeness of the people, nor the talk, nor the smells. She felt queerly comfortable and reassured, impressed.

Ralph was up again, cheering: the Finches had another single; two men on. Next came a pop-up, which the fielder caught; Ralph groaned, slapping his fist, as the crowd cheered. Then a single, but the man was out at third. Then what? Strike one; pitch—crack!— the ball rose high and higher, carrying into the stands. The first two men raced in to score; the last came trotting leisurely behind. Ralph went wild: the score was three to one! He shook her by the shoulder and called to Tom: "That's it! We did it! We're on our way, buddio!"

"Yah, siddown!" someone called behind him.

"Lefferts! Lefferts! Whattaya think of that! How about that?" He nudged her, sitting down. "How about that? Ever see anything like that? Having a good time, huh?" His face was flushed and eager, with round, shining eyes.

The next man up struck out; the teams changed places.

So inning after inning passed: two hours. Ralph, confident of winning, was as pleased and talkative as someone after a good meal, but Tom and Mary Lloyd refused to listen to him, concentrating on the game and drawing away, stonily, from his loud bragging and rejoicing. The score was five to one: Finches. The crowd stamped and hooted and clapped, but each time the Phillies came to bat, they struck out, hit foul balls, flied out or were thrown out, and when their turn came to field, they couldn't catch the balls the Finches hit, or dropped them, or couldn't throw them to the base in time; also they kept stopping the game to have conferences or to bring in new pitchers. Meanwhile their seats grew hard; the sun was lower, weaker, but glaring in her eyes; sea gulls looped and soared and now and then an airplane passed, still higher, bearing west. A great shadow engulfed one whole side of the stadium and crept across the infield.

"You got to be a sport, see?" Ralph was saying in a low voice to her ear. "Tom there, now, he's a lousy loser, a real sorehead." He crossed his leg and started scratching the ankle. "I mean, you got to have a sense of humor. But him, oh, no, he's going take it personal. You oughta see him lose at cards. You know, like his life's at stake, and you're some kind of enemy? Well, hell, I don't care he's my brother or what; you lose, you blame yourself, you don't blame the guy that wins. We were kids, you know . . . hey. . . ." All down the rows faces were turning to look up; Ralph looked and she did too several times before they saw him: "How about that guy?" Just over the park wall, she saw the tip of a billboard—like the bow of an ocean liner—and in the bow was a man with binoculars, watching the game for free. "How did he get up here? Mary Lloyd! Hey. . . ." He dismissed them: "Soreheads." And then: "See, Tom and me, we're different. He's got this thing, like he's the family pride and I'm the bum?"

She frowned: "Is it him that thinks that way, or you?"

"He's . . . what?" He sat up, eyeing her narrowly: "Wait a minute. Whatta you mean?" He glanced at Mary Lloyd and Tom.

"Nothing. I'm sorry; it's not my business, Ralph."

"What did she tell you? She's been saying things to you, hadn't she? What kind of things?"

"Nothing. Not a word. I just know the way you sound, that's all."

"Yeah, well, let me tell you this. I'm no prize, but I'm happy with my life and that's what counts. I live the way I live because I like it. Now Tom, he's different. He's your good, hardworking family man, married before he was twenty, got a trade, three kids, mortgage on the house, payments on the car. Stuck with it too, for twenty-five years. I respect him for it; don't get me wrong. But me? No. . . . I couldn't take a life like that. I'm just not the type. I like to move around, and see what's what, and try things out. I been overseas in Berlin, Germany; I been in every state but five or six—ask me some capitals. Why, I've had experiences, believe me, I wouldn't trade them for a family. I mean that. But my folks, see, and Tom, they got their minds made up I'm no account. I go home and all I hear about is Tom."

Without warning, the Phillies' hit that the whole crowd had been tensely willing, stamping, hooting and clapping for, miraculously happened. Tom, Mary Lloyd, the whole stadium leapt to their feet. Strangers were congratulating and hugging each other. She kept her seat beside Ralph, who sat stunned, affronted, refusing to get up and muttering: "So they got a hit, big deal! Sit down! Look at these jokers. What do they think they can do, bottom of the ninth?" But the Phillies, catching the crowd's enthusiasm, continued to rally with a series of base hits on Finch errors, with stolen bases, and with two home runs. The stands kept shrieking unrelieved. Ralph, ponderously, stood up to watch. Tom and Mary Lloyd were jumping up and down and hugging and shouting, and suddenly—as the tying run came in—Tom reached around to Ralph (who was shaking his head, gripping his fists) and punched him in the shoulder: "Hey, how about that; how about that one, buddio? Hah!" Ralph punched him back, tight-lipped and furious. Tom hit him again; they were both in tempers, about to jump for each other, but Mary Lloyd got between them and drew Tom aside, who kept on cheering wildly, as if he didn't know what he had done.

Ralph remained crouched and rigid, red as a beet, in the midst of all this cheering. She wasn't sure what to do, but feeling intensely embarrassed, she reached out and touched his arm. He jerked around, glaring; knocked her hand away. But seeming to recognize her, he grew confused, blinked, and shook his head—then sat down, finally, fuming. She sat down beside him. "It's all right, Ralph," she ventured.

Hunched over, he kept rubbing his face. "Look," he said, "Just let me alone, okay?"

Then he sat up and busied himself with putting on his shirt, buttoning up the front and stuffing the shirt tails into his trousers.

Grimly, they watched the game conclude: the winning run, the final out. Cheering subsided around them; some people sat down, others started moving down the aisles; advertisements for beer blared on all the radios.

"I'm not making up nothing to that bastard," Ralph promised.

On the far side of Mary Lloyd, Tom stood stretching, hat off, running his hand through sparse gray hair. He yawned, put his hat back on, sat down:

"Hey, you all want anything? Ice cream, drinks, pop, hot dog? I'm buying. What do you want? Hot dog? What? With everything? Okay, two cokes, grape? Hey," he called to Ralph, "c'mon. Let's go down and get some stuff. I'm buying." Ralph looked off across the crowd, refusing to answer. Tom's face hardened. "Okay, I'll go down alone. Thanks a lot!"

"I'll go," said Mary Lloyd, getting up.

"Naw. You stay here."

They watched him leave, nudging and shuffling and barging his way down to the front of the tier, and then across their section, to the stairs. They were alone. Overhead, on towers, grids of lights were coming on, and below them a maintenance crew was dragging some kind of sweeper around the infield, making everything look smooth and new.

"Fog's coming in," a voice commented behind her.

"Listen, that husband of yours, he can be pretty goddamn hard to take sometimes."

"Sometimes? Next to you, he's the most impossible person I ever hope to meet. . . ." Mary Lloyd was searching in her bag.

"Okay. Okay."

"Okay, nothing, Ralph—Excuse us, Anna Maye—Look, we came out here for a good time, didn't we? I mean, now here I bring my friend, how do you think she feels with you two carrying on like a couple of saps? I mean how about it? You want to leave? Because I think we better if you can't be a little more considerate and decent. You two want to spoil everything, fine. But don't expect us to sit here and suffer through your squabbles. I don't see the point."

"He started it," insisted Ralph.

"I don't care who started it. You promised me. Now why don't you try living up to your promises? Okay? You be nice to our guest here and quit fooling around, picking fights."

Ralph shifted and rocked, grimacing; Mary Lloyd was firm.

"I like the lights," she offered, to break the silence.

"They come on brighter later," Mary Lloyd told her, straining forward, then craning back to speak around him. "Bright as day, in fact. It gets real pretty. But how did you like the game, huh? Pretty exciting? I mean besides for these lugs"—she gave Ralph a push, good-naturedly. "Well, it's cooler anyway. You may want a sweater before we're through. . . . Hey, look!" She pointed out his hat. Tom was working his way back, slowly, starting up the aisle; he had a paper tray laden with hot dogs, cups, and cans of pop; his face looked flushed and sweaty, full of some experience.

Ralph got up without another word, climbed up and over, and sat down on her left. She moved closer to Mary Lloyd; then he moved closer too.

"Oh, man, you wouldn't believe it," Tom said. "You would not believe that down there!" He came edging into their row of seats and sat down next to Mary Lloyd, who helped him with the tray. "Here now. Careful," said Mary Lloyd, handing over a grape for her, a coke for Ralph, then dogs and napkins, which Ralph grudgingly acknowledged. He ate greedily, noisily, without a word for anyone; when he finished, he wiped his hands on his pants.

The second game was underway. The lights shone down through mist and rising smoke, making the grass look blue-green and the players shadowless, unreal. Matches flared like fireflies in the dark mass of the crowd across from her. The Finches were off to an early lead. Ralph leaned over once or twice to whisper: "I would've hauled off and hit him back if Mary Lloyd hadn't gotten in the way!"

and later: "If you hadn't touched me, I would've gone for him. I won't take that kind of crap." But she drew back, annoyed and scowling; there was no excuse for this. He baffled and offended her. All he cared about was his revenge: cheering and jeering extra loud, defiantly, together with another Finches fan two rows below, until finally someone threw a blob of ice cream at them and it splattered on her dress. They all stood up outraged, shocked, but there was no one to blame and all she could do was to wipe it off and say, "That's all right. I'll get it out. No, it's all right. I don't mind." She felt increasingly distressed, marooned. To her right, Mary Lloyd and Tom sat disgusted not only with Ralph but with the game itself. The crowd was restless, ugly, booing; at one close call, Tom stood up, tore his program, threw the pieces down. Ralph gloated, squirming close beside her on the left. The Phillies had simply collapsed; and people were filing down and trickling out even before the sixth inning ended. Tom and Mary Lloyd, however, were bitterly resigned to stay. The score was nine to two. A match flared and she glanced askance at Ralph, the glow of his cigar, then choked and turned her face away. She wanted to be home, away from this, safe in her own room; she was tired of people and unpleasantness.

"Well," said Mary Lloyd at last, "I guess we've had enough."

But Tom wouldn't budge; not until two more Phillies' errors, another Finches run.

"How about it," Mary Lloyd asked her. "You ready?" And then: "Ralph? Ralph! We're going to leave, okay?"

Ralph snorted and sat up, puffing his cigar: "Well," he began, "I don't know, now. . . ."

Tom led them down, step by step, slowly, to the exit, then on down the stairs, which were echoing and dark, with girders around and light bulbs glaring. Other people straggled down along with them, ahead and behind, shuffling aimlessly; no one hurrying or noisy, no one crowding. When they reached the bottom level, Mary Lloyd stepped purposely ahead to be with Tom, who crooked his arm around her neck, hugging her close and leaning on her. She and Ralph lagged farther and farther behind as they trailed on through trampled litter and out the gate, hearing the muffled shouting and booing behind them. She felt a pang to watch Tom and Mary Lloyd share each other's concern, reassuring, comforting each other. Ralph shuffled along, stoop-shouldered, scowling, grumbling to himself; she avoided him and he avoided her.

"Hey, wait!" called Ralph, as they started down a kiosk's steps. "You sure this is the right way?"

Tom waved his hand; Mary Lloyd looked back reproachfully. They kept on going down.

"Okay, okay . . . your show. Go on!" He looked disgusted. "This ain't the way we came," he appealed to her: "Is it?" She made no answer, trusting Tom.

"Say, we're in luck!" exclaimed Mary Lloyd, as an empty car appeared almost at once, headlight shining, and pulled up beside the deserted platform. They climbed on and took seats on opposite sides, still keeping their distance.

But the very next stop was Stadium itself; outside she saw a mob close in. She couldn't understand. People pressed up flat against the windows and doors, and the doors opened and they came pushing, shoving, shouldering, spilling, clamoring in. She glanced across at Tom and Mary Lloyd and then at Ralph, but he avoided her look, though he was bothered too, smoking his cigar. The crowd came scrambling in: faces of ruthlessness and determination, faces of rage, and the struggling bodies, arms, each one for himself. They clutched their baseball hats, and pennants and portable radios, and their animal feet shuffled closer as they jammed in tighter and tighter, with their red faces bending down, sweaty and glowering, and each one clinging to part of a loop, or a pole, or a hand on part of the window, until they were backed tight against her too. They reached around, bent over, crushed against her, separating her from Ralph and blocking any glimpse of Mary Lloyd. No one could move or breathe. She held her legs together, straining, doubled over and clutching her purse, and turned her head and bit her lip. Everything was swarming together, blurred and moving, swelling: too much, more than she could bear. She swallowed, fighting it back, gripping her arms, unable to contain herself. When suddenly Ralph was clutching towards her, pushing aside a man and shouting: "We got to get off, c'mon! We got to get off here!" She stared at him, then forced her way to her feet, blindly: she mustn't be abandoned. She clung tightly to her purse with one arm and lifted the other in the air: "Let me out!" she cried. "Please let me out here! I have to get off! Out!" She fought against bodies, flesh, impassively resisting, and Ralph was clearing a way by lunging ahead, and shouting to the driver who had shut the doors: "Wait a goddamn minute! We're getting off here!" She kept pushing on one person to force her way past another. People were laughing. Someone jabbed her painfully, and she glanced around, and someone else crushed her foot. Ralph and the driver were having words; Ralph pulled at her arm: "Got any change? Got a dollar? All I got is ten!" Everybody laughed. "Get that fatty off of here!" Shakily she groped in her purse, trying to find her wallet, which she finally drew out. She only had a five, so Ralph pulled out his ten and hustled her roughly past him towards the door. She climbed down the steps onto the platform where Tom and Mary Lloyd stood watching. Ralph came down behind her, muttering. The doors slammed shut and the car sped off.

They were on a dark, suburban platform with trees all around, stars overhead; crickets chirped in the shadows.

"Okay, now what? Where the hell are we anyhow, huh? What'd' you say?"

"Right track . . . wrong direction."

"Aw, well, that's fine, isn't it? You're one hell of a guide, aren't you? Jeezus, you and your wise ideas! No traffic. Easier."

"Oh, can it, Ralph! I mean it!"

Tom stalked away across the tracks to the side that would take them back in town. Mary Lloyd hurried after him. Ralph sucked and puffed the butt of his cigar, making it glow fiercely, then threw it away and started over after them. She didn't move. She stood there hugging her purse, still quivering and dizzy. Her side throbbed and ached. They were pushing, shoving. She was being pushed back, overpowered by a crush of bodies. She stepped back into the darkness and sank down on a bench where they couldn't see.

"Hey! Over here?" shouted Ralph.

"Yoo-hoo!"

"Now what's wrong?"

They were arguing about her.

After a few moments Mary Lloyd crossed over for a closer look. "What's wrong? Anna Maye?"

"Nothing," she gasped. "Go away. Don't touch me. Just go away."

Mary Lloyd left her. A short while later, she rose to her feet and tidied herself; then went over to join them. She sat down on the far end of their bench. They gave her slyly grudging, furtive looks, but no one tried to speak. No one said anything to anyone.

They turned down her street, cruised past parked cars and darkened houses, pulled up at her house. The downstairs was lit up, the porch light on outside.

"This one?"

"Yes." She gathered up her purse.

"Well, okay, sweetheart, now I'll see you Monday, right?" said Mary Lloyd, twisting around in the front seat.

"Yes. Monday. Thank you."

"Everything okay, now?"

"Fine. Yes. Thank you. Thank you, too, Tom. Thank you for everything." He grimaced and nodded, winking acknowledgement over his shoulder: "Yeah."

Absently fingering the door handle, Ralph watched her from across the seat. She glanced up, but couldn't see his face. He grunted, opened his door, then came around, dutifully, to open hers.

She gave a nodding, parting smile to Mary Lloyd and Tom.

"You got everything, now?

"Yes."

Ralph took her arm, to help her out, and followed as she stepped between the cars and around the trash cans and stopped at the bottom of her walk. "That's fine," she said, turning to face him. "It's been nice meeting you. You've been very kind to let me come along like this."

His face looked sickly in the streetlight. He rubbed his jaw and smoothed his hair: "Well, sure, that's okay. Nothing at all. Hell.

Good meeting you too. We'll try it again sometime, maybe. You just—uh—you take care of yourself. I don't get down here much, now, but you just take care." Their motor idled loudly, headlights shining down the street.

"Ralph, c'mon!"

"Well, goodnight, now."

Ralph went back; his door slammed and they pulled away with a toot. She stood there alone, looking after them. Streetlight shone overhead, gleaming on the leaves and casting shadows on the window of the children's room. She heard the television sounds. Coming up the walk, she saw Howard pass the doorway inside and start up the stairs, dimly, through the screen.

She climbed the three steps and opened the screen door, which yawned. Mary called out, unseen, from inside the living room: "That you?"

"Yes." She switched off the outside porch light, stooped down to pick up one of the children's plastic dolls.

"Hey, you're pretty late, aren't you? What'd you get lost or something? How was it, huh? Fun?" She squinted, stepping into the lighted living room, meeting Mary, who had risen from the couch. The television flickered and spoke loudly from the corner. She put down her purse, the doll, opened the closet door and put away her hat.

Mary leaned on the banister and called upstairs, softly: "Howard!" They heard the toilet flushing, steps; he peered down: "Yeah, what?"

"Anna!" she whispered. He was in his stocking feet, coming down, smiling. "Good time?" he asked.

She crossed the room and sank down on the couch.

"It was very nice."

Later, upstairs with the door securely shut, having undressed and having explored the fist-sized bruise on her right side, just under the breast, she opened the top middle drawer of her dresser and lifted out an ivory-colored jewelry chest. She carried this to her bed and began again the slow methodical appraisal of item after item: a broken railroad watch, some folded needle-point, tie-clasps, buttons, the bone-handled razor, a hand-carved wooden comb, a tarnished silver locket with a curl of fine blonde hair.

Confirmation

Five-thirty, Monday, just getting light. She turned over angrily and settled her body, tugged the sheet, changed the pillow and looked at Howard's sleeping face.

His eyes opened, blearily.

"What is it?"

"Nothing," she mumbled, "Anna Maye. Go back to sleep."

She listened to sounds of Anna Maye's dressing, bathroom, and downstairs to the kitchen, the clatterings, bumps and scrapes, and everything prolonged: come on, get it over with! Get out! Then—ah!—finally, the opening, closing of the front door. Silence, stillness. She was gone.

For now. All weekend Anna Maye had been more brooding than ever. She kept to herself, always in her room, not speaking.

Howard promised. But here they were still, after four months, with nothing changed. Except today she'd know. She'd seen the doctor Friday, said nothing to Howard except she wasn't feeling well, and had the physical and lab tests, and told the doctor it couldn't be this, she'd been careful, but he had said, well, it looked like it to him, but they'd wait and see the test results; his nurse would call Monday—today.

Did she want it? Was she glad? In a way she was. At first she hadn't wanted it—not this too! But then had thought: why not? What could he say now, with this? He couldn't argue, Anna couldn't either. A baby meant no more compromises, not with Anna or old Carl. Howard, finally, would have to face up to Carl: twenty-five thousand in that shop, maybe more if they got a good price. They would need it now. Just like they would need Anna Maye's room. But more than this, she had felt a yearning and fulfillment that surprised her—an answer from beyond her to a want she hadn't known to name.

She woke with a start to the children's voices. 7:25! It couldn't be. She groped for the alarm and found it shut off; sat up. Day bright, sunlight on the house next door.

"Howard!"

"Huh?"

"Come on. It's 7:30!"

"What?"

She pushed and shook him. "Come on."

She threw back the sheet, rolled out, stood up, naked, clumsy, heading for the dressing table and her robe. "It's your father," she muttered, pulling the robe on, pushing back hair.

"What happened to the alarm?" He swung his legs out, sat up.

"Just get moving, will you?"

Then sure enough, fifteen minutes later, the phone rang. Howard was in the bathroom. She was in the kitchen, cleaning up the kids' mess and waiting for coffee, while they were in the living room, bacon was cooking, and the food smells turned her stomach. Two rings, three.

"You up over there?" his voice demanded.

She clutched the front of her robe. "Yes, we're underway."

"Well, let me talk to Howard."

"He's in the bathroom right now, Carl. Hold on; he'll be right down—Howard! Your father!" she shouted, and left the phone on the table.

They were late, so what? Howard was supposed to be there by
seven, take the panel truck and drive across town to buy so many cuts
of beef, pork, lamb, and then the fish and poultry from wholesalers. So
he'd be an hour late. Shouting wouldn't change it. It wasn't their fault.

Back in the kitchen, she drained the bacon, heard him pounding down the stairs. "Pop? . . . Yeah, I know. . . . Look, I'm leaving
now. It's the clock didn't go off is all . . . yeah . . . sure. . . . I'm telling
you, I'll be right in. Fifteen minutes. . . . Yeah'll, okay." He came in,
frowning. "Got some coffee?" Undershirt, pants, stocking feet, hair
tousled, shaving cream on his cheeks. Ruthie crowded in behind
him. "Morning, princess."

"What's he, all worked up?" She gave him a mug of coffee.

"He's got reason. You don't go early, you get lousy cuts. Besides,
here he's opening at eight, what's he gonna sell? I go over, get the
truck, drive in; time I get back, it's noon. What's he do all morning?
He's got customers; he's got orders piling up, deliveries coming in."

She went to turn his eggs. "So that's my fault too, huh?"

"I'm not saying that."

"He couldn't take the truck himself, could he; and let you open
up when you get there?"

"It's too late. How could he know I wasn't coming? It's my job.
I should have been there."

She turned off the burner, faced him. "Well, why don't you go
get ready, then?"

He took his coffee and left.

But she was tired of hearing it. Carl kept bossing, calling up like
the world would stop, if it weren't for him. Seventy-two years old, a
widower for ten, he was keeping the shop for them, he always said. A
good shop. He had settled his estate right after they had married—
while he was still alive, he'd said, so there'd be no quarreling after-
ward—ten thousand outright to the daughter (who had a family up in
Boston), the shop for Howard, but only after he, Carl, had quit or died.
Howard had told her—one day Bobby, the dimwit storeboy, had tried
to take someone's order and Carl had blown up at him: "Look, I ain't
dead yet. I ain't out of the way yet. I'm still boss here, understand?"

And that's how it was. That shop and his customers were Carl's whole life. He wasn't thinking of Howard, or of their needs. He knew Howard wasn't fit to take over. The whole thing was him: like that time he was sick and Howard lost two big customers in one week— one of them a lady that Carl had had for eight years at one hundred a week or more. As a business, it was barely breaking even, with Howard only taking home a hundred a week, Carl living in the five rooms over the stores and working for nothing to save what it would cost for another butcher. But Carl wouldn't think of selling, wouldn't trust them with the twenty-five thousand, just sitting there, to start another business with—a business they could make a decent living at with a lot less trouble; something suited to them, not him. Oh no, this way Carl could keep bossing; keep blaming Howard for not working harder: here Carl had made it all from nothing; all they did was gripe. And Howard wouldn't stand up and say: it's you, it's you stopping us; give us what's ours and let us make our own way with it.

She stood at the stairs: "Howard!"

"Coming."

She got the girls dressed—feeling more and more edgy and unsteady: she had to lie down. Kept tasting bile, swallowing it back. Just lie down, keep quiet, maybe it would pass. She sent them back downstairs: "Susan, you look after her. You can play outside, but keep away from the street. Understand? I need to rest for a while. No fights." She flopped down, stretched out—eyes closed, one arm over her face; she was drifting, moving, the whole bed slowly swinging, first this way, then again. She couldn't think, except for this was happening; fighting it, hoping it would pass. She swallowed, sweating, feeling it worsen, still more certain, no, then yes, it's going to; she raged at it, wanting it over, not caring. Now. Up: it's going to. Unsteady on her feet, she had to hurry. First lurch, she swallowed back; she stumbled into the bathroom, sank to her knees at the toilet, certain: nothing. Bowing her head over the bowl, blindly, she thought of it, the hot convulsion, taste and gag: and then it was, a rush and pouring, all, and with the sight and smell, again, and nothing left but stomach juices, bile, sweet Jesus, not again: again. She choked and spit and swallowed, weeping, pulled the seat cover down, flushed; wearily slumped over and sank down, arm on the cover, head on her arm. Then she blinked, straightened, and gathered herself, pushed herself up, stood, cleared her hair back, wiped her face. Rinsed her mouth, brushed teeth, washed up. She felt better now; a little shaky maybe, but herself. She went back to the bedroom, sat on the bed. Time to get dressed, get on with day.

She'd been sick this way with Susan, but not Ruthie; but it had to be that she was pregnant. She thought of Carl: "You better have that kid!" She and Howard had been going steady, just kids in school, and then Howard had gone away. She'd set out, then, on her own: away from Anna Maye, from the factory, this house. She had done all right, found a good job, good times, and had money of her own. In time, she had grown tired of it, been hurt; when Howard came back, she had let him have her. That was fun too, but she didn't want to get married, not yet. She liked having him there, dependable and pleading, but she needed freedom too.

She thought of Jean, wryly, simple Jean, who'd played it right.

She stepped back, dressing, and studied her reflection. She cupped her breasts with the bra, fumbling for hooks. Where were her Bermudas? Okay. Yesterday's shirt. She still looked good, she thought; a little heavy. Thongs.

So that's how it had happened, her getting pregnant with Susan. She wasn't ready and hadn't wanted a baby, except Howard had; he kept on pleading and promising. Then they had fought. She'd had to ask herself what else there was? A life like Jean's? It wasn't that she didn't love Howard; only that she wanted time. Then when she'd gone to see Howard in the shop, he must've asked Carl for the money, because Carl had chased out the customers, slammed the door, put up the closed sign and shaken his fist in her face: "You better have that kid! Don't play smart with me. He wants to marry you, and you don't give an answer. Well, you ain't playing tricks with me!"

Something in her hadn't cared. She had hated Carl and every-thing imposed on her; she'd hated Howard too for standing by. If they wanted this, okay, then, but still she had her price. She had her own demands. It was her life that they would answer to, her needs that they would satisfy.

She went on with her day, beginning with a wash. She stripped the bed, sheets in pillowcases, stuffed laundry from the closet in a bag. Carried down the big bag, struggling.

"Susan!" TV on, but no one there. Outside. Dropped the bag. "Susan!"

"What?"

"C'mon! Come on in here!" She went out to the porch. "Hey! C'mere. Come on in here. C'mon." She held the screen open; Susan got up and scrambled up the steps; then Ruthie.

"Morning, Mary!"

She looked: Mrs. Bocosky, sweeping her walk. "How are you?" she called over, letting the screen shut and smiling through it. Ruthie clung and tugged at her.

"Lovely day!"

She glanced at sky, the brightness. "I'm doing a wash," she explained, and turned to herd the girls in.

"Okay, c'mon," she told them. "I need your help, okay? There's two bags of laundry up there. Top of the stairs. I'm taking this one. You bring those two down, okay? Go on. You too, Ruthie."

Susan reached the top, with Ruthie following. "Here?"

She waited until they'd started down, then led the way out through kitchen to the cellar door, opened it, turned on light. She started down carefully; the steps were narrow and steep, the wall on one side, railing on other.

The girls waited above her on the landing. Susan came down with her bag, but Ruthie held back, scared. She went up half-way, took the bag, Ruthie's hand, but still Ruthie pulled back. "Oh, come on. I got you." She led her on, then. "I got you." She led her down, impatient with each halting step.

While she worked at the washer sorting, the girls fooled around the workbench, pulled at something, which clattered, metal on the floor. She had picked up a hacksaw, stooped and gathered up the scattered chisels, a case of drills; then yanked open a drawer and shoved them in. Who had uncovered all this?

"Those were Grandpa's," she explained. "And look—both of you—no touching anything on this bench, understand? These things are dangerous. I don't want you getting cut." She frowned at the drill gun.

"Grampa's?"

"Grampa Potts." She looked around, dragged their coats off some things in the corner, heaped them on the bench. "He used to work down here. He made things."

"What things?"

"Forget it, Susan. Chairs and things like that."

Ruthie wouldn't know him; she was too young. They hadn't visited much, but when they had, he'd welcomed them like he could breathe again. She'd feel so guilty leaving, having to leave, like the first time all over, a twisting in her at the pity of it, nothing she could do. She hated Anna Maye for keeping them apart. She remembered how he'd fought against Mother, yet when Mother had died, how he had gone blank and dull inside, like it was his fault; how he'd let Anna Maye take over. She herself had been eleven then, Anna Maye eighteen.

Anna Maye had been even worse than Mother; had never even liked her; had envied her and tried to make her ashamed. Over and over, Anna Maye had told her she was selfish, foolish, irresponsible. If she had friends, especially boys, then she was too young or they were too old, but they were never good enough; her clothes were wrong, her language, manners, music were wrong; no grades in school, even if they were better than Anna's, were good enough; she couldn't be in the band—it would take too much time. She wouldn't help around the house. Then they would fight, or Anna would go complain to him behind her back. And if he never refused Anna, still he'd make her quit, and then he'd speak to her, Mary, like Anna was the queer one, the one to humor, while she was the one he really loved: go on, live your life, don't worry about her.

But she did worry. It hurt that this must be a secret between them, a feeling; that Anna Maye should have this power just because she was older and kept the house and worked and shopped and cooked and cleaned.

It wasn't all for them. Anna Maye had no friends; she didn't understand anything; all she had was family, them. So why had Father let her have her way? Why did he resign himself? Why, when he felt restless and stifled too; why must his feelings be kept secret? Why couldn't he just go ahead, like he kept saying; live his own life; make her take him like he was? Why was he afraid? Why was Anna so important?

"Me! You be realistic," she had shouted at Howard. "Look. You keep giving in to her, she's never going to leave. She doesn't care what she does to us. And I've had enough. I've had enough of her playing up to you and getting in my way and bribing the children and her poor, hurt sulks and she's so lonely, no place to go, and I'm some kind of no good bitch. What do you expect of me? What's going on, is this just me or is it us?"

"Aw, c'mon."

"No goddamit! We need this house; we've got every right here; we're a family; and she's got a perfectly good job—she can get an apartment anytime she wants to. She's not helpless."

"We can't just tell her move out."

"Why the hell not?"

"Because we can't. Because that's not our place. This is her house too and that's all there is to it. You knew that when we moved in here. Now shut up and listen to me. You keep harping, bringing this up. I don't see a problem here, except you make it a problem. She needs to think things out. Who are we coming in here, agreeing everything's okay, and here she's doing her best, giving us money, anything we ask, and then we're supposed to turn around and say, oh, sorry? We're not doing that to her."

"You just want her goddamn money! Where're we gonna go, some cramped apartment, hundred a week? If you aren't telling her, I am! Go on, stay with her, I don't need you!" She pushed him too far; she realized that; she was losing her hold; grudgingly, she had backed down, held back. Okay, she'd be more careful. No more threats. Just let him think he'd had his way.

Grateful, then, guilty, he had tried to make up. He'd said okay, he'd try; he'd ask Anna Maye what her plans were; maybe she would want to leave. They had left it like that, and of course he hadn't asked Anna Maye anything. The last few weeks had been like that, the whole thing gnawing at them. He couldn't blame her now.

She talked instead about their future. They had been driving out to Bob and Jean's: how they could move to the suburbs too, and what it would mean for the girls—the schools, and decent friends, and families their own age, the kind of place they really wanted. There were plenty of businesses; why, with what they could get from the house and the shop, just ask Bob. Howard had said nothing, but she knew he wanted it too.

And yet he kept on holding out; he couldn't choose. He was cowed by Carl and Anna Maye as much as by her. Well, let him find out what that cost.

In bed, all else withheld, her fury at his stubbornness, her own needs choked, she'd made him force her, everything be force, and if that cost her too, still, in their frenzied cleaving—her hate, his— held purposes and selves were lost. They'd never made love before like this, like it wasn't even them; and, left blank and dazed, she'd turn aside and struggle to gain hold, but couldn't.

The girls were fighting:

"Stop it, Ruthie! Gimme that!"

"No!"

"Give it to me!"

"Cut that out in there!" She sighed and pushed her chair back. Took a last sip of coffee.

"No!"

"Mom—mee!"

For chrissake. Goddamn colorforms again. Ruthie howling on the floor and Susan standing, looking angry, guilty, and triumphant, the scrap of yellow plastic in her hand.

"I told you cut it out! What did you do to her?"

"Nothing! I was playing with my colorforms and she keeps taking them away! I can't even find the parts I need. I try and make a picture, she just ruins it!"

"Ruthie, shh! It's all right." She lifted her up. "Where's her pappy?" Looked around; by the television. "Get it for me, Susan."

Susan got it, handed it to her, and Ruthie, silenced, burrowed close between her legs.

"Can't I leave you for five minutes? What did you, did you hit her?"

"She's supposed to keep away! She's not allowed."

"What did I tell you?"

"It was her!"

"All right, give me that. Give me the plastic. Susan!" Chased her to the couch.

"No, it's not fair! Mommy! Get away!"

Wrenched it from her. "You want a slap? . . . Okay." Tossed it in the box. "I told you: anymore squabbling, that's the end of it." She stooped, crouched, gathered up the other pieces, slapped on the box lid, glanced at Ruthie staring, whining—"It's not fair! It was her, not me! Don't Mommy! No!"—walked to the closet and pushed the box back on the cluttered top shelf, closed the door.

She was stuffing sheets and light things in the dryer, dark things in the wash, when dimly overhead: the phone? Tensed. "Sh!" Second ring. "Okay, listen, stay here! Don't touch anything! Just go ahead and finish up!" She hurried, ducked, lunged up the stairs—fourth ring—got it: "Hello?" Breathless.

"Mary?"

"Jean. . . . Hi, how are you?"

"You okay? I didn't break in on anything, did I?"

"No, no. . . . I was downstairs with the wash, that's all."

"I can call back—"

"No, that's okay. But, um, can you hold on a second? I left the kids downstairs; I want to get them up here first. Okay? Okay. Hold on." She couldn't talk for long. "Susan? Come on up here, bring Ruthie; come on! We'll do that later. I'm on the phone and I don't want you down there alone. Come on!" She waited while they came—c'mon, c'mon!—shooed them past, closed and bolted the door; turned, ignoring them, got cigarettes, matches, saucer, and on into the living room, took the phone and settled into Howard's chair, shoes off, knees drawn up, receiver cradled by her shoulder, cigarette in her lips.

"Now, hi. I'm all set now. What you doing?"

Jean: "Oh, nothing. Bob's gone. I'm just sitting here. I just can't get started; you know, sort of blah. Here alone, it's Monday. And I was thinking, you know, like we were talking, about a job,"—she lit up, her eye on Susan, who had wandered in; frowned at Ruthie, crowded by her arm—"but I tried telling Bob again last night and you shoulda heard him."

"Excuse me a minute," she interrupted; "Susan, turn down the TV. And Ruthie, look, both of you: keep quiet and find something to do, cause I'm busy talking, all right?—Sorry, Jean. What, did he give you that routine again: it doesn't look right, or what's his problem?"

"I dunno. It's sort of he wants to keep me here. He's proud and we don't need the money, and you know, my miscarriages and every-thing—well, we keep on trying—so if I do get a job, I'd have to quit as soon as I'm pregnant anyway: and that's what he keeps saying. He just won't listen; it's like I'm insulting him or something, being awful, because we got a nice place and he's working so hard so I won't have to, and it'd be different, you know, if I was pregnant and we did have kids, but we don't, and I can't help it—I get lonely. The only people we meet are Bob's business friends and they just make me nervous. And the neighbors are okay, like this girl, Barbie, down the street, but I dunno; she's got children, two in school and a baby, and she went to college and she's nice and all, but the others are old, and everybody's got their own life, and I just stay in and clean and shop and wait for Bob to come home. A job, at least I'd have something to do and I could make some friends—"

"Right. I agree," she put in, grimacing to herself: should she tell her? Thinking of those ten rooms, furnishings, new kitchen, bedroom set ("we're just beginning, but Bob wants everything nice"), thinking of the yard, two elms and the pine, a hedge, the quiet street of houses, trees everywhere, green everywhere, the block-long yard and Victorian mansion across the street, the sleek cars passing, slowly, down the hill, under the railroad, and the quiet business center down the highway. Yes, Mrs. Garton, what can we do for you today? Wrap it, send it, yes, Mrs. Garton. Houses like her mother used to take the trolley out to clean.

"He's got no right, then, telling me I'm wrong, does he?"

"Of course not."

She thought of Howard, awkward, sullen, in the butterfly chair outside, and Bob at the grille, while she and Jean were in the kitchen fixing hors d'oeuvres and highballs, and Jean's raunchy giggle: "Just like in The Topper, huh?"

"Well, I dunno, he feels so strong about it. It's like he's afraid someone'll make a pass at me or something, and he doesn't trust me? Well, I get to feeling guilty, you know. It's just this one thing, really, and he's so good to me and I want to make him happy. I don't know. Maybe it's me. I'm just making a big thing out of nothing, I don't know."

There was a pause, an appeal she couldn't rise to.

"But it was really great having you out here. Bob had a good time too, you know; he really likes you. And gee, if only things would work out and you could move out here. Like Bob was saying, a dry cleaner's or a meat franchise, and he can help you at the bank; I mean, Howard seems to want it."

Ruthie was back, clutching at herself, whining: "Mom—me! Pee-pee!"

"Excuse me, Jean—Susan, take her upstairs, will you? Go on: now! Will you please?" She watched them go up. "Yeah," she said to Jean, "but it's the same old story: he wants it, he doesn't want it. There's nothing I can do. We can't sell the shop because of his father; can't sell this place unless my sister gives it up. And he won't go against anybody; me, sure, but not anybody else. And meanwhile we just wait. I thought Bob would talk some sense to him; and if not me, at least he'd think about the kids. But he's so stubborn suddenly, I mean all the way home, nothing, not a word, and the more he wants it, the more he hates himself and blames me. . . . I mean you think you've got problems."

"But it's that sister of yours, isn't it? I just don't see how she can do it. You're a family, you got kids. She doesn't need a house. It's so unfair, it really makes me mad. She's got no right making a problem for you. I can see the whole thing so plain. If it was me, I'd take her aside and tell her: you need the house for yourself. You want to sell it, and as long as she's there, she doesn't mean to maybe, but she's making trouble between you and Howard, and you're sorry, but you're family and you can't go on living like this. So it would be a big help now, if she could make her own decision and save you all a lot of grief."

"Huh," she snorted, stubbing out her cigarette. "You don't know her. It isn't that easy, Jean."

"But going to her, person to person like that—how could she say no? I mean downright refuse you? What does she expect anyway? It's not like you're turning your back. Like you said, you've tried. I don't know how you've put up with it. But she's just blackmailing you, and where's it going to get her? You don't want her there, so what's she gonna do, drive you out? What good is that house to her?"

Weary, irritated: "I don't know; it's how she is. You just don't go to her, that's all. At least I can't. She never comes out and says anything, but every time, I mean I want to change the drapes or move furniture, or just to get the kitchen mine, it's been like I'm some kinda conniving, you know, heartless person, and I got it in for her. Anything I do, off she goes and sulks and acts all hurt, and then Howard finds her crying and how could I do that to her, look at what she's done for us, can't I show some common decency?"

"But that's not fair!"

"Oh, sure it is. It's me she does it to, not him. See, I'm the troublemaker, I'm the bitch. Let's just drop it. I don't want to talk about it."

"But he can't want her there."

"He doesn't." She sighed. "Oh, look, it isn't only him. It's her. She's never faced things, never had the nerve. It's like we're asking her to jump off a cliff. You just can't do it. It's not enough to say we need the house. We need some kind of reason, something, I don't know; something she can't argue with."

She glanced up, saw the children starting down.

"Mary, listen. It's none of my business, but it sounds like you're not facing things yourself. I mean what kind of choice have you got? You're a family. What more reason is there? Putting it off isn't sparing anybody anything. And what's so terrible? She doesn't have to live with you. You can help her find someplace. You're still there if she needs you. I mean this is a grown person, right? She works; it's a difficult change, maybe, but that's her problem, not yours. She's gotta make her own life, just like you. The longer you keep avoiding, the worse it's gonna get."

"Yeah," she said moodily, waving the kids off: play. "I know that. Try telling Howard."

"Well, he's got to back you up."

She snorted. "Sure."

"He does. You've got your happiness at stake. Either she comes first or you do. And look: you're being reasonable; maybe she won't take it that way, but that's her. You've got nothing to feel bad about. He's got to see that. It's best all around. Just tell her: you're ready to help; but no use pretending, this can't work out. The best thing for both of you, and the fair thing, is that she moves."

"Yeah. That's very good advice. Let's just leave it there. I told you, it's dumb. It's just more complicated than that, and I appreciate everything you've said, but I don't want to go into it, so let's just change the subject."

"Aw, hey, look, I'm sorry. I hope I didn't. I don't mean to stick my nose in. It's just I been thinking, you know, like we talked, and I know it's not my business, but I sort of thought maybe, well, my being an outsider, maybe it could help."

"I know. Really. It's just this is something, I'm not in the mood. There's no point. Nothing to do with you. I just, I got to work it out for myself. So let's leave it at that."

"Well, anyhow, anytime. You know I'm on your side."

"Look, it isn't this, but I better be getting off now anyway. I got this wash and I'm supposed to call Howard; I got the kids here after me. So how about I talk to you later?"

"Well, I hope I didn't get you down. Oh, look, before I forget: how about this weekend? Want to get together for a movie or something?"

"Sounds good. Yeah, that'd be great. Only, you know, we'll just have to see. I'll let you know, okay?"

"Well, I guess that's it then. I better get started too."

"Right. Well, look, you have a good day. I'll be talking to you now."

"You too, Mary."

"Okay. Byebye now."

She hung up, numbly furious, chagrined.

She imagined how she'd tell him. She would wait until after supper and she got the girls in bed; after Anna Maye went up. Then calmly, gravely, she would begin: ". . . I didn't want to say anything until I knew for sure. But I've seen the doctor and they called me back today: I'm pregnant."

"You're serious? You're sure?" He'd be angry: "How? For chrissake, can't you use that thing right?"

"Don't you want it?"

"Yeah, yeah, of course I want it. What're you saying? It's done, it's done; we can't change that, but yeah, sure, of course we want it. We would have anyway. It's just we got to think. I mean things are tough enough right now."

She would watch it close in on him, feeling satisfied that she had advantage back. He would be the one now forced to back down and defer.

Then she would tell Anna Maye, the fact, that's all, just casual, with Howard there.

If Anna Maye refused, then they'd have to go to her together, like Jean had said: ". . . we need the room, that's all; we need it for the baby. It'd just be too much. We need the house, we don't have anywhere else, so look, we can find you an apartment."

If Anna Maye refused: "I'm not going to leave. I've got a right," then she would have her answer, with Howard there to see: "Ashamed? Ashamed of what? Because I'm normal? Because I've got a husband and a family? Oh, you can't stand that, can you? Yes, I'm normal. Not cruel, not no good and irresponsible. No, I'm a mother with two children and a baby to think of, and a marriage, and a family life to think of: they're my right. So don't you talk about my decency. What about yourself?"

She was fixing lunch, when the phone rang.

"Okay. Both of you. Look, just stay here, go on and eat." She got it on the second ring. "Hello?"

"Mrs. Muller?"

She was all attentive: "Yes."

"This is Doctor Kramer's office. We have your results here from your A-Z last Friday?"

"That's right."

"Well, Mrs. Muller, your test was positive."

Dully, just like that, everything dropped out of her: "I see."

"Well, there's no doubt about it. The result confirms Doctor's examination. So he'd like to see you—let's see—you should have your first O.B., say, another month. Um, how about August 25, 9:15, okay?"

"Wait a minute. Did you say it wasn't positive?"

"No, no, Mrs. Muller, it's positive."

"Oh, I heard you wrong. I'm sorry. Oh, that's fine, yeah, thank you very much."

"Well, I said positive. I thought you sounded a little strange."

"No, I've been worried. But that's all I wanted to hear. I mean all weekend. You've got no idea. I was pretty sure, but I don't know, I've been half expecting something'd be wrong."

"No, no, you can relax, Mrs. Muller. I'm very happy for you. But that's funny, isn't it, I mean you really thought I said negative? I'll have to tell Doctor that one—Well, but what about this appointment now?"

"Oh, I'm sorry, yeah. What were you saying?"

"For your first O.B. August 25, is that all right?"

"Sure, wait a second. Let me get a pencil. . . . Okay, August 25. And what time was it? 9:15?"

"That's right. That's a Thursday."

"Sure. No problem."

"Okay, I'll just put you down here, then, and I'll send you a reminder in the mail. Well, that's about everything. Have you told your husband?"

"No, I wanted to make sure first."

"He'll have a happy surprise in store for him, then. Well, congratulations again, Mrs. Muller, and we'll be seeing you next month. Unless you have some questions?"

"No."

"Well, have a good day, now."

"Oh, yes, yes, I will. And really, thank you, thank you very much; and you too. Yeah. G'bye."

Decided, done. She felt relieved, empowered now, except that there was no way back: the change was final, the fact itself past choice or gladness or regret, the sureness of it strange. There was no use questioning; no use either in this calmer, shyer glow, remote from everything.

Susan stared at her from the doorway.

"What're you looking at? Go on back in, and finish your lunch."

She sighed, and pushed away, and went back to her children.

The Power Fails

Susan had told her about the baby. Then Mary had said tightly, yes, that they had wanted to tell her themselves; she'd only told Howard two days ago, and then she'd told the girls this afternoon.

Since then, for almost a week, she'd tried not to think about it, but she couldn't face them, either. She felt betrayed, not by Mary, but by Howard, who had understood, who'd cared. But then a baby changed everything. He had let this happen. Why? Why should Mary always be the one granted life?

After dinner now, she had settled in her chair beside the window. Her radio was playing low. There was a steady downpour outside, water running in the gutters, dripping; a warm, damp seethe pushed her shade, then sucked it back, tight against the screen. The rain only troubled and depressed her, along with all the other evening commotion—sounds of children, passing cars, air-conditioners, TVs, the Bocoskys arguing—that normally relaxed and reassured her. Her own walls and shelves, as she stared at them, seemed blank and unyielding.

She sighed, and laid back her head, eyes closed, thinking of the factory, of Rose Morgan, the way she was slovenly and short-tempered, making trouble, absent twice; of Louie and his problems, and how he came to her each morning now, just to her, to share about his wife, the future of his daughter, the ache of it from day to day. She thought about details at work tomorrow, errands; she would need a clean uniform.

She raised her head at that, gathered herself and stood up, walked over to the closet, was just parting her dresses.

Abruptly everything went black, still, and vast; except for the rain, which seemed to draw in closer.

She froze.

Distant, downstairs: "Hey!"

"What is it!"

"Daddy!"

"Blow a fuse?"

"Oh, for godssake."

"Daddy!"

"Shut up! Stay still."

"Out all over—"

"What happened?"

"—next door, up and down the street."

She wiped her palms, edged back, leaned and sat down on the bed. She wouldn't call, or move; just wait.

"Anna? Hey, Anna! You okay?" Mary called.

"Yes. . . . Yes!" she called back, voice loud in the room. She got up and groped barefoot towards the door, opened it. "Mary?" The hall was black.

From downstairs: "You okay?"

She made her way out to the landing, found the railing: "What happened?" Craned, searched the downstairs darkness.

"Scared! Mommy!"

"Shh! Get back!—Power failure."

"Here." Matchlight dimly showed up the wall, stairs and railing; then she saw the flame itself, small and pulsing, of his lighter, lighting up his hand, arm, face, shoulders. "Hey. Looks like a power failure. It's out all over the place. Why don't you come on down?"

"Ask her if there're candles!"

"There any candles or anything?"

She bit her lip, alert now. "I have to think. In the drawer, in the kitchen—the linen drawer. I'm not sure. Down underneath. There used to be a flashlight. Wait a minute, I'll be down. I just have to get some things on."

"Flashlight in the car too," he was saying. "Why don't you take this, see if you can find the candles?"

"I'll be right down," she repeated.

"We were watching television and I thought a fuse had blown or something, but it's out all over. That means something serious, not some off and on thing," Mary said.

"Well, we don't know," she replied. She had fixed four candles burning on their saucers. "They'll get it fixed; it's just a matter of time. Here, let's take these."

"Go on, Susan," Mary said. "Ruthie, how about you? Here, you have one too. Now, be careful. Let's go in the living room. Like a party, right? Watch your step, don't let it go out."

"Hey!" The screen door banged, and he came in the front, his flashlight shining at them, then down. "It is wet out there. Jesus. Got candles, good, huh? Everything's out, not just a block or two; it's all over the place. Soaking." He shook off his jacket.

They settled, her and the girls, on the couch, having placed their candles on the coffee table, the TV, and the table by Howard's chair.

"Wonder what the hell it is, must have been a generator, transformer or something blew," he was saying.

Susan went to him: "Daddy, where're the lights?" But Ruthie wriggled close to her. "Don't know, sweety," he said. "Have to do without them for a while—hold this?" He gave Mary the flashlight and bent to take off shoes and socks.

"I don't like it, Daddy!"

He carried Susan to the couch. "It won't be long. We've got candles, we're together here, how about we play some games or something? C'mon, hey"—he motioned to Mary, who sat down across from them. "Wait a minute, where's my beer? Here, okay"—sipped and put it back down on the table. "Let's see, now, how about this?" Nightmarishly huge, the shadow of his hand loomed on the ceiling; shrank, still large and sharp.

The phone rang. "Wait. Wait a minute, I'll get it," he said, serious again. "At least the phone works."

It was his father; he talked for several minutes (". . . yeah, here too . . . yeah, I know; don't worry about it . . . keep until morning . . . look, okay, doesn't come on, first thing, I'll get some ice . . .").

Mary made a face and looked at her: "Wouldn't you know? The minute there's anything, he's going to call here."

"He wants to know you're all right, probably."

"Well, I get tired of it. We're not his . . . I don't know."

Howard hung up and told them: "It's bigger than we thought. Pop says it's the whole of Germantown; he heard it on his portable. The central power plant or something."

"What's that about ice?"

He sat down again.

"The shop," he said. "We've got five hundred bucks of meat in the locker, okay? It's all right overnight, but if the power's off tomorrow, then it could start spoiling on us. So first thing tomorrow, if the power's still off, I have to find some ice, and that means 6:00, 6:30; there'll be a rush on before eight. Anybody with perishables, they'll be at every dry ice dealer around." Mary said nothing. "It'll be on, don't worry about it; mainly he just wants to talk—What? What's going on here?"

"Play our game?"

He did. His two hands twisting over the flame made a shadow like an elephant.

They settled down, and here in the candlelight, they all seemed out of time and free, laughing and fooling for the children. Even Mary joined in, suggesting they eat the ice cream before it melted, and later leading them in singing songs. But none of it counted really. The charm would fail, the children tire, or mention of the baby come. Then time and lives and differences would all come back, more crushing than before.

They had had trouble getting the girls to bed; then Howard and Mary had settled down again and talked with her, politely. There was no use waiting; it wasn't coming on tonight. Better figure on the worst. Look, her alarm was wind-up, could she wake them when she left, then? Had to make sure on that ice.

She had excused herself, taking a candle. She had wished them good night, and come upstairs; then back in her room, she had laid out her uniform, wound her clock, taken off her dress and gotten into bed. The rain kept on. She heard them downstairs in the kitchen, their locking up, then finally they had come up too, had moved around in their room with voices low, agreeing, then each to and from the bathroom, then settled into bed, more talk, silence, nothing.

She alone lay waking with her thoughts:

About the busses or if she'd have to call a cab; about them; about the factory, and whether the black out had reached that far; she had her scheduling to do, first thing; the canteen order had been left half done; about her talk with Mary Lloyd two days ago.

"Well, what? What next, Anna Maye? You have to think what next."

"I'll stay with them."

"What's going to come of that, huh? There's no future like that. You deserve better. And there is, there's something, if you'd just get out and get away from that. I mean, lookit, you're younger than me, you're a fine, decent person. I don't think you realize but there's lots of good people around that would be glad to meet a person like you."

"Please. . . . " She'd turned away, and waved for her to stop.

But Mary Lloyd went on: "I know that Ralph thing was all wrong. It was stupid, it was dumb of me, and I should have known better. But just cause one thing didn't work, don't quit on people; don't go back in your shell. I wouldn't be saying this, except you've been so low lately. And I'm your friend. I can't sit by and watch you get like this. If you'll let me, well, I can't promise miracles, but that's not the point; the point is you get out and build some confidence. Like there's this friend of Tom's, for instance, he's a contractor, he's— I don't know—forty, he's divorced, he's—"

"Please. I don't want to talk about it. I know you're being kind, but this whole conversation, I'm sorry, I don't want to go on with it—no, I don't want to go on with it! Please, just leave me with my problems to myself."

They hadn't spoken to each other since.

She thought, then, about Louie, about how he had changed, how he was facing a grief and hurt so much larger than anything she faced. His wife was home from another operation, an invalid and suffering, like she had aged twenty-five years, he had said. Soon she would have to go back in.

"No, I'm a different man," he had told her. Instead of the proud things, he was telling her about how he'd failed and been mixed up. She would wince at each admission, each hard, shameful thing, then judging (wishing that this wasn't him), she realized that she couldn't judge, or say anything, even, for fear of showing her unworthiness. She wasn't versed enough in love, in weakness, or in the cruelties he'd experienced, to be his equal; to take the hurt and take the courage too, and know him from inside his life.

The more they talked, the more his life began to claim and weigh on her. She felt so close to him sometimes that she must check the impulse to reach out and touch. But she also felt that shamefully, compared to his, her own life lacked real claim or consequence.

She woke to: lights! Radio!

Hurriedly, she fumbled, reached and turned the radio off. She sank back, saw the window black. There was no more rain, but she heard music now and other sounds, as if just after dinner. She realized with relief: the power had come back on. But everything had to be turned off now: did they hear? She listened: all asleep. She got up and put on her wrap and slippers; quietly, opened door to the hall light and a hum downstairs, and no sound from the children's room (still dark); and finally, creaking, started down.

She found everything alive, but without lives: lights, colors, TV test pattern, fan, Howard's beer cans, toys, newspaper, stubs of candles. She turned things off: the TV first, then the fan, and then taking beer cans into the kitchen, the kitchen lights, then lamps. She opened the front door, clutching her wrap against the chill, and turned out the porch light; then stood for a moment watching the empty street, street lights gleaming off of wet cars, and houses lit like it was 7:00 P.M.— some remained that way; others now, like hers, sound by sound (next door, abruptly, music stopped), light by light, returned to darkness, still of night.

Factory Changes

Manville's was supplying a new Leinhardt item—
a chocolate mint packaged for supermarkets.
Leinhardt's was a famous company with advertise-
ments on TV and in all the magazines and had a reputation for making only the finest (and most expensive) chocolates. Normally
people thought of giving their best-known item—the assorted
chocolates—as a special gift. Now here she was packing boxes and
cartons bearing this name and trademark. They had supplied certain
items to larger companies before, continuing to run the usual
Manville lines too, but never to such a famous company.

Soon after they began to run this item, Bill O'Neill, head of
mechanics, had quit; he'd simply vanished, without warning or ceremony. They hardly had time to discuss it over coffee, when three
young men from Leinhardt's had appeared, one of who (a Mr. Bonzer)
took over Bill's old job. Another had something to do with the
bookkeeping and production records, and the third, Mr. Walsh, was

introduced as their superior; he'd be acting as assistant plant manager
with the present general manager, Mr. Spence.

Now this morning Mr. Manville had come around to announce
a meeting at four o'clock. She'd had no chance to talk to anyone about
this, except Mary Lloyd, briefly, at lunch. Mary Lloyd agreed it had to
be about Leinhardt's and the new men, but couldn't guess what.

She left her girls in charge of Mrs. Shaner and met Mary Lloyd
at 3:40. They entered the front offices together; Mrs. Pinkerton, the
office secretary, told them to go right into Mr. Manville's private office.

Ralph Sheets was the only one there, chewing on his toothpick,
jiggling his foot over his knee; he looked up from a magazine (one of
many arrayed on a table before the large mahogany desk).

"You'll catch your death," Mary Lloyd warned. He blinked, with
shiny glasses. "Shouldn't sit so close to the air-conditioning," Mary
Lloyd said.

He stood up, tossed his magazine on the table, slid his hands in
baggy pockets.

Mary Lloyd stepped closer and glanced at things on the desk.
"Where's Mr. Manville?"

Ralph folded his arms and whispered, with a jerk of his head:
"Next door. He's over there with Spence!"

Mary Lloyd raised eyebrows, pursed her lips, then sat in one of
the leather-backed chairs, beneath the golf cartoons.

She sat too, in the chair closest to the door, knocking the hat
rack and making hangers rattle; she stiffened, then sighing, smoothed
her dress. Mary Lloyd snorted.

"What? What is it?" Ralph asked, hitching his trousers and sitting next to her.

"Nothing, Ralph." Mary Lloyd said. "Want a cigarette?"

"What's this? Coffee break?" Louie stood in the doorway, hands
on his hips, hat tilted up, his mouth twisted. Dave Case appeared
behind him.

"I thought you were Mr. Manville!" said Mary Lloyd.

He pushed his hat up farther, shook his head, then passed in
front of Ralph over to the air-conditioner, where he cooled his palms
in the draft.

"Ninety-eight out to the loading platform," said Ralph.

"Yeah, it's about a-hundred and eight up there with them moguls, too," Dave Case told them from the doorway. His uniform was white and had smudges on his legs; but he looked nice. He was taller than Louie, younger, thinner; always courteous. He had unusually blue eyes and wore a hearing aid. Mary Lloyd, hand cupped under her cigarette, asked if he saw an ashtray. "Hah, sure," he said, coming in, and gave her the heavy copper ashtray off of Mr. Manville's desk.

Louie took his hat off and sank into the chair next to the air-conditioner. He rubbed his face with his hand. His hair was matted to his forehead and over the bald spot; he kept toying with his hat between his knees. "We got to have these meetings, he could start on time—where is he?"

"Shh! He's right next door!" hissed Mary Lloyd.

Louie was rude again in reply; he waved his hat at Mary Lloyd, then dropped it on the floor; leaned back into the draft, eyes closed. Mary Lloyd stubbed out her cigarette. But she herself was watching his throat, his knobby chin, his mustache, nostrils.

Louie looked up: "What?"

She looked at her lap and felt Mary Lloyd's eyes.

"You been busy today?" he asked.

"I guess she has!" said Ralph, shifting his weight towards her, taking out a handkerchief. "My truck boy thinks so anyways!"

She smiled. "We finished six pallets this morning, but there's some trouble with the cellophane wrap this afternoon." And in her turn, asked Louie: "You been busy?"

"Jesus. You wouldn't believe what can happen," he complained; and over Mary Lloyd ("We're all busy with this Leinhardt thing, aren't we, Dave?"), went on to say he was short-handed, started late; the dark vanilla never came that Leinhardt's promised by noon yesterday; Bonzer never fixed the hotbox door; Tommy, the enrober operator upstairs, got stung by a wasp out back during lunch, then wanted the afternoon off to go show it to a doctor—"And now, as if I got nothing better to do—'Important meeting.' I told him, I said, 'Look, I don't have time for meetings, I got a real busy day today; besides, I wanta get home early.' Goddamn, thirty years of this job—I know what's important, what isn't. You don't tell me, 'Four o'clock! You be there!' He's not finding nobody else to give him the job I do. I gave his old man a good job. But you don't get big with me. I know my job; there's plenty places that need good chocolate men—"

They heard the hearty laughter, masculine—the opening of the office door, and with it, Mr. Manville's voice: "Harry, seriously now, see that's—Go on, go on!"

"No, sir, you go first!"

"—that's—the point." Then in he came; heavily, briskly, without looking at anyone until he was behind his desk, had run his hands inside his belt to smooth the shirt around his waist, and touched the knot of his dark tie, and sat down slowly in his chair, which creaked. He folded his glasses and put them in his shirt pocket; looked up, finally, frowning.

The others came in, found seats. The door was closed.

He cleared his throat and scratched his cheek.

"All right," he began, "I asked you here to discuss both the future of the Manville Company and our future continued employment, yours and mine. I haven't wanted to alarm any of you, I mean, before this. But frankly things haven't been looking very bright. We're a small family business, as you know, family owned and managed, and the problem is, if small family concerns like this are going to survive nowadays, they grow big fast—like Davis Chocolate did, for instance." He nodded, frowning, towards Louie. "Some of you remember they weren't half as big as we are, but now they got a real consumer name, new equipment, specialized personnel." He glanced at Mr. Walsh, who was leaning against the filing cabinet. "Another thing you can do is try to tie up with some outfit already big, but that's not easy. And see, there aren't many chances for that sort of thing. So there you have the general picture. You either do one of these things or the other or you have to call it a day, close up shop, and liquidate. That's been the trend all over the industry." Suddenly, he was looking directly to her: "Now, I'm explaining this to all of you, because I want you to know where we stand. Now, I've been negotiating for some time, as you know, with Leinhardt Chocolates." He glanced again at Mr. Walsh. "What they want is a low-cost plant, in addition to their big place, where they can experiment with a full, new commercial line. Now the news I have is this: this chocolate mint we've been running has proved successful enough, that now Leinhardt's has agreed to sign a contract, on a test basis, for the next three years. When that's over, they'll have the option to renew for another three years, or to buy Manville's outright. If they decide against renewing, or the purchase, then we'll have to liquidate, the way I've just described."

"Understand, nobody can guarantee the success of this line, or that Leinhardt's will ever want this as a permanent deal. But if you ask me—and I've looked at this carefully—I'm convinced we've got an opportunity here, an exciting opportunity. And this arrangement is going to lead to your security."

She listened numbly to his droning words. He cleared his throat again, looking for reactions.

"Before I continue. . . ." She looked up at his lips, which were swelling, shrinking, curling, changing shape, at his scowl, at the wobbling cheeks and double chin, his nervous eyes. "I must announce at this time, the official retirement of John Spence. . . ." John Spence stood by solemnly, head bowed. "Mr. Walsh," continued Mr. Manville, with a jerk of his thumb, "is to be your new boss, effective tomorrow morning."

Her skin felt tight and clammy, and she squirmed; Ralph Sheets stirred beside her.

"It's up to you to see that you report to him; you satisfy him from now on. Understood? You fail to cooperate or satisfy him—all I can say is that I've filled my obligation to you. I can't do any more."

He asked if there were questions.

"Well, so who's working for who? Who's paying my check? It stays the same, or what?" asked Louie; and he was answered in an irritated monotone.

Mary Lloyd, also looking concerned and alert, asked: "What about you, Mr. Manville?"

He frowned and took a breath: "My duties will be primarily of an advisory nature from now on," he said. "Now, I want to turn this meeting over to Mr. Walsh. Harry?"

"They're going to fire me."

"Oh, calm down. Come on," said Mary Lloyd, leaning closer and hugging her shoulders. "They won't do any such thing."

They were back in her office; Mary Lloyd, having changed to street clothes, had stopped in on the way home. She sat in her chair and Mary Lloyd stood beside her, leaning back against the desk. Outside the glass partition, her department was closed down; the last of her girls had left some time ago.

"An experienced, loyal, hard worker like you. You're valuable. How could they get along around here without you?" She gave her shoulders a squeeze and stood back, smiling, arms crossed.

"We're just nobody, strangers," she said, looking down. "I've worked for Manville's nineteen years. Mr. Manville knows me. I've never worked anywhere else."

"No one says you have to! That's the point. That's why Mr. Manville brought in Leinhardt's. They'll be changes, sure. You heard Mr. Walsh. New work, new machinery and modernizing. They're fixing the place up; they'll be giving us new benefits. We'll get the same as their regular employees over at the big place. They got the money, the brains, and this will be a better place to work, you'll see."

Mary Lloyd snorted at her and pushed away from the desk, stopping in front of the mirror to pat her hair.

"That Harry Walsh. He's smart. And young? I bet he isn't even thirty."

"It's different for you," she said.

Mary Lloyd faced her. "Why's it so different? I've worked here as long as you, or almost. I have my job at stake too. That's why I like this Leinhardt's. I mean, Mr. Manville's getting old. Like he said, if it weren't Leinhardt's, he'd have to liquidate, which means we're on the street tomorrow. Don't think an outfit like Leinhardt's is coming in here for nothing. They're going to buy, and that means permanent work."

She didn't know. She sat there long after Mary Lloyd had left. Arthur, the night watchman, looked in about seven. "Still here, huh? Working late?" He shuffled off about his rounds. The factory was quiet.

Mr. Walsh had spoken of supervisory training sessions, increased production, quality control. She'd be replaced because she couldn't adjust. Where would she be, what could she do if she were fired?

More and more the purpose of her life seemed cut off with the past and her future seemed meaningless and barren. She was thirty-six. She knew no other life.

She took off her sweater, hung it beside the mirror, powdered her face, straightened her hair, took up her purse, and turned off the office lights. Outside, she checked the temperature and humidity gauges, shut down the last of her lights and pushed open the heavy door. The sultry heat of evening warmed her flesh as she turned wearily down the main concourse of the building towards the freight elevator, to the water fountain for a drink. The building was empty and dark, not even Arthur to be seen, as she came back; the concrete floor echoed dully, moist and tacky underfoot; skids of fifty gallon drums were stacked in tiers all along to her right; then skids of sugar bags and starch; overhead was a maze of steam pipes and electrical fittings. She couldn't understand how all of this could be in jeopardy. She didn't want to think about it. The company was here and solid; had been, would be—bricks and concrete, steel, people, business flowing daily; supplies coming in, candy made, orders placed and orders filled.

She had turned the corner by the time clock and had started up the dark front corridor, when she heard a door open, footsteps scuffling. She looked back and saw Mr. Manville standing under the light.

"Mr. Manville?"

He squinted at her through his glasses, glanced down at his watch. She came closer, embarrassed, holding her purse.

"Just starting home?" He scowled at her, perplexed. He was in his shirt sleeves, tie loosened, a few white strands of hair astray. He held a sheet of paper in his hand.

"Yes, Mr. Manville"—she blinked, looked down. "I had some work to do."

"Seen Arthur anywhere?"

She looked at him searchingly. "Yes. He stopped in, it must have been seven. He's upstairs now, probably."

"See this?" He rattled the paper, stepped over and pinned it to the notice board. "Another meeting. Tomorrow morning." He stood back and looked at her, rubbing the back of his neck, alarming her with his sagging face and stubbled cheeks: not like himself at all, but somehow pleading, needing her to stay. "Well," he said, "how long's it been? Twenty years?"

"Nineteen years."

"Um," he nodded, and sucked his lip. "You started with us back before the war. You were working as a general helper. Nora Ransom was forelady, and after her, who? Margarite Bell. Who else was there? Phil Jenks, remember him? Cantankerous old Irisher, retired ten years ago. How about my father; remember him, do you?"

"Well, not exactly, sir. He'd passed away."

"Before your time. That's right. He'd retired; didn't die, really, 'til '46—heart attack. Spence came in in '45. Cousin, Bill, in '47 . . . well, that's all some time ago, isn't it? Lot of things have changed since then; hard keeping track. Doesn't seem like twenty years." His voice grew remote; he put his hands in his back pockets and frowned down at his polished, tapping shoe. "Built this company up to twice the size. Got us through some hard years. Gave my boys a chance to come in, if they wanted, but I'm glad they didn't. They each chose their own careers. Doing fine, too, even Charles, you know, the youngest."

"He's in New York?"

"Yes. He's with *Time Magazine* there, you know. Brought a nice girl with him down here just last month. I'm pleased the way they all turned out." He scratched his arm, absently, and ran his hand around inside his collar. "You never know. Things happen. You do the best you can; try to make the right decisions. . . ." He took his cigarettes from his shirt pocket.

"Nobody could do better than you, Mr. Manville," she found herself insisting.

Fumbling with his lighter, he lit the cigarette; exhaled, cleared his throat. "This Harry Walsh"—he nodded towards the notices— "young fella, but he knows the ropes. Big shots over there think he's tops: young, alert, ambitious—outstanding young fella. They're a top-notch outfit too, you know, not some fly-by-night. I never would've gone ahead with this otherwise, you understand. No guarantee, but this tie-up ought to make for something good for all of you, with or without me, or any member of the Manville family. You work as hard for Harry as you have for me, you won't have any trouble. He's your new boss. You please him, you'll do all right." He brought his hand to his lips, drew on the cigarette, exhaled; put his other hand in his pocket and jingled his change.

Fists clenched, her nails dug into her palms; her muscles ached; she shifted her weight to her other foot. The time clock clicked.

"Beg pardon?"

"You got that cellophane wrap fixed all right?"

"Yes, sir. Mr. Bonzer fixed it fine. Just one of the sprockets was jammed, he said."

"How's it working out at home? You're living with your sister now?"

She nodded. "Yessir."

"Well, don't let me keep you"—he rubbed his eyes, up under his glasses—"it's getting pretty late. You'll want to get started. Didn't mean to keep you here, listening to the old man jaw." He snorted humorously, then grew solemn: "You're a good employee, Anna Maye." He dropped his cigarette and ground it with his shoe.

"Thank you, sir."

"Well, look, you go on home. I'm on my way out too, just got a few things I want to check on. Think I'll look upstairs for Arthur."

"Well, goodnight then, Mr. Manville," she said, giving him a last uncertain look.

"Goodnight."

As she walked away down the corridor, he didn't move—just stood there watching her go; and later, all alone and waiting for the bus, his image haunted her. She'd never seen him quite this way before.

Hospital

He reached the plant earlier than usual, a little after six. The side gate was open, which meant probably Bonzer was in already, and as he pulled up the alley into the back lot, sure enough, Bonzer's new pickup was there. He parked alongside, took his lunch, locked up and let himself in.

The shop lights were on, but he had no time for Bonzer (who must turn up the boilers, oil and grease the equipment, and check out the refrigeration). He went around right and found the concourse lit, and past his own darkened department, past the hotbox, wash tubs, this side of the elevator, he ran into Bonzer anyway, in his Leinhardt mint-greens, up on a ladder, hammering a valve. Doors to the compressor compartment were open opposite and big motors humming.

"Louie. Hiya," Bonzer called down, and hit again.

"What's that? Trouble?"

He tried with his wrench, straining. "Froze," he said, and quit a second.

"Case in yet?"

"Unh, haven't seen him." Frowning, tried: "C'mon, that's, that's it, there—jeez. There, that got her." He was turning by hand now. "Naw, I don't know, just got in, I been down here."

He hesitated, watching. "Yeah, well, I'll see ya."

He still felt awkward with the guy. He was Leinhardt's. He'd come in here like that, taken over O'Neill's job; and all of them, they stuck together, old pals from the big plant. Bonzer and his helper, Gillis, would take their coffee and lunch breaks either out back or up the front office with Walsh. They put him off: young guys, strangers, coming in and running things—and in their company uniforms (Walsh wore a manager's white suit and hat, like a doctor)—like being Leinhardt's, working for some big-time outfit, they were specialists, and Manville's was just a bunch of amateurs. Maybe he had welcomed that at first, because he agreed that this place was half-assed, from Manville on down. But then these new guys, with all their college boy degrees and bullshit rules, they didn't know about a plant this size. All he asked was for them to do their jobs and keep out of his way. You want results, you let him do his way.

He dropped off his lunch, checked his schedule. He climbed the front stairs. He walked through Mary Lloyd's, and into glow and heat and smells of chocolate, starch, and batches in the vats: ran down the windows, started up the fans, and set about tempering. Meanwhile he greased up and checked belts and screens; and on each enrober, he set the timing, belt to belt and belts to screens, and spaced right at the transfer points; he adjusted the blowers and screenshakers to give right thickness. All of this was tricky, delicate, and different for each machine, and different for each type of candy.

"Hey, Lou! Hey!" he heard, over the racket.

Spotting Case, he waved, and shut down Number Three; then checked a few mints at the cooling tunnel. Case came over: fresh white uniform, hair slicked, bright pink sunburn. "Bright and early. How's it doing? How's the weekend?"—speaking loud and one hand to his hearing aid.

"All right." He wiped his hands on a rag. "You?"

Others were in now. He met Leo downstairs. Gillis was in helping Bonzer. His own man, Buster, came in, and he'd finished the
tempering downstairs, so he left him greasing, timing, and the screen
to fix on Number Six.

Anna Maye was in her office, working on papers.

"Hey, hey there."

"Hi. Well—" She pushed around, smiling, then intent. "How
you doing?"

He grimaced and came in, slumped in a chair, took his hat off,
turned it in his hands. "Took her in."

"Louie—"

"Yeah, you know. Yesterday. She won't be coming back, we
both know that. The doctor says to operate again will help the pain,
maybe give her another month, two months. But there's no way to
keep her home anymore."

She held his eyes, like cowed. "It's what you had to."

"Should have been me, not her."

"Don't say that, Louie."

"She's forty-six. Worn out, she's lost fifty pounds. I carry her, it's
like carrying Josie. Drove her myself, just the two of us. Frank and
Nancy took Josie, the night before. We figured that was best, for now,
anyway. She didn't want the kids. And just she laid her head back,
looking, you know, all the way like that. I got her settled, stayed for
dinner. But like she's someplace I can't reach. Gets you, that's all."

She listened, knuckles to her mouth.

"I'm never letting Josie go. I told her, that's my worry now.
We'll work it out. It's just I wish, you know, for her sake, she felt easier. But all I got is promises."

"No, you've got deeper. You've got love. She's got to see that.
But even if she doesn't, it's what you have inside. You have to trust
yourself."

"Yeah." He breathed, eyes down. "Tell you, if wasn't for you sometimes, I mean having you listen and talk like this, I don't know if I could handle it. I really don't."

"You can and you do," she said, acting flustered. "I'm glad if I can help. But you're a good man. You're strong. And just, you make me feel so small, when I think of all the things you live with, and how each time you've cared. You've kept on, known what to do. I truly respect you."

"Hey. Wait," he said. "We're talking about you now, aren't we? I mean what are you saying, you don't have it?"

"Not me." She held her hand up. "Not now. No, I appreciate, but look, it's late. We have to stop now." She straightened her papers and stood up, waiting for a moment, like an appeal.

Towards three, Walsh came around. The coating operations had been going good, except for a screen downstairs that he'd had to shut down five, ten minutes to replace. Otherwise, the packaging had held him up. Walsh checked a mint, looked satisfied. "Looks good," he said. "Got that screen fixed downstairs, huh?"

"Yeah, nothing serious. Running good."

They both watched Tommy and the women. "You got a minute, Lou? Something I've been wanting to talk to you."

He nodded. "Sure, yeah, they're okay." He followed him out through the kitchen, past the moguls, to the outside landing, where Walsh offered him a smoke.

Then Walsh was asking about Anna Maye: "I don't mean like she's a nice lady, or she's loyal, or you're all fond of her and all; but does she do a job?"

He told him, sure, you bet she does. As good or better than Mary Lloyd. Then he asked him, why, what's the problem? Walsh said discipline, for one thing; overall efficiency. She tried to run her department like a social club; and he was top help; he knew the whole place had to run to capacity, and that packaging was holding it up. Look at the slow downs today. She's got absenteeism, slacking off; her scheduling's been off.

"Okay, lookit, Harry"—he defended her—"you're asking me? There's no one working harder in this place. She deserves real credit, she's running as good as she is. The same with Mary Lloyd; they're both of them running the best you'll get. The problem ain't with them—it's who they're working with. It's low grade help you're getting now; and either you can put on more, or you can raise your wage to where you're getting better—but these school kids and these shiftless types—takes you three to give you one. And same with the equipment. Get some new stuff in, and get your guys in there and figure out some different layout. Then you'll get your volume up. But don't go blaming Anna Maye. They're doing first rate with what they got; weren't for them, those operations wouldn't be going half of what they are."

Walsh listened, weighing what he said, but saying nothing back. Then left off with just "Thanks," and "We can keep this just between us, okay? I'll think about it."

Afterwards, he had no chance to tell her. What with winding up and trying to get out early. He had to get back, brief the men, and make sure Tommy here, and downstairs, Buster, would supervise the shut down; and no more foul ups, like with pans. They had to wash down, clean up, set the chocolate right. He'd talk to her tomorrow.

The traffic was heavy and he got home late. He called Frank's, and made sure that Dom and Victor would pick up Josie. He took a quick shower, changed, had a can of chili for dinner; made it to the hospital a little after seven.

Then he sat in the parking lot a while, trying to sort himself and put the day behind him. The last of the sun was shifting through the trees, and high up (he peered out the window), he watched a pigeon bright against the deepening sky. For a moment all seemed his; all timelessness and leisure, stirring trees, the lawn, the traffic casual, the people strolling past along the street, and the hospital itself just as blank and harmless looking as a school. Then a station wagon pulled in, parked two down; a lady got out, in her forties, dressed up for the visit, face intent and frowning as she passed.

Paula shared a room, windowless, with an old Polish woman, Mrs. Mocek, who'd watched them come in yesterday, eyes alert as the nurse introduced them, but who had only managed, "Yes," and then had grasped for the nurse and whispered; "Here, all right, I'll be with you in a minute," the nurse had told her, "I have to see Mrs. Miscello now."

Rearranging Mrs. Mocek's pillows, the nurse had drawn a curtain around the bed. "She's a very sick woman," the nurse had said, as the orderly fixed Paula's bed, and Paula, in the wheelchair, had tightly gripped his hand.

She was on the fourth floor, in a different wing from the other times, so he walked past admittance, down a strange corridor, and turned left, the way they'd come in yesterday. He took a different elevator, making room for a guy rolled in on a stretcher (just a kid really, out cold, his head all bandaged), the doctor, the nurse, and they were talking like he wasn't there—suturing and hypo-this and Dinah someone on assist and what about in A and E? They stopped at four. They wheeled the kid out, turning left; he turned right, remembering, with dinging overhead and paging Dr. Buck, past kitchen-like, past lab-like rooms, with stainless steel counters, microscopes, medicines and stuff, past a room with large, forbidding rigs—life support or X-rays, he didn't know—and on down the hall to the ward at the end, where he turned down a double row with some doors open, others closed. He tried not to look; they were all strangers, all bad off, this one lying fleshless, wasted, all hooked up, another—woman, younger—cards and flowers everywhere, and an older woman, the mother maybe, visiting, who gave him a sharp, indignant glance). At another door, a nurse came out, carrying a tray, closing the door behind her: "Help you, sir?" She was a stocky redhead, fifties, all in white with a special cap.

"Visiting," he said. "My wife, Miscello. Four-twenty-nine."

She nodded, solemn, sympathetic: "Mrs. Miscello, yes. I was just there. She's got the surgery tomorrow, doesn't she?"

"Yeah. Stomach."

She nodded: "She had a bad night, and then tests today, but she got some rest this afternoon, and she's on a very strong drug now, it's helping with the pain. But don't be surprised, if she's a little groggy."

"Yeah," he said. Any problem, just call her, Mrs. Downs, she told him; she was the floor nurse; Dr. Tollerman should stop in later. "Yeah, thanks," he said, feeling bashful and obliged.

Her—his—in all of this, in a strange room, in a strange bed and gown, with her hair tied back. They'd cranked her up part way and propped her with pillows, and her arm was bandaged. She wasn't looking at him, but towards the wall, and he couldn't tell if she was asleep. He tapped lightly at the door, glancing at the other, Mrs. Mocek, who was watching, head back, eyes unsettling.

"Hey," he said—and nodded, smiling, to Mrs. Mocek—came on in, just as Paula turned and met him with a troubled smile. "Well, how's it doin', huh?"—her hand squeezed his, and gingerly, he bent to kiss her.

"Not so good."

He nodded. "Here, let me get a chair."

"Pain's been bad," she said. "They gave me codeine, but it didn't last. Just a small dose, every four hours, and they wouldn't give me any-more. I couldn't sleep. Poor Mrs. Mocek had to listen to me all night long. Finally, the doctor, this morning, gave me something knocked me out, and they've got me on something stronger now, makes me feel all thick and dizzy. But I don't know, I can't go through much more. Just can't."

"I know. But look, the operation's going to fix all that. They're going to get the worst out. You're going to be a whole lot better."

"I don't know," she said, with that bleak, fixed look, until she winced, her face knotted and she shook her head with tears.

"It's tough. I know it's tough," he said. He watched her, feeling winded and abashed. Then he got up: "Let me get that curtain."

"Yes, you visit," Mrs. Mocek urged, as he pulled it across. Then he turned on the light, and it was just the two of them, private, close. He gently stroked her hand.

"Where're the children?"

"Coming," he said. "Frank's got to work, but Dom and Victor are picking Josie up. Talking to Dom, I don't know, about an hour ago and they were just starting. Shouldn't take them very long."

"Has Josie been all right?"

He faltered. "Yeah. Called Nancy. Pretty much like you'd expect. Says she's acting kind of homesick and confused, not eating much or playing or anything, but it's only been three nights. Been a couple of tantrums, but they handled it okay. Nancy says like not to worry—they love her; they're going to give her the best home that they can."

She looked, then closed her eyes, scowling. "It's not right," she said. "I know they'll try, but they got the baby. They're just starting out. She's just too much for them."

"They're going to be all right. For now, anyway. It's what they wanted; they're going to try. We got to give them a chance. Not much else to do, right? I mean, I thought we settled that. And it's hard some ways, but still it's better. Nancy home all day, and being there with family."

"It's later."

Angry, hurt, he held it back. "Later's going to be okay," he said. "We'll work it out. We're going to pull together. I was telling Frank, like I can sell the house, and all of us together, we could take a bigger place. Or they don't want that, I could take a place nearby, you know, for Josie and me, find her a good school, quit the job and take something differ-ent, so I could leave her off mornings and Nancy take her afternoons, and I'd be back by five. Or still, you know, there's those parents' groups and stuff; we just don't know until we look. Maybe someone with their own kid, they could take her afternoons. But it's not just nothing. There's plenty of ways. The main thing is we stick together, and we love her, and she's going be with us. Like before you kept us going; now we gotta do that for each other. And I know, I've been more trouble than anything else. But I love them too. They're going to be okay."

For a moment, this time, he thought she might accept. But as she gripped his hand: "It won't work out," she said. "You have to work; and you can't keep a home. She needs full-time care. Someplace steady, not this back and forth. You have to think of her future, five years from now, ten. Frank and Nancy have their own lives; they can't plan their lives for her. And no matter what you tell yourself, or you want to try, Louie, you simply aren't enough alone. You're going to have to put her somewhere."

"Hey, c'mon. What are you saying?"—the shock and wound could wait; the main thing was his alarm for her, for how low she'd gotten and turned against hope. "You don't mean that. We none of us want that. You seen those places; you seen like before. I mean, how can you give up on the chance? Any chance that we can keep her. Give us some credit, honey. We're not quitting, never quitting. That's the same as give up on ourselves."

She blinked and turned her face. "It's no good," she said dully. "I don't want it either. But it's what you are. It's how you're going to be. It's what's the best for all of you. There's no use fighting." She met his eyes and he looked down. "It's nothing you should blame yourself. Don't be set against it. All those places, you don't know. You have to look, ask for help. There's the social worker here. Maybe there're good places. You could visit, have her weekends. But she'd have things there you can't give her. You should want that, Louie, for her; for you too. You know she's all right, then you'll be free. The children free to live the way they should. That's all I'm saying. It's a chance for you too, and the others."

He sat silent, no heart to reproach, and at the same time feeling sunken with shame. "You never wanted this before. I mean, all along, we've felt the same. Now why, why all of a sudden like this?"

"There's no more time."

"No call thinking like that," he pleaded. "I mean, look, we done all right so far, ain't we? Think about us, think about our feelings in this. We got a right, honey." He swallowed. "Sure, those places, there's Therese, the nuns, and if we got to, we'll look. But it doesn't have to come to that. I mean, that's our part now."

Through the curtain, Mrs. Mocek was coughing, muffled, followed by the clatter of a water glass.

"I don't want that weight on you," she said. "I don't want you going through all that, or putting the children through it. It's not going to help, Louie. There's only so much, any of you. You can't keep living from day to day and hoping somehow it'll all work out. It took the both of us, Louie; we were younger and the boys were on their own. But that was hard, even for us, even when I could give her all my time. You can't ask that of them now, or yourself. It's not the same. The more you fight, the less you're going to do for her and you're going to upset all your lives. I don't want that, Louie. You have to think what's reasonable. You want her safe, and if anything happens to you, she's still no worry on the children."

"You want her put away."

She lay back, breathing slowly, worn out by the strain. "I may not come out of that tomorrow," she said. "I need to know it's something firm, and won't be something that drags you down, or be a shadow on your lives. You're only clinging to false hopes. Be honest. What's the good for her?"

He realized that all the things he meant (no burden, no grief; they were stronger; their hopes were no more false than her doubt; they'd be all together; they had to try), now made no use. This wasn't his need anymore, but hers, and it was final and apart. While vowing all the more deeply to himself, and bearing all his lifetime's faults, he had to grant her the only answer that she could trust.

"Okay," he muttered, choking on it as hard as on the truth. "It's what you want. It's right, I guess. And like you say, the kids; and probably it's the best for her."

"Louie?"

"I'll ask the people here, if you want me to." He hung in silence for a moment, while she studied him; then doubt gave way, and in her eyes he saw apology, and then the gratitude, relief.

For him: there was no costlier, more wretched, or more faithful lie.

Later, the kids had come. Josie, scared probably from her own visits here, pulled loose of Victor, and came stumbling, battling with the curtain, to his arms. She wore her party dress and shiny shoes, and smelled of fresh soap and sweat.

He hushed her: "Hey, here, here, baby. Quiet, quiet for the lady now. Shh, now. Here, now look, here's Mommy."

The boys said hello shyly. Paula struggled up—"Get her pillow," he told Victor. He moved the chair so Josie could climb up, and with him to steady her, Paula could hold her tight and kiss her. "Miss you so much, love you so much"—then Paula sank back, holding Josie's hands, stroking her hair. "That's a real pretty ribbon. Nancy give you that?"

He waved in Dom to take his place; cleared back the curtain to make room; asked Mrs. Mocek, did she want him to pull hers? (She didn't, eyes on Josie; then closed.) Mostly he just stood back, leaving room for Paula and the boys, except that Josie craned and whined for him, so then he moved alongside Dom, where he could hold and rub her from behind.

She spoke to Victor, who was dressed like a punk, cheap flashy suit, trying to look big time. He'd been back four months and nothing had changed. He never visited. He'd had a couple of jobs, night clerk, used cars, running around with wiseguys down in the neighborhood. No matter all that Victor hurt her, she kept hoping he'd come back to stay. "Good job, yeah," he was saying. "Joe Iagulli, you know, from back school, says he knows some guys. Sharp guys, buying in this lighting supply. And what they're looking, someone do road sales. Says it's gravy, all these little lighting shops, and what they got's top line. Any good at all, you're making three, four hundred, and these guys, these are the kind of guys, they're into a lot of things. Think you got good stuff, you're set. That's what he says. So, I don't know, I call them up, go down. Hit it off real good, you know? Shoot the breeze, talking like I done sales out in Vegas. And like he says, these guys are sharp. They're putting money in, they're gonna take this outfit, make it go. So what they want the road guy, someone bright, can operate alone, and push like old accounts and bring in lots of new ones, upstate, west. Start me on commissions, give me car, expenses. Do good enough, they'll pay me a salary later."

"That's good. That's right for you," she said, unquestioning. "Sounds like something, you can make a start."

Then there was Dom, more quiet, serious, never any wise stuff, acting tough, but just as closed and turned away. Dom had told her to divorce him, but when she'd taken him back, both boys had put a wall up: Victor going out of reach, bumming; and Dom in his own way, getting his own place, working for the same contractor, hard work, but like something had frozen inside and there was nothing else he wanted, nothing he was looking for out of life. Maybe they would be different, both of them, if he had given them something to respect, but it was too late now: twenty-seven, twenty-nine. Anything he would say, would just give them worse offense. Only Frank had gone ahead.

"Yeah, not like keeping hours," Victor was saying. "My own time, my kind of thing, meeting people, get around. Can't keep boarding off of Dom here, spoiling it for all his broads."

Dom complained: "What broads, your broads."

Paula asked Dom, suddenly serious: "What about Lucy D'Alsonso, you still dating her?"

He hadn't known that Dom and her had been talking about girls.

"Her and some Irish trick," Victor put in.

And Dom: "Naw, Ma, her and me, she's marrying some college guy, a lawyer, something, out of Baltimore."

"Nothing you want anyway," Victor sneered.

But Paula, distressed: "They're good people, the D'Alsonsos. I thought you had it real special for her."

Dom mumbled, "I dunno, she got fed up when I never asked her."

She kept looking: "That's not right, a good girl like that. Both of you, you're no kids. Time you quit this fooling around, and thought more serious. A decent girl, someone you can count on; you don't sneer at that. It's what you need. The both of you: responsibility, and something more than just yourselves. Maybe you think you're too good, you're never going to get tied down, but that's just missing out. It's only gonna twist you up inside."

Victor tried to reassure her: "Hey, c'mon, Ma. It'll happen when it does. Just give it time, that's all."

"I wanted see you settled, wanted to know your wives."

"We're going to," Victor said. "We'll be okay. But won't be no one half of you."

Josie got restless and started whining. Paula asked her about her new room and Nancy, the baby, things she liked, but Josie lolled back and reached around for him. The boys talked about tomorrow, faces set, uncertain: We'll be here, Ma. Just rest up now, get over that tomorrow, we'll be back as soon as you feel up to it. Love you, Ma. Goodbyes. She held Josie.

While they waited for him in the hall, he'd said his own good-bye: "It'll be okay. I'll come straight from work."

"You'll start looking," she insisted, so he promised her again.

Outside then with Josie, the boys still separate from him and hostile to him in their grief. They stood watching while he hugged Josie and told her: "You're going home to Nancy now, it's going to be okay, and I'll be seeing you real soon." She whined and clung— fought with him finally; it ended in a tantrum, Victor holding her as they drove off.

He drove back through the night, the town and lit up storefronts, street lights, traffic, taking turns, stop, start, slow down, waiting for the guy ahead; down darker streets with houses lit and chirring crickets, sleeping trees, to his neighborhood, his own dark house and yard.

Pulled in. And like an echo or a reflex, he had no force left, but was carried by his motions.

Out of the car, grass wet, crickets, sweep of stars, Leavitt's porch light in the trees; scrape of the screen door, key, opening onto musty dark.

His mind was all one pounding blur: of Josie, clinging to him; boys, like crippled by their hate; of Anna Maye, of Walsh and the job; of Paula, without hope; of him, with nothing left except to lie, and even in the saying, even going through the motions, he was risking she was right, and that he'd be same he'd always proved. He had to hold against that now, and think his talk with Anna Maye. Here, as he paced from room to room, he must keep intact, keep simple, ordinary—wash the dishes, clean up the kitchen, watch TV, and maybe get a drink to calm his nerves, a good night's sleep, an early start; but all the things he should and owed, and all the movements of that man (so clear in mind, whom nothing could dissuade or break) went hollow, flimsy, no one left to firm against.

Moving Out

"Saturday? The Y? This Saturday?" Mary demanded, disbelieving, putting down her fork. "You can't be serious."

She looked down at her plate and nodded. "Yes. Yes, I am."

And Howard: "Aw, no, no. Now wait a minute. What is it? You don't want to do that."

"Well, we won't let you. You can't. There's no reason. You want to find another place, well, that's one thing, but to just spring this on us like this, and the Y, what Y? North Philly? Have you ever seen it? Do you even know what you're talking about? I mean you don't mention it. You just go ahead without asking us. And there's no call. We can help. You're no hardship case. No one's pushing you. You've got plenty time; you've got money. It's just you don't want to admit it, isn't it? It's gotta be you stay with us or nothing; and if you can't stay, then you're gonna make the worst of it, and it's all our fault, right? Well, it's not our fault, and you know it. It's how things are. And if we can't change that, it doesn't mean we don't care. We do. We want to help; we want to see you settled someplace decent;

someplace comfortable and safe, and where you can have your privacy at least, and not some dump of a YWCA. We're not kicking you out on the street."

"Okay, hold it, willya?" Howard intervened. "What Mary's saying, there's just no reason. We don't want you leaving that way. So first off, let's just call the Y and cancel—they don't care. Then let's settle down, let's talk about it, let's try'n see what's best for everyone."

She shook her head, all quavery, fighting back tears. "No. I'm leaving. I don't want to stay. I don't want to talk. My mind's made up. It doesn't matter to me now. The house is yours; I'm out of your way now. It's not your worry. It's nothing more to do with you. I only want what's easiest. I want to go, I want it over with."

"Mommy?"

"Shush, Susan. Look, you and Ruthie, you're excused. Go in the living room. Go on! We're talking."

And when they'd gone, first Howard, "Anna Maye . . . ," then Mary, overriding him: "You're just doing it for spite, for stubbornness and spite. You won't listen, you won't even talk about it—"

"Cut it out!"

"No, I won't!—All these months and now just suddenly, like that, you can't wait to move out. YWCA, you don't care. No reason. No consideration. How do you think we feel? Here, take it all, just kick me out, I'm nothing to you anyway. Well, that isn't how it is. We're not taking anything from you. We don't want you anywhere you don't want to be. We need the house, yes, we need the room— and there's no sense kidding ourselves—we're different people and we can't go on living on top of each other—but we're not turning our backs, and it's not like there's no place else. There're plenty places, places you'd be perfectly happy and a lot better off than here. But no, you don't want to hear about them. You don't want to take the time. You don't want to admit there's anyplace else. You just want to rub our faces in it. But it's not our faces, it's yours. You're the one we're thinking of. And this is no good—you know it. You just can't stand we're right; you've got to sneak off and pull some stupid trick rather than give up your pathetic self-pity and resentments. Well, go on, go ahead, do it. Don't listen to us. Don't let us help, aw no. You wanta be miserable, fine, but don't expect us to feel bad about it. You got no one but yourself to blame."

"I don't blame anyone," she said sternly, and with indignation now, not tears. "I don't blame you or Howard. I want you to have the house. I know I've been a burden on you. But this is very hard for me. I don't care what you think. It's not for you to tell me anything, not you, no." And glanced at Howard. "This is my decision, what I'm doing, what I have to do. And it's hard enough without arguing about it. I'm sorry if you can't respect it, but it's nothing to do with you—it's me. And all I was hoping was you could drive me, and I have to pack and I'll have to store some things here. But I didn't want any bad feelings; I didn't mean to be a problem. It's just this had to be; it's for me to work, and me to go through, and this is the least painful way for me."

And then their silence: Howard leaning forward, forehead in his palm; and Mary—Mary snorted, looked away, glanced back, eyes wide, mouth twisted, then away again, and shook her head.

"Okay," he conceded, grudgingly. "It's what you really want—"

"No!" Mary put in.

"Shut up!—It's what you want. I don't like it. I think you oughta wait and find the right place first. But you feel this strongly about it, your mind's made up, you got yourself a place, that's good enough for me. Maybe this kind of thing, it's better you work it out alone, I don't know. That's up to you. But anything you want, drive you, help you pack, sure—and more'n that, anything you need from us, just say the word. Okay? We're ready to help out anyway we can. And look, you change your mind, I mean there's still time, that's okay; or you go ahead and once you're there, you don't like it, that's okay too. All you gotta do is call."

"Oh, swell. Pat her on the back. Let her go someplace like that, when you know it's stupid and she knows it's stupid, and the only reason is she wants to throw it in our face—"

"You're wrong," she said.

"That's all it is. Your stupid pride. Your grudge. You hold it all against us—yes, you do. You're gonna go off, and gonna make yourself miserable. And why? Because we can't keep you here, that's all; you don't care why. You don't care there's any other way. You won't listen to reason; you won't take any help. All you want, you wanta make it the worst you can, and then say this is what we did to you. Well, it's not us. It's you. It's spite. And I won't have anymore to do with it." And glanced from her to him, and breathed; then pushed away, stood up, and left.

And now. Saturday.

She'd woken from her fretful sleep at dawn, had taken her things and used the bathroom and fixed her hair and touched up the redness and dark of her eyes, had put on the house dress she'd laid out, and quietly as on workdays, went down for her solitary breakfast.

She'd settled down and eaten, while six had come and gone; and she was all awake, and planning, when she heard the children: scuttling, whispers, giggle on the stairs. And then they'd found her, both of them in panties: Susan startled, Ruthie grinning, reaching for her hug. "Well, good morning! How are you? Hi, darling . . . we're up early, aren't we? Want some breakfast? I just finished mine."

"How come you're up?"

"Well, I've got lots to do today," she'd said. "But how about a really special breakfast? How'd you like some pancakes?" She kept on being happy, normal, and she made their breakfast. But they sensed, they knew: Ruth with her clinging, Susan with her sullen pout.

"You're going away today."

"That's right. But not until later. Your Daddy's going to take me."

"And you're packing all your things, and you aren't going to live here anymore; and we aren't ever going to see you anymore?"

"Of course, you'll see me. I'll visit, and I'll sit with you, and we can do things together; and when your Mommy has the baby, then I'll probably come, and I'll take care of you. But this is your house now. And I have to have my own place too, where I live."

"But why don't you wanta stay with us?"

"I do, sweety, and I'll miss you very, very much. You know that. You know I love you, both of you, and I'll always love you, even when I'm not here. But I can't stay, because it wouldn't be right any-more. I'd just be in the way. And I want you to be happy, and with your Mommy and Daddy, and have the whole house to yourselves, so you can be together."

"No! I don't want you to go! Please, Aunt Anna!" And Ruthie joined in too, and came and burrowed in her lap.

"Shh, now, shh! I'm not going yet."

"Mommy says you don't even like us anymore!"

"She knows better than that, and so do you. You know I love you, and I'm very sad, and I wish I could be with you for always and always."

"But why can't you stay?"

"Because I can't, Susan. I have to go. And it's hard—it's very hard to say goodbye. But I know we won't stop loving each other, and we'll still see each other; we'll just be living different places, that's all. You'll be happy here, and I'll be happy where I'm going too, and there'll be lots of other ladies there, and I'm going to tell them all about you. And that'll make me very proud. So it's not so bad. And we have the whole morning now, and you know what I was hoping? I was hoping we could go upstairs and you could help me pack. Could you do that? Cause I still have all my things to get ready, and I don't know if I can do it by myself. But we'll have to be real quiet, so we don't wake your Mommy and Daddy."

And so they'd followed her upstairs—shh, quiet—Ruthie clutch-ing the newspaper she'd asked her to carry, and Susan frowning and glum, but both of them excited by this trust. The sight of her room upset them—boxes, bareness, drastic change; but right away, she'd said: "See how much I've done? This one has my shoes, see where it says? And this one . . . but what we have to do now is clear off my knick-knack shelves and pack away each of my little statues. And we'll have to be real careful and wrap each one in newspaper, so it doesn't break. Okay? So why don't you get up on the bed there, and we'll use this box. . . . Ruthie, here, let's spread out your paper. . . . Well, which one shall we start with?" She wrapped the china spaniel over and over and put it in the box. "Okay, you do this one"—a crystal cat for Ruthie—"And Susan"—old man sitting on a stump. "What's he doing?" "Well, he's an old man. See his beard? And he's been walking, but now he's tired." She watched each time for special fascination and attachment, for she'd never let them handle them before ("Those aren't toys; those are my statues; they're just to look at, not touch"). "You know what this one is?" "She's dancing." "That's right, she's a gypsy dancer, isn't she pretty?" But they didn't seem to like her enough, nor the shepherdess, nor robin, nor coolie, nor brother and sister. And Ruthie liked animals, but it wasn't until the baby rabbit, crouched with his pink nose and flattened ears, that she murmured, stroked, and guiltily looked up. "You can have him, but you'll have to be good to him and remember he's not a toy, and if you drop him, he'll break." She turned to Susan: "I want you to have one too." And Susan brightened and looked: "That little girl?" "This one? Yes. She's very special. See her pretty face and the funny dress and bonnet?" "What's she doing?" "Well, she's picking flowers, see the basket? And know why she's special? Because she was your grandmother's—my mother's and your Mommy's mother's—and she brought her here from another country a long time ago, and far, far away, and little girls there used to dress like that." "Where's she from?" "It's a place called 'Lithuania,' can you say that?" "She's mine now, for keeps?" She nodded. "Ruthie, look—she was grandma's from 'L-Luwaynya,' and she had a little basket, see?" Ruthie jealously clutched tight her own. "But both of you, you know I love you. And I hope you love them too, because they're very fragile, and you can't just treat them like toys, okay? You want to keep them in a nice safe place where they can't get broken." "I do, and I'll take very good care of her!" "I know you will, honey, and Ruthie will too, won't you, Ruthie?" And fraught with all she wished the gifts to mean, she leaned over a last enfolding hug and kiss.

Then Mary had come, frowning and mussed, clutching her robe. "Good lord, what have you been doing?"

She kept on with her wrapping. "Good morning, Mary."

"Mommy!"

"Look, Mommy, look what Aunt Anna gave me!"

"It's not even eight o'clock—What, Susan?" Then she'd seen, examined it, mouth set in a grimace.

"She was grandma's."

"I know, dear."

"See my bunny!"

"I wanted them each to have something," she'd said, meeting and firmly holding Mary's baleful stare. And Mary shook her head, and whatever she'd been about to say, gave it up.

"Well, that was very nice of Aunt Anna, wasn't it? Did you thank her? . . . Good. Because I want you to come on now. I don't want you bothering her."

"We were helping!"

"No backtalk. Just come on. Come on! You can go down and watch TV or something, and I'll be down in a minute and make your breakfast."

"We had breakfast."

"Go on." She hesitated at the door, scowling down at nothing for a moment. "I'll see you later." Quietly shut the door behind her.

She'd finished everything.

She'd left the box with figurines, radio, clock, two small plants, and toiletries open on the dresser. She'd stripped the bed. She'd hefted the suitcases and dress bag onto the bed and laid out her good dress and shoes. She'd gone down for the broom and mop and bucket, carrying the first and lightest box, and despite Howard's protests (he was eating), taking it on down to the cellar. And when she'd come up, first Howard: "Look, don't do anymore of that. I'll be up in a minute"; then Mary had seen the bucket: "What are you doing? Now come on. For godssake! Gimme that!" "I want to clean." "I can clean it!" "I want to clean my room," she'd insisted. And she had, while Howard took down box after box; she'd swept and dusted, mopped the floor (especially the closet was filthy), sponged clean window sill and moldings. And then she'd carried down her trash. "Well, that's everything," she'd told them, together on the couch and with the children. "I want to shower and change. And then could we leave in about an hour?" "Aunt Anna?" "Okay," Howard said flatly. "Don't you want some lunch?" Mary had asked. "No, I can't. Thank you." And she'd showered, careful not to wet her hair, and back in her room, had powdered and made up, brushed and pinned her hair, and dressed, and everything ready, everything settled and accounted for (money in her purse), had nothing left to do but sit here, stunned by fact.

And now.

"Anna?" Howard stood in her doorway, biting his lip. "About ready?"

"Well, yes," she said. "I suppose I am."

"Don't want any lunch?"

"No, it's better this way," she said, and was on her feet, and straightening her dress. "We have to get started."

"Take these first?"

"Not both. Wait." But he dragged both suitcases free, grunting with their unexpected weight—"S'all right"—and bumped out the door, around the railing, down the stairs. Meanwhile she retouched her face and hair, pinned on her hat, snapped shut her purse. Then he was back, a little flushed and short of breath.

"Well, that's everything," she said. "If you could take this box— I'll bring the dress bag. But be careful, it's got my figurines and bottles and things; maybe we could put it on the front seat."

"Okay, I got it. Hey, look"—he turned—"leave the dress bag. I'll get it. Just c'mon and say goodbye. They're waiting for you." He wouldn't move until she nodded and stepped forward, though she hung back briefly—a last look at this room without her. Then out and started down behind him, her low heels clacking and empty-handed but for her purse. And there they were, and Howard went ahead, and as she stepped off the stairs, the screen door banged, and she was all alone, the children staring, Mary, arms folded, smiling.

"All set?" Mary asked.

"Yes." She put her purse on the phone table, and bent down, beckoning to the girls. Ruthie came gladly, but Susan followed glum again.

"Are you going now?" Susan asked.

"That's right. I'm all packed. Time to say goodbye now." She gave Ruthie her hug and kiss. "Careful of my hat—Susan?" And Susan's specially tight hug surprised her. "Susan . . . you be good . . . you be a good girl," she said, kissing her hair, squeezing back. Then firmly eased apart, and stood, and looked at Mary.

"Here. C'mon. Remember what I told you," Mary said, coming closer and drawing them to her. "You'll be seeing her again."

Then Howard was back. "I'll just get the dress bag." He went upstairs.

"I just can't believe it. I mean you're going through with this. But I hope it works out for you all right. And anything I said, well, I had no business and I'm sorry. I just wish it could be different. And I hope you don't feel too bitter against us, cause you matter to us very much. And we want to see you settled. And if you need us, well, you know we're here."

And Howard came down, dress bag rustling, and shifted his grip, and went on out.

"I told you. I don't bear any grudges, Mary. This is my decision."

She picked up her purse. And out on the porch, then, she saw him slam down the trunk lid and start up the walk.

"Well, goodbye," she said, reaching for a stiff embrace.

"Take care of yourself, Anna."

And quick goodbyes for the children.

"Stay back. Stay here, kids!"

Howard held the door, and she stepped out and down, and he helped her.

"Bye!"

"Bye, Aunt Anna!"

"I'll be back in about an hour," he told them, and down the walk, and sun everywhere, and then he held the car door, and after she got in, slammed it. And she sat there: no tears, just clenched and suffocating silence, looking down. And deaf to shrill cries of her name, and blind to watching eyes and waves.

"Hey, you okay?"

She swallowed and wiped tears again: "Don't mind me. I'm sorry . . . ," and then was done, had passed, dull readiness returned. "I'll be all right," she said.

He was busy driving, jaw clenched, nothing else to say. Down Washington, towards Germantown, her route to work, through family neighborhoods with children playing and people on porches, and then onto Germantown, and not like riding to work, but Saturday and noon, and brightness, heat, not air blowing in her face, stops, starts, traffic lights and traffic, and brick and cobblestone and trolley tracks (she steadied the open carton between them), and businesses and people everywhere, and then the poorer sections, bars, the lounging groups of men and boys, the park, and handsome buildings of the private school, and rising behind them, the big, new apartments, and down the hill towards Stenton (the factory just two blocks away), the long, blank factory walls and gates and loading platforms (Jenkins Pipe and Supply, Liberty Printing, Coca Cola), and wedged between or facing, the narrow, blistered row houses, with their steep steps, and all black families now, and then the intersection, U.S. Steel stretching for blocks down to the right, and sharply to the left—"That's my bus stop," she said. "Factory's just up there." He grunted. A tractor trailer rumbled past; then the light changed, and they kept on Germantown and under the bridge, and this was stranger, more forbidding, City to her now, and all unknown: street narrow, traffic jammed, double parking, people swarming everywhere (and mostly black), and endless little storefronts, shops and businesses, cafes, laundries, neon even in the daylight, nightclubs, too much, on and on, and still more complex, motley and perpetual.

"Shouldn't have any trouble getting a bus down here, anyway," he said, with a quick glance, then braked hard as a truck shot ahead from a side street—"Jerk!" And muttered and shook his head. "I mean, from Broad, they probably got one turns on Germantown. You ask 'em at the Y." She nodded, wanting to keep up the small talk, make it easier, but couldn't think. "I'm grateful you're driving me," she said, and he gave her a look. "No, it's very good of you, and all the help you've been. . . ." And then should stop, but kept on: "You understand, I'm not upset with you or Mary. It's just I've been wrong and I know it; I've been selfish. . . ." "C'mon," he rebuked her. "Yes, I have; I've been too weak. I've just been holding on and holding on and shutting my eyes to it. I should have done this months ago. And I'm ashamed for the trouble I've been, because I wasn't thinking of you; I was only thinking of myself. And my problems aren't yours. I have to help myself. I have to have some self-respect." He kept on driving, silent, almost like he hadn't heard. "Look, don't try'n explain. There's nothing to explain," he said. "But don't go telling me you're selfish either. That's as cockeyed as you can get. I mean, lookit, we're the takers. And we're grateful, we'll always be grateful. But we can't help feeling lousy either. That's all Mary was saying—Jesus!—I'm sorry," he said, and sighed. "Okay . . . it's nothing to feel ashamed for. It's something, you got to get your bearings, get your life set, that's not asking too much. It's just, well—I don't know—we're what we are, and we let you down. And I understand. You wanta work this out alone. But lookit, well—we don't want you shutting us out. I mean, okay, you say self-respect, and there's plenty other reasons too. But I just don't want you feeling, well, ashamed, or like you need us and you can't come to us, or we don't want you, or we're try'n tell you what to do. Cause we aren't. We're gonna miss you. And we wanta know you're set. And this isn't the right thing, you won't hold it back, okay? Cause there're other places and we can help you look, or it's too much rent or whatever, I mean anything we can do, don't let it stop you, cause we're more than willing. You're a very special person to us, Anna. We wanta see you like you oughta be."

"This is what I want to do," she insisted.

"Okay. I'm sorry," he said.

"No, I don't want you feeling—"

"I know. It's okay," he said.

And then they turned on Broad, six lanes, graver and more urgent, and Howard tense and silent with it, traffic bearing down, keep in your lane, keep moving, no time for hesitation or mistake, watch out for stops, for swerving; then wildly working towards them, a red police car, siren high, lights flashing, through a red light, traffic yielding, louder—there (glimpse of uniforms, stern faces)—past. And on ahead, from the rise of a hill, the vista of blocks stretching all the way downtown, sudden, close, the downtown buildings, PSFS, City Hall with William Penn on top. And no more houses, shops, but city buildings, brick and stone and concrete, whole blocks long and six floors high, like banks and hospitals and office buildings, and plate glass windows to the street, showrooms with new cars, or televisions and appliances, or furniture, and canopied entrances, and gas stations, an official-looking building with columns, high stone stairs and arching windows, and this block, a modern, boxy building, all tinted glass ("IBM"—big letters on the side), then brick again, and rows of single windows, restaurant, drugstore, rug sales, men's shop, floors of offices above.

"What was it? Allegheny, right?"

"That's right, Allegheny at Broad." She opened her purse for the paper, her heart quickening.

"Watch out for street signs. Didn't say anything it was near, did they?"

"No. Just 2050 Allegheny, just off Broad."

"Keep an eye out. Oughta be pretty close."

Venango, she read. Tioga. Ontario. Then one was missing; then squinting she wasn't sure, but as they passed: "Allegheny! There!" He glanced in the mirror, signaled, swerved into the turning lane— a horn blew angrily—stopped at the light, then turned right, down a residential block—parked cars, scattered trees and shade, and people on the stoops and sidewalk, casual, a janitor bringing in ash cans, a stylish woman walking poodles, young men in Bermuda shorts—and right again and down a shorter block, and then again, on Allegheny. "Okay, 2100 going down. It's just across Broad." They waited at the light: "There you are." And both with sinking and relief, she saw: higher than the building and stores on the corner, farther down that block, the high brick wall, its faded sign, white letters against black.

Inside was dark and cool, and silent off the street, a worn and scrubbed tile floor, smell of mustiness and disinfectant, faded posters like a movie lobby, elevators on both sides, and by the open one an old Negro man tilted back in a chair and reading (he didn't look up or offer to help), and a tall office fan blowing, a double doorway opening on a lounge room to the right (some women sitting there, some looking up), and then the big main desk. And after Howard brought the luggage up, they waited for the girl in charge to finish her private conversation on the switchboard telephone, while from a corridor to the right (a sign pointed "Cafeteria") drifted smells of cooking, sounds of dishes.

"Don't wait, Howard. You don't have to. Really I'll be fine now," she was saying suddenly. "Why don't you start on back?"

"Well, we wanta see you got your room and everything here first, huh?"

"No, that's all right. I'll be fine now. Please, I can manage the rest. And I'll call later tonight."

"Wait a minute. Here, she's coming." He nodded towards the desk girl.

"Yes?" the girl asked, a little stern towards Howard. She was angular and plain, with a worn, peevish face, hair tied back, white button-down blouse.

He took her things to the elevator, which was busy, the operator gone ("No male visitors upstairs!" the desk girl called; "Okay, okay, I'm just helping her," he answered, bringing the suitcases this time), and if any of the women were giving them looks, she didn't care, for all that mattered now was their goodbye.

He glanced up at the jerky progress of the elevator dial. "What's your room number?"

"608."

Glanced down and frowned. "You'll call tonight and tell us how you're doing, huh?"

She nodded.

"And anything you need or want, you let us know, all right?"

"I'll be fine," she said, holding his eyes, and her own helplessly starting to tear.

"Look, you know I feel lousy."

"Don't Howard. Please. I'm sorry. I just, I want you to give my love to Mary and the children. Don't worry about me. I'll get settled.

And I want you to be happy now, I wish you all the best. And I want to say goodbye now."

"Okay then."

Shifting her purse on her arm, she gripped his hand in both hers, gripped harder than she meant; so awkwardly he raised his left to her shoulder, reached around, and drew her close and kissed her cheek, and she kissed his, and turned her face against his shoulder, eyes wet, pressing close, and sensing his embarrassment, yet needing so much, even pity now seemed like belonging and relief. "We're gonna miss you," he said. The elevator hummed; doors rattled open. They drew apart before the sudden stares of women, who hesitated, then stepped out and around.

"Here," he told the elevator man. "Can you help her with these?" And lifted up the dress bag and one of the suitcases, while the old man, grumbling, struggled with the other. Then Howard got the box and set that in. The old man waited. A trembling smile, a glance, she stepped in then herself, when—"Hey!" called a woman crossing from the lounge. "Going up!" And brassily stepped in. And still, edging back beside her luggage, she smiled at Howard, who kept watching her. The old man worked the lever, closed the doors.

The room was small and close and bare. Double locker (she must buy a lock apparently), metal bunk bed, single mattress on flat springs, cheap white cotton spread (she'd want her own), coarse wool blanket, table desk and straight chair, dresser, arm chair by the window, radiator, throw rug on linoleum, fixture hanging overhead. The curtains, white gauze, stirred; city noises drew her to the window. Parting the curtains (they felt tacky), she glanced across at buildings, flat, tarred roofs, and windows, down, six stories down, leaned closer, craned to see—tops of cars and tiny passersby—and figured where the entrance was, and farther down, across, found the garage, but he'd be gone, halfway home, and gulf and din, implacability of size unsettled her; she dropped the curtain, wiped her hands, turned back. Unpinned her hat, watching in the spotted mirror on the door. Hung up her dress bag first; unzipped, shook out her dresses, spaced them on their hangers. Then could do no more. Sank down, bed sagging beneath her; sat, elbows on her knees, face in hand, just weak, no will, a ringing through her. Dropped her hand, stared dully at her luggage, listening, not to street sounds, but to footsteps in the corridor, click of a lock, bumpings in the room next door, and farther off a radio, muffled rattle of the elevator, voices loud and casual (there had been one or two open doors as they'd struggled with her luggage from the elevator, and glimpses of rooms, women looking up, someone calling—"Georgy, hey! Hey lover! Hey, c'mon, we're waitin' for ya!"—laughing, teasing, and others in the hallways, tight-lipped as they passed).

No matter she was hot and grimy, nor her bladder ached, nor stomach cramped; she couldn't risk the strangeness here, to find the bathroom, go down to the cafeteria. Must wait, must hold the temporary safety of this room, catch up, regain herself inside. Except she couldn't. Part of her seemed gone, and worse than fear was uselessness, just weight, just flesh, no strength to move, effort ghostly as a memory, empty of effect. . . . Stop it. Closed her eyes and shook her head. Was fine. Was perfectly all right. Would keep on going just the same. Would change her dress. Go out, come back. Unpack. Had paid up in advance. And they were only women, no worse than the factory women; mind her business here, keep out of their way. And lock her door. And work out her routines. Today, tomorrow, clean first (ask for bucket, brushes at the desk). Arrange her things. Make a list of other things she'd need for when she called. Monday, then, she'd go to work; she'd catch the bus right at the corner, and get off at Stenton, all of that still the same. Just think ordinary, simple; people here just people, lives just lives. No more at stake in doing but itself; think that, think as she was and what remained. The rest was nonsense, in her head. Just give herself the credit, have the faith. But then the void of it came over her: she couldn't! What was wrong? Her legs! They had to help; she couldn't be expected, not her fault. . . . Yet she'd have to. Did, finally: stood, began. With terrible effort, yet with none at all.

She'd been down earlier for a snack, so felt easier now, knowing where things were, what to expect; stood shuffling in line for dinner, with her tray and silverware. Had come down in the crowded elevator, and several women from her floor, familiar, chattering, then more and more from lower floors, until they all fell silent, jammed together, waiting, dropping, past another floor, another, to the surging halt, the doors scraped open and release. Hubbub, then, and everything seemed busy, active, though the dinner line was only backed a little into the hall. She took her place behind the big, broad-hipped brunette (shirttail out, rolled up dungarees) and her smaller, swarthy friend, who wore a tan jumper, had close-cropped hair, and a crabbed, sour face (both from her floor, both in their thirties, both, for all their veteran haughtiness and ease, somehow slatternly and shiftless): ". . . Know what she said to me, that bitch? You're not invited, that's why—it's a private party!" "So what, let's just go to the Rail or something." "I'm sick of that place, I dunno what you see in that place." "Better'n sitting round this bunch of shitheads. Saturday night, been a helluva weekend so far, hasn't it?" Mustn't listen, look; keep blank inside. But covertly kept peering, taking stock: the others here, especially as she turned the corner, saw them mixed and crowded, eating, and the noise, the smells, big fans blowing, saw all ages, kinds: old women, white-haired, gnomish, shabby dresses, bloated ankles, faces set, and younger girls, some eighteen, nineteen, not rude like factory girls, but quiet, nicely groomed and dressed, though skinny, plain, or acne-scarred or fat (one with a blue birthmark over half her face); mostly they seemed her age, older, sullen, not like working women, with families, households, other lives to care for, but derelict, like refugees, and no one but themselves alone, and each with private hurt and flaw, and no clear faces, calm or reconciled. Except she wasn't: not like them. "Go on, go on"—the old woman behind her impatient— she'd reached the counter now, so slid her tray along, chose salad, chocolate pudding; then waiting at the steaming pans of sauerkraut and wieners, meat loaf, noodle casserole, and the serving ladies harried, cross, one looking up: "Well, what do you want?" and another handing a meatloaf plate to the close-cropped hair, decided: "Meatloaf, please," and had to say it louder, gravy, yes, and peas not beans, and then a glass of milk from the machine, and waiting to pay; paid, and pocketed her change, and turned with tray, hoping for a table to herself, but seemed they all had somebody, and edging between and around, and everybody talking or solitary, eating, saw one, but the close-cropped hair and big brunette were taking it, and looked again, and farther back, wall table: someone getting up and leaving. Worked her way over, and once dirty dishes stacked, and hers off the tray, once seated, settled, looking for the busgirl (giving up), began to eat, attending just to this, eyes up each time she took a bite, then down again, and chewing, swallow, then another forkful. "S'cuse me." Looked up, startled by the busgirl, who cleared the dirty dishes, wiped around her with a rag, and no sooner rolled her cart away, when a dark-haired woman, green scarf around her hair, and wearing glasses, sweatshirt, sweatpants, was putting down her tray, dropped her purse in the chair, put plates on the table, tray aside, sat down, and no acknowledgement, just started eating (she did too, with tension in her like a blush), then stopped, pulled a book from her purse, held it open as she ate. Herself, she kept her eyes down, yet sipping milk, read "*Kiss Me Deadly*, Mickey Spillane," and there was a naked girl on a bed; the other caught her eyes, held them, still chewing, then snorted and relaxed: "Ever read him?"

"Excuse me?"

"Spillane. Mystery writer, here"—she pointed at the cover.

Apologized, smiling: "No, no, I don't read much."

"You ought to. This'll really get you hot, I'll tell you that. There's this Mike Hammer, he's the detective, see, and he's nice and sexy, but he doesn't take anything from anybody, y'know? And these Mafia guys, big guys, they kill this really sexy girl he picks up and almost kill him too, and he's not gonna sit for that. I mean, this guy's a wild man, and just hates crooks, y'know, and the cops can't do anything, so he goes right after 'em and he's not scared of anything, I mean, this guy, and he fights dirtier'n they do and they don't expect that, see; he just wades right in and he kills 'em with his bare hands and it's all this really raw stuff. I mean, that's what I like. And all these sexy girls keep falling for him, and it's all this really hot stuff, y'know? Here, listen to this"—she flipped a page—

"Please, it's not my kind of story, I don't think."

"Oh . . . well, okay, guess not, but I tell you—you're missing something."

Smiled and took another forkful.

"New here, or what?"

"I moved in today, yes."

"Permanent?"

She nodded. The other grimaced.

"Well, it's what you make of it." And went back looking at the book and took a bite. "Me, it's cheap, it's safe. Got the gym. I like my sports. Not like these oddballs here, been here for years; just you need someplace, you know, 'til you get to know the city, meet some people—got a job? Yeah, I didn't, first came here; do now. Me'n a friend, we're looking for a place, gonna be roommates, but I'll tell you, even you split it, anything you want, y'know, it's sixty, eighty apiece, and other places, you're better off here. This part of town anyway. I mean, I know; I've been looking all summer. Nothing worth the rents they soak you. So now we're thinking down South Philly somewhere, but we only got weekends, and that means subway or something, back and forth cross town."

She nodded, nothing to reply, food growing cold. The conversation hung a moment, failed. The other shrugged. Then back to eating, back to reading, each ignoring other.

Undressed, slipped on her nightgown, then her robe, her slippers; gathered up her own towels and facecloth, and soap, shampoo, toothpaste and brush, hairbrush, comb, powder, putting all but the towels in her spare purse; then waited, listened, till the voices passed, the hall seemed empty; then opened her door, stepped out and locked it with her key, and no one there, other doors shut, except for music from down past the elevator, a bawdy shriek and laughter, some kind of party; steeled herself inside, starting in the opposite direction, hoping time was right, that everyone would be back there or down-stairs at the movie, that the bathroom too would be deserted, but if it wasn't still must go ahead, not mind, just go about her business. Away from their noise, around the corner, slowly pushed the swing-ing door: and no one was, just sinks and mirrors, fluorescent light, open window, stalls empty, benches, showers empty (and with cur-tains), all now to herself. She brushed her teeth first, used the toilet (trying to ignore the scrawls); then back to the bench, her bag, soap out, shampoo, towels within reach. And hung up her robe, and glancing around, pulled her nightgown up and over, and out of her slippers, tile cool to her feet, pushed back the curtain, reached in for the spigots, when she glimpsed, drew back, and sickened, outraged, stared: like dog's, but fatter, human turd.

Three days passed, and, outline of routine worked out, she was doing fine. Too early Monday, so Tuesday up at 5:30 (all her floor still sleep-ing and deserted), breakfast in the cafeteria, bus caught 6:15 (instead of six, wan fellowship with two or three others now, who left same time, direction), factory by 6:35, and not even Louie told yet or guess-ing. Just the same as always—coffee, then her scheduling, her girls arriving, bell at eight and day begun, and worked (the Christmas line beginning full production), and keeping to her job, and everything like Mr. Walsh had told her, though ache, a kind of dizziness remained, and she must struggle sometimes to act as she would act, to think, to say. And if she'd hoped the work might carry her—that it was only strain and dread of failure, dread of missing, doing wrong, or some more seri-ous debility, but did, got through, with no one noticing; and would, and each day surer, better. Bus stop, then, 5:35, and if not first, then second bus, and crushing, jolting ride to Broad, which made her faint, and then more breathing room, and worry over landmarks, off right stop, and city all around her, frenzied, thronging, and the Y—relief, and finally her room, and off with clinging uniform, tight shoes, and six perhaps now, cleaning up and changing. And seven, when the line was shorter, down for supper. And after, back, preparing for tomorrow (doing laundry in the bathroom). Bed by 9:30. Yet no matter weary, lights out, she couldn't sleep for radios and footsteps, voices, elevator doors, or traffic, sirens. So she spent long sessions sitting at the window, coolness stirring, and past the void of street, dark roofs, past other banks of windows, lighted billboards, neon signs; she gazed at taller buildings, jeweled by distance, thinking all she'd been, and loved, and strength in lives depending, their sake hers, and all she was or could be called upon and given—to provide, to keep, to answer harm with loyalty and gentleness and being there and feeling wrong and filling loss, and all the little things, and no one else to know or love or give so naturally, so totally, so much.

Woke to ringing of alarm, and anxious as if still at home, groped blinking for it in the dark, pitch dark, fumbled, heard it crash, and ringing still, and threw back her covers, and missing slippers, eased out, down on hands and knees, and reaching, found (beneath the chair), and silenced, just as it was running down. And clutched it tight and eased back up and only, feeling for the bed, seeing nothing, no shapes, not even as she sat, the desperate hardness in her hands. Heard ticking: no dial; heard traffic: no outline of window—felt like 5:30 (couldn't be the clock), no crack of light beneath her door (they never turned out hall lights), and rubbed her eyes, thought power failure, something wrong. And clutching clock still, stood up in darkness—keep her wits, keep calm—and strangely lost for balance, doubtful where things were, as if the floor were tilting, gulfs before her, found the edge, the desk, and felt from there to flat of door, doorknob, chair, and up to lock, the light switch—on, off, on—nothing, set down the clock, tried again, more frantically, and fearing more than darkness, heart pounding, scrabbled at the lock. Stepped back, opened—nothing there—and inching forward, doorjamb, listened—no one—out, and felt back for her doorway, and didn't matter, slippers, robe, sickening into panic, groped alone to next door, hands flat against it, hesitated, then started batting with her palm—"Please! Please!"—and listened— "Wake up! Please!"—and hand closed into fist was beating: "Help me! Please. Wake up!"

"Get away! Shut up!" Voice gravelly and muffled.

"Please, no please, there's something wrong. Please. Come out."

"Go away!"

"I'm from next door!" And pressing hard against the flatness, batting, until sounds of movement; then closer, through the door:

"Wait a minute, wait a minute. Okay. What the hell? What do you want?"

"I'm from next door. Please!"

And angry rattling with a lock, then click, then feeling it give way and stepping back.

"Okay, okay"—gravelly, tight voice, direct—"What now, what's goin' on? Whatta you banging on doors, six o'clock in the morning?" Then: "Hey . . . hey, wait a minute. You okay? What's wrong? Hey, here."

"My eyes . . . something." Groped, was caught, was clutching. "I can't . . . it's black. I can't see! I can't see anything! Please!"

"I have you, here now, here. What happened? You hurt?"

And other doors unlatching, other voices: What is it? What's wrong? She drunk? Thought it was a fire. What's the racket? And steady, firm, the person close, the arm to cling to; yet all belied, and there not there, and known unknown, and others terrifying, different, only wrong with her, and smothering, and simplest natural thing denied, and all beyond.

"Here, it's okay. We're here. We'll help you."

"What is it, dear?" Another voice, touch.

"Says she's blind."

"Get her to her room—Here, here dear, let's go to your room." Was urged, was guided, led, and crowd around, the whispers: moved in Saturday; what's she, blind? Dunno, crackin' up.

"Why? What's wrong with me? Lights . . . can't, can't see!"

"Calm down now, we're helping; we're with you. Here's the door now"—through the door, bumping chair. "Okay, here, here's your bed now"—staggered, fell back into, was sitting. The other sat beside her.

"One of you, go on, call the desk, get a doctor," gravel voice insisted.

"Wet towel, get a wet towel—Here, look this way, look at me." Warm hands held her head and, gently, fingers prodded wide her lids (accent flat, breath stale). "Can't see anything, nothing, not even blurry?"

"No!"

"Shh. It's okay now. This ever happen before to you?"

"I don't know. . . . I've never had trouble. I just woke up, all dark. I have to get to work."

"No, now, keep calm. Doctor'll be here. But this just happened sudden like this, no headaches or eyes hurting you or anything? Hit your head or anything? Any pain?"

"She's been taking something, betcha." And from doorway: "Lookita room, lookita stuff." And gravel voice: "Out, c'mon, we'll take care of it."

"Please, listen. I can't. I have to work. Supervisor, I have twenty-five girls. Have to be there, no one'll know, lose the day, blame me. Please."

"Don't you worry about work. Can't go like this now, just keep calm and we'll wait for the doctor. Not your fault. No one can blame you. What's your name?"

"Anna Maye. Anna Maye Potts."

"Listen, don't worry about it, Anna Maye. When you sposed to be there?"

"Six-thirty, 7:00. Scheduling, I have to schedule. Starts at 8:00."

"Okay, that's plenty time. We can call in for you. Now where is this?"

"Manville. Confectioners."

"Okay, they're in the book; then; we'll call . . . no, sit still, here."

"Please, my robe. Have my robe?"

Gravel voice: "Hold on. . . . I got it." And she stood, and they helped her into it, and damp, cool, they had a towel, that's it, lie back, put your feet up, just keep quiet, and soothing coolness over forehead, eyes, and gravel voice was Elly, and on the chair beside her, tending, Mrs. Donovan, and then a knock, and not the doctor, house director, Mrs. Turpin, and what was wrong here, who was she, and yes, doctor was coming, and asking her (she lay weak, submissive, yet still flailing in the fact, in now, or hospital, or job lost, all at mercy, unknown as the dark; yet must keep clear, attend, reply): was fine, just eyes, just couldn't see, no, didn't know, no reason, sorry to be trouble. Well, they'd stay with her, then, good, but Elly had to leave 8:30? Mrs. Donovan could stay? Good. Well, she'd stop back after doctor had been; oh, how about family, should she notify anyone? No, please, not yet, she didn't want to bother them (felt more and more ashamed, aware of how she sounded, looked, and of her room and life all unde-fended from their unseen eyes; yet she was strangely glad to have them know, as if defenseless she were safe), but factory, had to call, to tell them—now, what time?—ask Louie, ask for Louie, Mr. Miscello, be there now, tell him, tell Mary Lloyd to schedule for her, and Mr. Walsh, that she was sick, just something sudden, not that she was blind, not that they should worry, and didn't know about tomorrow, but later, afternoon, would call. Wait, what factory? Where? But Elly knew, yes, she'd take care of it, get dressed, go call right now. And Mrs. Donovan would stay. And Elly, yes, would say just like she said, would write it down. And Mrs. Turpin, leaving, call if any problem, not to worry, just keep quiet, doctor soon.

"Real cute figurines," Mrs. Donovan was saying. "Mind if I look—what, do you collect these, or what?"

"I didn't have shelves. All the others, they're in the carton."

"Just moving in, yeah. When you come, Saturday?"

"Saturday." She nodded.

"Yeah, hadn't seen you, once or twice. Person before, she moved out, oh, two, two-three weeks ago. Where'd you move from?"

The question bothered, yet seemed careful and sincere. "Home," she said. "Germantown." Mrs. Donovan was back, was sitting down. "Am I blind? Am I going to be like this? Can it just happen like this?"

"No, no, don't think about it. Can't tell now, none of us, not till doctor comes. Could be anything. I mean, like blackouts and

migraines, that kinda thing, like this friend of mine told me, a friend
of hers, her eye nerves crossed, some kinda spasm, so they gave her
some drug and some treatments, and a couple weeks, whatever it was,
you know, they straightened out and relaxed, and she was fine. So
you never know, it might not be so serious."

"I can't. Two weeks, no, you—"

"Shh, I told you, don't worry, please now, just relax, we'll wait
now, it'll be all right now. That's it. Here." And she changed the
towel over, so it was cool and moist again. "So you were living with
family, huh?"

"My sister. My father died. I was living there with him. I cared.
Years. My sister, she's married, and her family, they didn't have a
house; I couldn't stay there alone, so they moved in. They're all I
have. I wanted, I thought we could live together, but I wasn't being
fair . . . even when I knew . . . I was in the way . . . wasn't them, but
I kept blaming them, but they were family to themselves, had their
happiness, their problems too"—seemed floating, talking to herself—
"and then they had the baby coming, and I knew, they'd need the
room. . . . I had to, didn't matter, had to . . . work out for myself, and
I'm not, I'm not a normal person. I've never faced my life alone. Have
to face things for yourself, and still be someone, even when there's
nothing."

"Shh, dear, don't. Don't talk like that. There's never nothing.
Here, here, now, you're all right. Listen, I know; believe me. I know
how they treat you. Caring for your father like that, and probly she
couldn't even go off, get married, wasn't for you. And he dies: they
want your house. I know, family's worst of all. Like my daughter, same
thing, her'n and that husband. Gave 'em my insurance money, savings, for a house, just like you, and I was gonna live there, gave up
my apartment, quit my job, and I was gonna keep the children; she
was working, got a good job, but just like you, they turn on you.
Wasn't six months, shouting, blaming me, treat me like dirt. Just use
love against you, worse'n strangers, and minute they don't need you,
then they turn you out. Well, better off without them, better same as
if they're dead. That's how I think. Two years since I moved here.
Work. I'm a presser in a laundry down here, nights. Friends, I meet

people. Like it here. . . . Family goes against you, that's an awful thing, but that's them, them, that's what I'm saying. Don't let 'em; don't look back. There's you. You're a decent person, that's what matters, and there's people. Don't give up on people."

Embarrassed for reply, she swallowed, dizzy, must avoid, yet mustn't give offense, and felt the waiting, watching pressure of concern; and outside sounds were busier, and couldn't, what if, and she had to call: "I can't, can't be blind."

"No one says you're blind. Don't know what this is now."

"Can't go back to them. . . . Please, what, what time?"

"Just after seven."

Then: hey, here, here you are. And Elly was back—scuffle, bustle of her coming in, and throaty voice: "Everything's okay. I talked to that Louie guy. He says he'll take care of it, someone'll fill in. But he was real concerned about you, kept asking, you know, what was wrong and how bad and what're you doing here, thought you lived with your sister or something, and all I could tell him was you were sick and didn't know how serious, and you'd be calling in later about tomorrow. Anyway, he says he hopes you're better, and when you call in, he wants you to call him personal."

Later, after Elly had left for work, after Mrs. Donovan had helped her to the bathroom and she felt better, cleaned up and presentable, and after Mrs. Donovan had dressed and come back, and must be eight at least, came the knock, the male voice startling: "This the patient? This Miss Potts?"

It wasn't blindness, and relieved, she also felt humiliated and ashamed. The doctor wanted her to rest, and go to the clinic tomorrow for more tests, but said nothing was wrong, nothing physical, as far as he could see. And sometimes under severe stress, well, things like this can happen, and nothing physical; eyes can see and picture's going to the mind, but mind refuses to respond. And this was a way, sometimes, trying to tell yourself you need time out, or time to readjust, or it's too much for you alone, and maybe you need professional help. Nothing to be ashamed of, but you have to respect, and realize you're upset; it's a bad time you're going through, and you can't deny and act like nothing's wrong, cause like any illness, more you neglect, the worse it's going to get. That's the problem, not your eyes. Get good rest, take the pills, you'll wake up tomorrow or next day with your vision back. But it'll just be something else later, stomach problems or headaches, unless you get some help with your emotions. Because that's what this is: you're under severe emotional stress. Counseling can help. There're excellent facilities at the clinic. You go in there tomorrow. I think you should ask for an appointment. Tell them I said that. Ask for Dr. Lopes, okay?

And he was alone with her, saying that. And told the others: nothing serious, just temporary, she'd be all right in a day or so, and she should stay in bed and rest. Hospital wasn't necessary. Only someone should stay near, and help if she needed. And bring her up trays. And tomorrow she'd need someone to take her to the clinic and back. And house director said all right; and Mrs. Donovan, she'd watch out for her. And again, after he'd gone, they asked: any family she wanted notified? Yes, my sister, she'd said; tell her, please, temporary blindness, and I'm all right here, but I'd like her to come over.

She was sitting in her chair, Mrs. Donovan's radio playing low, and the fan blowing softly and hotness in her hair and robe and on one arm, and from the window sultry breeze, hot tar and concrete, city smells and unaccustomed weekday sounds. And Mrs. Donovan brought in her lunch, her tray. "Here's soup now, tomato, and macaroni and cheese, and milk and cake." She balanced the tray: "Here, want me to help?" "No please, I just have to know where things are, if you can show me." Was guided: spoon, soup here, milk, and feeling foolish, laughing at it—careful, hot—and lifting to her mouth, uncertain; and then she'd gotten the knack, and groping, finding, and lifting to her mouth or putting down, cautiously, was eating, and radio with its tinny, excited drone, and bite each time or swallow, taste, surprising in her mouth, and greedily to savor and consume. And then asked Mrs. Donovan, did she have her lunch? "That's all right, I'll get some later." Here, have some of this? Sure? "No, no—well, maybe just a bit of cake. I'll eat when I take down your tray."

And that's how Mary found her; knock, voice: "Anna?"

"Mary? Mary, that you?"

"Come in, come in"—and bustle of her getting up—"I'm Mrs. Donovan."

"I came as soon as I could. I had to leave the girls with Mrs. Bocosky."

"Here, here. I'll just be across the hall. I'll leave you."

"Mrs. Donovan?"

"S'all right. Have a nice visit. I'll get your tray later."

Silence then, except for radio.

"Mary? Here, could you take this tray?"

"No, no, don't mind me. Go on eating." Radio went silent; purse put down, door shut; sat down on the bed.

She tried, forkful to her mouth.

"My god, what is it? What happened?"

Swallowed. "It's temporary, not serious. Just—doctor said it's my nerves."

"Nerves?"

"Well, he wants me to go in for some tests tomorrow to be sure. But he says I'll be all right; it's just a day or two. And I should rest."

"You can't see? Nothing?"

"No, black, just like the lights are out. That's what I thought when I woke up. I thought the lights were out. And then I realized, and I didn't know, I thought I was blind. But everybody here's been very good, called the factory, and the doctor for me."

"But how's that 'nerves'? You're gonna be all right; it's gonna happen again, what?"

Faltered, feeling close and trapped, and tray impossible. "I'm fine. Nothing wrong, he said." She stood, and started with the tray towards the desk.

"Here, stop. I have it. Now, c'mon, Anna, sit down. Now, come on, what is it? What's the story?"

"I don't know." Back in chair now, and sunlight over her again, she glanced back and up and into what must be the sun. "He said it was in my mind, like shell shock with the soldiers."

"What do you mean?"

She clutched the smooth burl of the chair arms. "It's, I don't know, it's just it's all no use. I don't belong with you, I know that. It wasn't you, but just that Father's all I had, and he did; he needed me, and all those years I gave. But since he died, it's—I'm not helpless, I know, and I don't want to be. But more I try, it's this feeling love's worth nothing; nothing I can do is me, and it's all so senseless, like great iron doors are closed against me, and they're inside me too, and someone has to help, but no one can. And I don't know, it's when you feel like that and don't know why, and just you have to go on, it's something happens in your mind, and makes you so you're really sick, so you don't have to go on, and then it's not just feelings anymore."

She sensed the consternated, intent gaze; the measured breath.

"He told you this, huh?"

"Some. I know it anyway." And turned her head, and felt her robe. "I'm—I realize now. There are reasons. I don't have to put it on others. And I'm at no one's mercy but my own. That's what this has shown me. This morning, see, I thought I was really blind. And I couldn't work, and couldn't manage by myself, and all the things I really can do, I couldn't. And I'd have to turn to you, or someone, and be a burden. And who I am, I realize now, how much that means. I'm not like this. I'm not pathetic. I'm a plain, single woman who stayed at home instead of marrying, and now I'm alone, but I'm no different than thousands of others; my troubles are no different. And they are scared too, but still they learn, and still they matter to themselves, and so do I; I don't need to beg. I don't need pity. It's my troubles; they're mainly, they're in me. It's for me to face, and not ask others what I can only ask myself."

Silence.

"Wait a minute." Mary lit a cigarette. "Look, okay . . . , self-respect, right? That's what you told Howard. Well, it's not self-respect, turning your back on everything and putting yourself in the worst situation you can. I mean, look at you, look at this place, that filthy little woman. Why? For self-respect? That's not self-respect; it's pride. Pride you don't need anybody when you do, and pride there's no place when you know there is. I mean, it's all or nothing with you. We can't keep you, so just like that, you take it all on yourself. Doesn't matter we're your family. Oh, no, it's gotta be this. It's gotta be you push yourself right into a nervous breakdown first, before you'll admit you can't be alone, and that you're not alone. I mean, self-respect is you have limits; and you want to help yourself, fine, but take help when you need it, and quit pretending we're not there. We are."

"I can't go home."

"I'm not saying that. Look, if this was blindness, then we'd find some way. But it's not. It's your denying; first you won't try anything, then you wanta try too much; it's still denying. Let's get you out of here. Let's find you someplace like you're used to, and you're closer to us, and it's still the neighborhood, and people aren't misfits and trash and God knows what; they're decent, normal people, people like yourself. Doesn't that make sense? We'll still be there and we'll still be part of each other's lives. That doesn't stop."

Imagined seeing; yet, sight's memory dim, shape, form, color seemed like phosphorescence in the dark. And Mary sitting, wearing what? Some summer dress, and hair curled tight, and squirming forward, legs bent sharply, what expressions, gestures? What was she saying? Why?

"What do you want me to do?"

"Okay, now. Look. Best thing is you stay here for now, and rest, and I'll take you for your tests tomorrow. Let's just hope this clears up, you know, like the doctor said. Meanwhile I'll start looking for an apartment, and you're okay by Saturday, we can look together, and the sooner we get you out of here, the better—what? What is it?"

She was turning her head. "I don't know. I have to think."

"Why? What's there to think about, Anna? I mean, let's get it settled. You wanta be like this?"

"I'm not saying that. It's just I'm here, and that moving again."

"You're serious, aren't you. You still won't—my God, what's it take?" Mary jumped up, moved around. "You're blind, you've got a nervous condition. You say you want to help yourself. Now what is it? Me? You can't stand it's me? Quit it, Anna. This is no time for that. You want to hate me, go ahead, but don't think you're getting back at me by hurting yourself."

"I don't. It's not you."

"Then why do you refuse us? Why can't you be reasonable?"

"I'm not. I'm not saying no. I only said I want to think."

Silence.

"I'm not going to argue about it." Mary sat down again, was scrabbling in her purse. "You go on, you think all you want to think. I'm going to start looking tomorrow anyway. We can talk about it later."

Almost feeling sorry for her: "Yes, we'll talk about it later."

Courtship

The seasons closed in without his noticing, except as a grimness coming on—tired drift from August heat through Labor Day (Christmas rush on at the plant), and still hot shirtsleeve days, and maybe a little cooler, and then the kids were back in school, and late September, first trees changing. A couple mornings, he wore a sweater; a couple nights put on the heat: but fall still seemed something to come later. And then was everywhere the changing leaves, all golds and scarlet, and weekends he would rake and burn. He found a place for Josie, since it wasn't any good with Frank and Nancy, and that's what Paula wanted: got her back in Belmont, at least until the rest was over and he could figure something else. And then his birthday (fifty-seven). He finished painting the house (and bills came in, ignored), and had his car inspected (oughta winterize). And for a week or two, it was back Indian Summer, but vees of birds like heading south; and then from crisp days to days of rain and bite, trees bare, football, heavy coats.

Paula died November, week before Thanksgiving.

She only went twice to the clinic, while she kept up everything else the same. She went through telling the harried secretary and then the nurse (this was Saturday, first thing): her problem was emotional, and the doctor at the Y had told her Dr. Lopes. She completed the forms and got her slip. There was a long wait, crowded room, hard chairs, and all sick people, mothers, children, threadbare and unshaven men (and hacking coughs and spitting into handkerchief), children crying, others groaning, talking to themselves, and crutches, bandages. And then a nurse would come, and all look up, as a name was called. Finally the name was hers. The nurse led her past examination rooms, to one for her—scale, curtain, table, old bare desk—and told her to wait: he'd see her soon. He was a big man, light mulatto: came in briskly, but attentive and his voice refined, and sat down at the desk and asked her questions, studying her sheet, older than her maybe, graying hair. She told him what had happened, about her blindness and how sight came back, like the doctor had said, in next two days, and she was worried if it happened again, she'd lose her job. And she didn't want to be any trouble on anyone, when it wasn't physical, but only something in her head. Well, let's let me be the judge of that, he'd said; and first examined her eyes, then told her to undress. And was humiliation, as if first time (it was, for several years); shame of body and exposure; startle as he touched. But then was all official, and her body her, but other than herself; and odd relief, apart from any shame or judgments, just to stand there commonplace, and problem health, and touch impersonal and sure and gentle all at once. And even the worst part (which she dreaded and went clammy: up on table, feet in stirrups, forced to slide down while he pushed down on her abdomen, fingers were inside and then syringe), he did quickly and without hesitating, like was regular, and asking her last period, and making her concentrate and help, and then was over, before shock could register.

He told her to get down, dress (throwing out his gloves, washing hands)—fine health, far as he could see, except the overweight, blood pressure low. And once she dressed and settled down, he was asking more. Now this is recent, no headaches, pains, no stomach or menstrual trouble, nothing before? He wanted facts: her family, job, her situation at the Y. And as she told, it was like confession, something blameful, and just to say things sounded foolish, foreign, like some playback of her voice. Yet he listened and took her seriously (and the same time it felt like a mistake and what she'd longed for, both). And kindly, he told her, look, it's not unusual; I mean you're going through difficult times—you've got the shock of your father, your family failing you, changes at work, and suddenly you're left alone, and it's no surprise under those conditions you suffer a nervous attack. But what's important is that you understand that you've got reasons. You don't need a physical problem for an excuse. I mean, that's what this sounds like, doesn't it? This blindness: it's you feel disabled and upset, and you have every reason to be. And you have to respect those reasons, not feel guilty about them, or that somehow they don't count. They have to count. It's by admitting, sure, you're hurt and you're afraid, and you resent being left alone; and you got every right to, especially when your whole life's revolved around family and home. But once you admit those feelings—and I don't say that's easy, but that's where I come in—then you've got a chance to work them out and realize their positive side. That you wouldn't feel helpless if you weren't strong, or so alone if you weren't a deeply caring person with a real capacity to give. And I think once you realize that, you'll start to find new ways and chances and put those strengths to use and feel like life's more meaningful again.

And second visit, after she'd had time to think, he'd started prying deeper, asking about Father, how she'd felt when she was needed home, and before that, what she'd wanted for herself, what plans and dreams, and what it meant to give them up. And part of her would answer, trying to cooperate ("you must've had expectations that you'd go on like other girls and marry and start a home of your own"), but part held back—aware of more (that even then she'd felt afraid and different; and difference had to do with looks, and feeling the same as Mother felt, as if by nature they belonged to someplace far off and unreachable, and that the world around them was ignorant and harsh, as Father had become too, and Mother all her life had fought), but was no reason to subject, and too bound up and personal to let him touch. And what made sense, she already knew for herself, and it seemed stupid and degrading to be told; while the rest he said was for some troubles too mixed up and different from her own. She felt impatient that she'd come. The problem was too obvious, past need to talk; and hers alone, to act on for herself.

He'd kept on warning her about Walsh. And then she'd been out sick three days—had moved to a North Philly Y, for Chrissake. And when he'd gotten that call, he told the girl to tell her call him back, but she didn't, nor the next day neither, though she must have called the office, because they had her helper in to take her place. Then after work, he'd called himself, but all he worried (what about her eyes? how serious? and what'd happened? what'd gone on with her sister? why'd she move out all of a sudden to a place like the Y?), it was suddenly he realized, at the startle and reluctance in her voice, that this was more than just their talking gave him right. And simple questions, and she thanked him—nothing, no, was fine, she'd be all right, she'd be back in by Monday—and it was better that he leave the rest unasked: just he'd been worried for her (like they all were, all had been asking), and he hoped it would be okay. But bothered him, that she was in real trouble and she closed him out, and all he'd looked to her, there was so much else behind her life, and things that mattered that she never told.

And when she'd come back Monday, she was the same as on the phone, as if afraid to talk and pleading for him let it pass. She told the others (Mary Lloyd kept fussing at her): Just a little dizzy spell and doctor says I'm okay. And then she was working harder than just to make up, or even to keep off Walsh, but like the work was everything and left no room to talk. But there were things he needed to talk about, and same for her; he couldn't let this be a block, or be like anything so serious and personal that friendship had no claim. So the second day back, the second day of small talk, interruptions, workday offering them no chance, he went and told her: Look, I wanta know what's happening. I want know like's going on, and what's this moving and this being sick? It matters to me, understand? So how about like after work tonight? I mean, we meet and go someplace for dinner, round to Ernie's, someplace? No big deal, just give us a chance to talk—okay? Got my car, drop you off at your place later. What do you say? Her answer was yes, as brief and solemn as his asking.

Ernie's was a spiffed-up modern diner, couple blocks away, where sometimes supervisors ate. They got a big booth by the window.

"Got a good veal parmesan," he said. "Want a little music?"

"No," she said. Then: "What about Paula? How's she doing, Louie?"

He shook his head. "Not good. . . . While there, after operation, she was better, and it helped her, y'know, like we settled about Josie. . . . But then the pain came back—took out all her stomach, keeps on spreading, nothing they can do but dope her up. . . . I go in, she don't know me half the time, and all she says is why can't it be over, and see her like that, you want it too . . . body won't let go; it's gotta burn itself out first, and every bit's like keeping her in pain."

They were silent. "What about you?"

"Me. I dunno. I'm getting by. Saw Josie last weekend. She's coming along. Took her out for a hamburger; walked in the park. Gonna take her a while, but they give her good care, and the other kids there and all. School. Probably best thing for her."

"You mean for later too?"

Looked down. "I dunno."

Waitress coming broke it off. Ordered.

"Now what's this with you? When'd you move?"

"Two weeks ago."

"Have some kind of argument?"

"No. Nothing like that . . . please, Louie."

"I wanta hear about it," he insisted. And as she told, he got the picture, bothered and impressed. "That's a pretty big break for you, though, isn't it? I mean, burning all your bridges. . . . Sure it's right?"

"There were no bridges anyway; just wishes, and things I wouldn't face about myself."

"And what was that last week?"

"Nothing really. Nothing worth discussing. Just I got there, things caught up with me. My nerves gave way. But I'm all right."

He waited, taken back by "nerves" and family stuff, as if too personal to get mixed up in, but then the way she talked, she wasn't asking that. He raised his eyebrows: "Here's the food."

And after waitress left: "Well, this Y. You keep on staying there?"

"For now, yes. It's still too soon to know what else. Apartment, I don't know. And maybe in a week or two I can. But there's work and all this still to sort out, and I'm better where I am. When I'm ready, then I'll look."

"You'll find someplace."

Later, he asked about her job ("Walsh say anything, I mean your being out?"), but mostly she was right, and wasn't left for him to warn or reassure or ask, but just to understand and share its weight.

Early October, she'd studied the listings, called and made appointments, and on one weekend, as well as on several evenings home from work, she had taken the bus or walked, and gone to look, mainly in the blocks from Allegheny down to Germantown. She wanted something close to the bus, and safe, and maybe one room with a kitchen, bath (not the rooming houses where you had to share) and didn't matter furnished (she could take things from home), but even the cheapest were one hundred twenty, and searching out strange addresses—west off Broad and closer down towards Germantown—the neighborhoods were crowded, poor, and mostly black, and places that she saw—one over a barbershop, three others all in tenements—were cramped and dingy, windows opening on

brick walls, yellowed, peeling paper, cooking smells and families shouting, flights on flights of stairs, and broken locks, and scribbled walls, and
nowhere she could see herself as better than the Y. And meanwhile, for
other, nicer places, closer to the Y, or off Broad east or by the university,
the rents were far too high.

Louie told her, okay, lookit, quit the bargain hunting for one
thing. Probably what you want, you're talking more one-fifty or one-
sixty, and it's worth it someplace comfortable; and you can manage
that, can't you? Sure you can. And this ain't something now, you want
to hold out on yourself. Another thing, too, now, why keep looking
in the city? I mean, North Philly, I lived there fifteen years and I can
tell you: do a lot better you look around here, out Germantown or
back the other side of Stenton, or even out towards White Marsh,
you'd still be close to the factory; it's residential. And 'stead of looking in papers, call some agencies around here.

Then and there, from the factory, he'd looked up agencies with
her and called, and the second place a Mr. DeVincent of Germantown Realty said yes, they had several places she might like; she could
meet him after work or make an appointment for Saturday.

So she had found: the second floor rear of a large frame house
(near a bus stop on Wadsworth, which took her to Germantown and
then a change and ride to her old bus stop, and maybe two miles the
other way from home). The lady who owned it lived downstairs with
her husband, who worked, and two teenage sons, one in school, one
working; and she was a staunch, important, proper woman, in her
forties, whose care was everywhere, from the neatly clipped hedge,
swept walk, mulched and tied garden, vines up front, to gauzy curtains, to warm vestibule, patterned paper, pier glass with hat pegs,
carpeting, handsome polished banister, and upstairs pictures of horses
and cats. And there was a new tile bathroom (all in beige), a living
room, a small bedroom off right, kitchen off left, and windows with
a fire escape and orange of tree outside and looking down on the
back driveway and cinderblock garage and over that more trees and
backs of houses and triple deckers. And they still had the kitchen to
paint, counters to finish and some work in the bathroom, but it
would be ready for November first; the rent was one-fifty. A retired

man had the front apartment, and two girls (a secretary and a lab technician) the apartment upstairs.

Moving again the biggest problem was the furnishings—her bed from home, and bureau, bedroom chair, plus other things—and soon as she'd settled with DeVincent and had ridden the buses back to the Y, she'd had to call up Mary to explain, which was hard. But Mary surprised her, stern at first, and skeptical, but as she heard then, suddenly all eager and convinced. The weekend following, she had gone to sort with them and pack; and she felt awkward still, and strained, with all their questions—they wanted to go see it—and with Mary's irritations over this piece, that; and she had drawn a floor plan; and Howard offered her the upstairs rug and other things, but she refused. Then Saturday the twenty-second—they'd hired two men with a van for fifteen dollars per hour, plus Howard helping (Mrs. Gould had said it was fine)—they'd moved it all in one trip and Mary followed after them, with her and the girls. She'd been embarrassed before Mrs. Gould for so much confusion, for the girls' whining and chasing, for the van outside, for struggling in with the heavy mattress and other things up and down the stairs. But then it was done—and Mary kept admiring, satisfied as if the doing were all hers: "Oh, yes. You can do a lot with this. This is perfect for you, Anna. You ought to be real happy here." What about for curtains, lamps? She made it clear that she would work it out herself, and if she needed more from home, she'd ask; and the rest, she'd look for used furniture and fix it up as she went; and one concession (she hadn't thought of it, but they'd persuaded her), she'd have to get a telephone. And everything seemed different now, her efforts even as they tired, seemed like assent, and fresh, and filled with strength. Then on the thirtieth—a Sunday and two days early (again Mrs. Gould was kind)—she'd check out of the Y, and Howard helped her with the car, and when they got there, he brought things up, and she got the keys, and then the work was settling in. She thanked him. He shouldn't stay. And promised she'd call Tuesday, as soon as her phone was in.

She cooked for herself that night. Showered, brand new bathroom to herself. Eased into and pulled up the covers of her bed. There had been music faintly, earlier, and footsteps overhead, but only radiators now, a car in the driveway, garage door. The silence, privacy, and space both joyed and baffled her, like undue luxury and someone else's right. Except the right was hers. And only at great distance, as if dulled: old guilts, resentments, memory of the girls, Howard like a stranger, Mary's gains of pregnancy.

At work, with new determination, no matter her fears for her job or Harry's personal dislike, all fall (since the Y), she'd struggled to do her best and given all her energy. She'd brought up her volume by 12 percent. She'd studied how to quicken and improve each part of her operations—sorting candy off the belts, filling and storing boards, supplying boards to three different stations for teams to fold up boxes, fill, weigh, and pass to two cellophane wrap units, where machines wrapped, and then wrapped boxes must be packed in cartons (and making cartons at the treadle stapler was a full time job), and cartons run through sealing machine and packed on skids; and then there was a fourth team working on a gift assortment with a different box, special insert, and wax cups for every piece, and with a separate wrap machine, and larger cartons to accommodate. She'd also planned more carefully, taking Harry's quotas for both month and week, and scheduling two weeks at a time; she'd check on the progress every night and with each team, so she could give them quotas for the next day, and have the teams compete, and teams ahead of quota could leave early. Then at the end of the week, she'd rotate assignments (except for weighers and wrap operators), so the teams were never the same, and whether sorting, filling, packing, sealing, making cartons, or helping in the sample room, they all took turns, the younger girls as well as regulars, and this helped them to understand how different jobs depended on each other, and helped to ease monotony. And watching needs, she made sure she was never short of supplies; if low on candy, cellophane or boxes, she had the girls report instead of waiting to run out; and same with maintenance, at the slightest falter of equipment, she must know, and keep insisting after Bonzer's men before it turned to trouble. But as Louie and Mary Lloyd both told her, the most important and difficult thing was the discipline. She had to ask her women to feel, as she felt, the pressure of responsibility; that the factory must step up now in order to go on; that each of them must do their best in their parts; that the job was the question and depended on each one of them, and no more gossiping or breaks or absences with no fair warning or excuse; and any letting down or negligence would hold up teams and the whole department, and there was too much they must do for that; and either they all pulled together and kept up, or Leinhardt's would take over with people of their own. Anyone who wasn't willing now, and ready, she'd told them, they should quit, because she wasn't going to fight, and they had a job to do, and there was no place for anyone who wouldn't do her best.

Two teenaged girls, then, when teams complained, she'd had to fire and then replace. She hired a Cuban girl (whose father was an exiled doctor, Louie said, and worked out back with the roasters), and an older woman, black, and neither had experience, but both worked conscientiously, intent, and caught on right away.

But Rose Morgan's working out gratified her the most, for it had been a risk, with Harry noticing and Louie like the others all insisting she should fire her. And no one thought that Rose was worth it, but Rose had been here for years, was serious, and only since her husband had left, and threatened, and refused support (she had three young children), had she been trouble on the job, as if embittered by the work and they were somehow all to blame; and absent, slovenly, or late, Rose not only dared her to report her, but she quarreled and accused others for their errors, slowdowns, or for piling her with work. And guilty because she understood, and frightened of what Rose would do, and what would happen if she were fired, but forced to think of the whole department: she'd stood up to her and had it out.

She told her private troubles had no place; that she knew it was hard, and that was why she'd been as patient as she had been; but this was something Rose had to settle for herself; that there were rules and a job to do; that people had complained; that absences hurt work; that her temper had made an ugly situation; and if she was anybody else, she'd have been fired long before, but she was giving her a last chance, to go home now and think, and not come back unless she changed her attitude and came in ready to cooperate and be reliable and follow rules.

There had been outrage and contempt and slamming out. But Rose came back in the next day—on time, fresh uniform—and ever since, if closed and stonily remote, she'd made an effort and worked well. And she had made her weigher for the gift assortments. And she was never again any problem; and never again, even when she tried to praise her, was there the slightest sign of personal response.

The death and funeral came and passed.

She'd been in a coma the final weeks, and she never came out of it. Every night he'd been there. The last week, the doctors had told him, she couldn't last for so many hours, forty-eight, thirty-six, and she'd never regain consciousness, and if her body twisted, moaned or shouted out, it wasn't her—she couldn't feel and wasn't suffering—but all unconscious, as in dream. But that was the hardest part: memory of those cries, that agony, all closed to him, and past where he could touch or speak, or she could ever recognize.

Four-ten in the morning, pitch black, still, and out of dazed and muffling sleep, the phone had rung and rung. They told him she was gone. And come tomorrow they could make arrangements.

As if this weren't expected, even wished for, for her sake, there was still the shock and disbelief, and memory not of how he'd seen her just that night, but as they'd lived, and as she was when she was well, her presence, voice, and look, and always busy, tending Josie, cooking, cleaning, sewing (with him watching TV), planting in the garden; girl she'd been and years they'd come, and force of love, supporting and rebuking him and surer than his harm; her pride and worry for the boys, and fiercer still for Josie; gladness when they'd moved, and closer than since years before, and chance to look ahead and see lives settle, boys work out and all of them as they should be, coming close like family again. Her will in that, and like she'd never quit (or let them quit) on they were worth and they deserved. She'd been so sure and never done. He couldn't grasp now she was gone, as if desire were life, and incomplete. And though he'd seen the sickness wear her down, and spirit go resigned, remote, and failure easier than hope, and need for finish too abrupt; she still was all that energy and part, too constant, present to arrest. She seemed as vivid as himself, as close as whisper in the dark, and worried for him, listening, watching what he did, and no more stopped or gone than times when he'd run off and realized loss, and she'd be there, more'n harm, or distance back, or he had right.

"She's better off now, Pop; better than she's been for a long, long time, and she's at peace now, Pop," Frank had said, when he had called and woken them, and needed to make words, and same time feared, as if to speak confirmed.

Later he'd called Tony, standby for him on the job and ready for this last two weeks. And Tony, suddenly alert and brusque: Yeah, he'd start in right now, set up. Take care of everything; and sorry, Lou; and dontcha worry 'bout the job.

Then all like trance: showered, dressed; called up a funeral director out of yellow pages, local guy, and told him nice, but reasonable. He went to the hospital first, for the last look, signing papers; then over to the funeral home, nearby, and looked okay, pisan; and guy'd bring her body over here; they'd keep it simple, closed casket (oxygen mask and stuff had left her bruised), just him and boys, graveside service; nodded, yeah, Catholic graveyard outside Moorestown, make it a family plot. Two days after tomorrow. He tried to keep it businesslike, part of him bargaining and sharp on getting took. Newspaper notices, flowers, plot, limo, five hundred this, eight hundred that. Have her ready tomorrow; he should come back in the morning if he could, approve arrangements, pick out the casket.

Partly he was grateful, glad to have it seen to, fixed; and only left to him, as swept along, to keep up his part, take the calls, clean up the house (flowers came with a card from Harry, Mary Lloyd, Sheets, Bonzer, Tony, Frank and his crew; separate flowers came from Anna Maye, and from Manville and his wife), and work out family stuff. He wanted Josie there; Frank and Nancy would get her and keep her overnight. Nancy would cook (over at their place, for dinner the next night, she gave him a list to shop). They'd come down early. Dom and Victor would come, 11:00; 12:30, the limo would take them all to the cemetery; and afterwards, they'd eat. Then there was the crap with the priest—they'd neither of them been to Church (she'd gotten last rites at the hospital). He didn't want the visitation or the mass before, just service at the grave, and memorial later. Keep it simple, not prolong; kids all busy, loss for each too different to share; and each with lives, and only his bewildered now and hurt turned all question, deeper, larger than they'd want or he could bear to have them touch. Then plans and errands weren't enough. There still were gaps of time, and nothing but to feel or realize when he didn't. Thursday, then, he picked his suit up, shopped (Therese called, upset she couldn't come); cleared out medicines, and left for Nancy, dressing table, drawers— clothes, he'd call Salvation Army—and then just need to get out, walk, and like he had with Josie, farther, out one neighborhood to the next, and hunched against the chill, and as if motion only searched its lack, and world went on, and sky, and houses, yards, and school teams scrimmaging, and lives, but curious and blank, his grief alone as fact; and then for moments, nothing else, just coach and boys and whistle blown and one kid angling out for pass, and world without him, homes they'd go to, mothers cooking, old man home from work, all natural, enduring, and intact.

The next day, then: the kids, the limousine, and panic as they rode, and he was trying to think like this was simple too, and known, and as agreed, just car, just funeral, and somewhere through strange turnings, in fixed time, would be the cemetery, gates, the casket at the grave. They stopped at the office; the priest came out and followed in his car. The panic passed (he couldn't have them see). And on through streets and turnings, acres filled with monuments and stones and statues, still, and full as city in itself. They stopped. Her. Got out, and he went with them up incline, and distance off and back with other graves, breaths in their faces. They came to the casket, bigger, polished gray, and flowers arranged, and green mat over dirt and hole, and none of it seemed his, but just mistake, and they were guests, and they were lining up, taking hands, going through the motions—service, prayer, and trying to do right—but all for other's grief. Not for that was Paula in there, or who she was, or this was the last they'd see her; or force and beauty of that life, and size, and terrible difference now, and still for each of them unrealized and untried. He wanted more, not the priest, not formulas or funeral guy; but something large as loss, and true, and words or actions to express. But had no place; and anxious as if his only chance, found nothing he could speak, acknowledge, or provide.

He'd asked her to come with him, meet Josie.

Weeks had passed, and back at work, he brushed off all condolences—things happened, yeah, was okay, thanks—and thanked her for her flowers, but otherwise avoided her. He wasn't ready yet. She must respect his need, and wait. And it wasn't only his loss, but their friendship too: whether there could be more, and whether either of them meant more, or whether the question would confuse them. She must be wary, as of threat of weakness, not to think of him as a man, or of the pull she felt, or doubts, or of his hurt as opportunity. Yet, guiltily, she couldn't help imagining just how she'd feel, and for herself. Then all she knew of him seemed strange; too hard, and serious, too much to choose.

Then in a day or two, he'd stopped and asked, simply, how about dinner; maybe tomorrow? Someplace nice this time and quiet, where they could talk. And she was glad, yet also shy. She wanted to clean up, and couldn't wear just her uniform, or have him drive her back to change, so she brought her dress along the next day and freshened up and changed in the supervisors' ladies' room (Mary Lloyd came in, and when she heard, looked sour and disturbed, but held her peace). They met at 5:45—he'd changed to sweater, slacks—put on their coats, and went out to his car, fixed on no one's business but their own. He took her out Wayne Avenue to Barto's Steak House.

Talking was difficult: about her, the job, her apartment, how it had all been working out. She told him fine; she was settled now.

She told him about the people there, the neighborhood, and little incidents, like Mr. Gould (who worked for the post office) dropping her at Germantown the day it snowed, or the man who ran the laundromat, the corner grocer and his wife. He listened to her dully, tolerant, seeming to approve: what about her sister? She told him: she'd gone over Thanksgiving, and once again to baby sit. They were talking about selling the house, and she would get half. He frowned: what did she think about that. I don't know, she'd said. It's Mary's new idea. She wants a house in the suburbs, and her father-in-law to sell his butcher business, so they can start a business of their own. Howard, her husband, doesn't want to, and his father won't sell now, but if Howard pulls out, then he'd have to. It's the same all over, with Mary pushing and blaming everyone. I can't let it touch me anymore. And he said: Yeah, it's like my kids. They're goin' their own way, and only way to deal with them is leave 'em go. Whatever happens, it's over, far as you're concerned. Anything else, it has to come from them. He fell silent; then gradually, looking off or down, and as if speaking mostly to himself, he told. The hurt of how they'd kept apart, with nothing anymore as family for each other. How it was his fault, the way she died, with all she'd lived to see, no good. Victor was a bum; Dom closed off and no ambition for himself; Frank too busy on his own, and Josie better off with the state than with him; and nothing he'd done made any difference.

"That's not true," she said. "You all of you were hers, and gave her life, and gave her meaning to her life. She did the best she could. And like you've told me, how she stuck by you, how hard you worked in bringing up the boys, and later with Josie, the problems you faced. That's not failed. Or she kept worrying for you and had the courage to accept and not ask more than you or anyone could do. That's not hopelessness. It's wanting you free. She knew what you'd face, and the same for Josie—not that she was left alone, but she was cared for and safe. And if you could give her better later, then you would."

"Yeah, I don't know. I guess," he said. "Would have been a lot worse all the way around. Probably just be harder on Josie anyway, and she'd end up someplace no where near as good. I don't know."

"But that's not failing, is it? And I think that's how Paula felt—that it wasn't giving up, but being proud and strong and faithful to your lives."

He'd been listening, but when she finished, after a moment's silence, abruptly he got up and walked through tables out of sight to the left. She waited, worried, food half-touched. Then there he was, with a new beer, sitting down, as if he'd only gone for that.

"Better settle down and do some eating, huh?"

"It's good; it's just too much," she said, still watching and confused. "It's always easy for the other person, saying how to feel. I'm sorry."

"Naw, naw, that's okay. You're probably right."

She frowned, but held her peace.

"Has it been hard for Josie; I mean, since she's been there?"

"Yeah. Pretty bad, especially at first. She's doing a little better now, and kind of settled down. But I don't know; it ain't the same. It ain't like love."

"But you still see her. She has your love."

He shook his head. "I see her weekends. That's her life, not me."

And still she mainly listened and absorbed, and left him free to follow where he needed to. They ate. He talked of food and asked her: what do you do for relaxation anyway? I mean usually? What sort of things you like? But still there was the undertow, and on and off through the evening he'd come back to Josie, as an individual, "my little girl," and as he loved her. The way, "see, hear that she's retarded, I mean back when she's like three, and think why you, and feel like you been cheated"; the way "you gotta learn and hope for her the way she is"; and, "never with the boys, never anyone like that, like I was giving life, and everything was new for her." And she was thinking, while he spoke, of color snapshots that he'd shown her once: Paula and Josie outside their house, Josie in a pool, the slightly pug and slant-eyed, wildly grinning face. "And just you see her opening out," he was saying, "and not all scared or acting crazy anymore, but starting really to be a person. That's what's hard to quit. And once you've seen it, once you know."

Later, outside her apartment house, in his heated, idling car, he turned and gently took and pressed her hand. "I want to ask you something," he said; "hope you don't mind, or think it's funny or something, but just I'd really like you to meet Josie sometime, and come out to the school with me, and maybe spend an afternoon. I mean, you mind, just say so. Isn't pretty. But just I'd really like for you to meet her." Shaken, yet as firmly as if she'd already answered this, she'd replied: "I'd like to very much." He'd asked this Saturday. He'd pick her up at two, and they could stop for dinner on way back. And she'd said, let her make him dinner here. No, please, really, she'd like to make him a good meal.

So Saturday they'd gone. The night before, she'd cleaned and planned; this morning she had shopped, and started stew, all eager to be doing this, yet apprehensive too, and trying not to think of him, of child, of witnessing and what that posed. Then he had come, and she was ready with her coat and purse. And he seemed strangely scrubbed and meek, and moody as they drove.

They worked through Germantown, through side streets, out to Wissahickon Drive and creek and woods and Fairmont Park, all new to her and on for miles and finally up a street with big houses and yards, and then all open on the left, like any other school, with a modern, glassed-in building and parking lot set back on acreage from the street. Then a big gate and a sign that said "Walter Belmont School," and a car was coming out as they turned in, and there were wider fields on the right, and older houses and brick buildings scattered ahead, and down the road, shuffling, a man in an Army overcoat, whose hair was grizzled, crewcut, and who grinned toothlessly and waved as they drove past (one of them, she realized), and then they turned into the parking lot and parked. "Go in here first," he said. "Her building's ways down there, but like you to check in here with the supervisor first."

So they went in: to flush and dryness of heat, tiled modern foyer, and corridors with brightly painted cinderblock walls, and a lady sitting at a table for a reception desk. And as he explained he was Josie Miscello's father, in Farrell Hall, and asked was Miss Stromley here, a thin young girl with glasses appeared, and dragging a black boy, maybe nine or sixteen (she couldn't tell), whose frantic bellowing—baw-wah!—both Louie and the lady frowningly ignored, as if this were normal here, and she must too, though the force and rawness of the cries struck deep in her. And the girl was shouting, "It's all right, Ronnie; calm down," and dragged him past and into a room off the corridor and shut that door.

Miss Stromley hadn't been there, but he'd gotten his parking pass and left a note, and walking back to the car explained how she was a college girl and smart and had taken interest in Josie, and each time he came out, she'd give him a report. Maybe they'd run into her—like you to meet her—different from the usual staff. She'd see. Then as they drove, slowly, deeper into the grounds, was like a series of schools, buildings set back separate somehow, three storied, flat-roofed, with high screened windows, dirty brick, and leafless trees and hedges between; and outside one, there was rundown playground equipment, and outside another, a cracked cement courtyard and netless basketball hoop, or a tennis court with a sagging fence. And no matter the cold, there were more stray walkers, men and boys, and in the distance, with their spastic motions and clownish scarves and caps, a group with a ball; and then the shock of a normal boy, upright and agile, as they turned downhill, who crossed the road to a deliv-ery truck, and farther down, drawing back to let them pass, first women that she saw, and then a small church (sign said: "Chapel of the Holy Innocents"), and over a stream and around a bed was a one-story complex, with woods behind and parking area in front, where they pulled up by several other cars, and the landscaping was still bare dirt. This was Farrell Hall, and just for children Josie's age and younger, while others (she'd learn later) were for the other groups, the older adolescents, adults, especially handicapped, and violent cases, and always men's apart from women's, and worsening with the problems of each group, as if there were less that anyone could do or care (and later he would tell her: Farrell's one thing, but he was wor-ried when Josie's birthday came, they'd transfer her to a building up the hill, and you could see her future here, laid out like on a map).

They asked for Josie at the office (there were muted voices singing, piano pounding) and a smallish young woman came out to welcome them, a little awkwardly, yes, Mr. Miscello, how are you today? And she was Karen Bader. And Louie introduced her, Miss

Potts, friend of mine (she shook her hand). Miss Bader's in charge of Farrell, he told her. For a moment they talked. No, he wasn't signing Josie out today, just thought they'd visit some and talk and maybe take her out around the grounds, and asked how she'd been, and if Miss Stromley'd been by and they could see her before they left; been in this morning, yes, but didn't know if she'd gone home, but she would tell her if she saw her. She showed them a rack to hang their coats. And led them down a hall to double doors and in: to a large, bright room, like a kindergarten, with sofas and chairs at this end, and round tables and wooden chairs, and toys everywhere, and brightly colored platforms and playhouses to climb on and crawl through, and a huge doll house against one wall; and at the far end, an upright piano, where all the children were, fifteen boys and girls perhaps, sitting in a half-circle, and each with a triangle or tambourine or drum, and several parents watching, and the teacher playing: "clippity-clop—that's it, Larry!—big billygoat went over the bridge, and . . . where's the troll? Come on, Kevin, 'Who's that walking on my bridge?'" The first boy kept beating on his drum, and the other boy, grinning: "Who's on-a bridge?" Then hoarsely, to bass notes of the piano: "Who's at?" And they were all excited, banging on their instruments and laughing. "Come on, billygoat—no, now Donna's Gruff." . . . "Eatem up!" And only children afterall and simpler than she'd feared; which was Josie? "There," Louie said, as if guessing her thoughts, as they came near, and Miss Bader moved ahead to one little girl, who turned and looked agape (she looked like she had in the photograph, but skinnier and smaller, with curly black hair); and then her eyes went wide on seeing him, and a huge grin, but as if pleading in its eagerness, and the others craned around—"No, go on, everyone; it's Josie's father here," Miss Bader said, and the teacher kept on. And Josie jumped down; Miss Bader led her out, and then rushed forward, up, and he was holding tight and kissing her: "Hey, baby, hey, baby," and turning from the others, eyes clenched. "Daddy loves you. Daddy's here." Then lifted her down: "Look, there's a lady come to meet you, here. This is Anna Maye."

Josie looked, but turned her face and clung to him.

"You want more privacy, there's the lounge," Miss Bader said. "You know the way." He said, "Yeah, I guess we will." And if they wanted to take her out, just ask, and Miss Bader would get Josie's things; and then she left. And he helped Josie tie her shoe, and the three of them went out to the hall, with the room's commotion left behind, and him and Josie hand-in-hand (Josie leaning back to look), he was saying, "Anna Maye's a real nice lady; and she's come out special to meet you." She said: "Hello, Josie. It's very good to meet you. Your Daddy's told me lots about you." And Josie looked, and up at him, but once they'd gotten settled in the lounge, with him on the couch and Josie in his lap, and her in a nearby chair (and the only others here, a woman with two children playing in the far corner, by the TV), they had more chance to take each other in.

"Missed you, sweety. Missed you very much." He tucked in her blouse, which was small on her, with frills at the wrists, and coming out of her slacks. "She's dressing herself, and making her own bed, and learning how to write and spell her name. And playing different sports, aren't you, honey?" And she said, "Oh!" impressed, and asked what kind of sports? Josie looked at her, slack-jawed, and rolled her eyes: "Ball!" she said, with a lopsided grin. And asked, "What else?" Thick-tongued, Josie told her: "Wo-way, wo-waw." She had to guess: "Red rover, red rover? Uh-huh, I know that one; and what else, kickball?" And Josie: "Yuh!"

"And bowling, right?" he asked.

And more excited: "Bowling!"

"Got a regular alley here—And swimming too, right, once a week, and you like swimming, don't you? And what day's that? When's your swimming day?"

"Thur'day."

"Right. Good. And where you go to swim?"

Weaving, and for her now: "Gym!"

"And you been learning how to kick, and you can stay up by yourself now, can't you?—Really. Told me. Only one in her whole class."

"That's very good."

"Daa-ee, love my Daa-ee!" she said, too big, and reaching arms around his neck, and head laid on his shoulder. "See, heah, 'ocket.

Daa-ee got." She reached in her neck and brought out a chain with a locket.

"Let's see, yes." Getting up and bending close to look, she saw a tiny picture, Louie with Josie, just heads.

"Da-ee got!"

"Something for you here," he said, lifting her back. Dug in his pants pockets—"Here we are." He gave her a package the size of cigarettes; she tore the wrapping off and it turned out to be crayons, two rows.

"Aw baw!" Grinning, she tried to take them out.

"Crayons, yeah. You like those, right. Wait—." But she had shaken them all out. "Whoop. Okay, that's okay. Here, here you go. Let's pick 'em up." They'd gotten paper from a cabinet, along with a scribbled-over coloring book. Josie sat cross-legged on the floor, arms up on the table. And mindless of her dress, she got down beside her, while on the other side, on the couch, Louie leaned close. A purple crayon gripped in her first, Josie scrawled and zigzagged over the outline of a tree. "That's a pretty color," she said, as she might with Ruthie, and Josie turned and stared; then dropped the crayon and stroked her sweater sleeve and then her collar and the front of her dress. "That's maroon. Maroon," she said, smiling. "Look, look, here's maroon." She picked out the crayon, which Josie grabbed and bore down with. "That's it, see? Maroon. It's just the same, and different from the purple, see?"

"Moon?"

"Maroon. That's right."

"Ma-oon!" Josie crowed, as if it were an accomplishment, and something proud and special that they shared. She asked her, then, her Daddy's shirt, what color's that? Which crayon? And as they played (after colors, he began with letters, write her name, and then write hers, and then they drew together, houses, boats), that catch of interest, frowning effort, then appeal, then exultation as confirmed— "That's good, that's right"—was what she kept on working for, and with all patience, gentleness, and seeking Josie's rhythm in the play, which Louie helped her learn, but more so Josie asked. And when it came, she felt the warmth and glow of Josie's happiness as deeply as she felt the deprivation and neglect, the struggle limits posed, the apathy, the distance from contact. And that she was of use, and they played so well (impulsively, she'd smooth Josie's hair, or touch her hand or arm, as Josie did hers, squirming closer), and that she recognized her specialness: all made her doubly proud in front of him, aware that he approved, and gratefully, as if she'd answered, where he felt fiercest and most lost.

And later (other children had come in, curious and bold and wanting to join in, and grabbing crayons and making a fuss), they'd gotten Josie's things, and bundled up, and gone out for a walk, freer now and closer in the cold, and Josie holding both their hands, and slowing down to Josie's pace, and him and Josie showing her, around behind the buildings, up a dirt path through the woods, all bare and tangled in their undergrowth, where they saw squirrels, and grackles in the branches overhead, and Louie stopped to point them out, naming, explaining, or suddenly Josie would pull away, absorbed with finding pebbles to collect, or a twisted stick, or a leaf, and stuffing them in her parka's pockets like prizes (he made her throw the stick away). The path led to a road above and open fields, and a campsite cleared on this side, with a shelter, bathrooms, stone fireplaces, weathered seesaws, swings, and all in wintry disrepair, and this was where they'd come for cookouts and parties when the weather got warm, and grass and trees turned green, and there'd be flowers, right, and different kinds of birds would be back, robins, cardinals, blue jays, pretty birds and different songs—and butterflies— and they could play outside and all the outside games (and hearing him go on like this, as if around them everywhere, in details now and even cold itself, and time, and season's change, was wonder rich and full as love, she felt both touched and drawn); and Josie wanted to try the swing, so he hooked up a seat, brushed it off, and pushed her to the cry of rusted fastenings. Josie tried to look in the bathrooms, but the doors were locked. Then on down the road, the shed-like building at the field's end was the technical instruction shop (she thought she saw machinery through the glass) and for the older kids, the trainables, to teach them a trade and help them find a job outside.

The road turned down through the woods—"How doin', sweety, warm enough? Here, now wait a minute. Let's wipe that nose"—and came below the bridge, on the road they'd taken the other way to Josie's (and facing the rest of the grounds, up hill, with all the buildings scattered out). And here, set back in trees, was the gym, imposing as a bank, with steps and a porchlike entrance and marquee; and just for a moment, they went in, through heavy metal doors, into a heated lobby, with trophy cases all along one wall, and all the smells, and Josie pulled them towards open doors, and shouts, and the thud of sneakers, whistle, and there was an echoing court with a volleyball net up, and five or six men on each side (one hairy, obese boy with his shirt off and sweatpants on instead of trunks; one tall and gangling gray-haired man, with trunks pulled higher than his hips), and they were wildly batting the ball or bouncing it off their heads—"Hitaball! Hitaball! Looka 'Tolami! Asshole! Watcha! Getaball!"—or some just standing there with eager grins and gesturing, until the attendant gave one a special turn. Then a stocky man, like the others, except fully dressed, had seen and started towards them, with a clubbed-wrist dismissive wave: "Naw, naw! This ward thirteen, ward thirteen!" Officious and imperative. And Louie said: "Okay, okay, just looking. We're leaving now—Josie." On their way out (the man still watching with concern), he told her: "Pool's downstairs, y'know, and showers, special therapy and stuff." And she said yes, to him and Josie both, it's very nice.

Then tiring (she was anyway) and more uncomfortable in the cold, they followed the road alongside the stream to a second bridge, where the stream fed into a thawing pond, with ice floes at the far end. They stood at the railing looking down, with the sun dropped low in the trees, and grasses, trees and sky reflected upside-down, and blackness in the shadowed parts, and Louie tossed in stones, and the mood turned sad, with the sense they'd come to an end, and nothing left but turning back, the same as they'd begun. Then as she bent with her handkerchief and wiped Josie's nose, where Jose had been using her sleeve, she told her, solemn as an adult confidence: "My Mummy's sick. She went away." She glanced at Louie, and though alarmed and stricken by what this meant, she straightened up, and equally solemn and matter-of-fact: "Yes, I know, dear. I know," she said; and held her close through clothing's bulk.

He looked drawn and somehow lost. "Yeah," he said. "Time we started back."

Leaving was the hardest part. Them keeping on their coats, while Louie helped Miss Bader take off Josie's, and emptied her pockets into a little box, along with the crayons. And sounds of other children reached the hall, and adult voices and hoarse cries. And Josie just gone limp, withdrawn, as if their leaving meant not coming back, and nothing different in her world. She told her how she'd enjoyed today, how glad she was she'd come, and hoped to see her soon again, and tried with kiss and hug to seal the things they'd felt, but there was no response. The same for him. And worse than clinging, tears, or fight, that crushed obedience and vacancy, as if routine, upset her like a failing in herself. And leaving, carried the hurt, for him, for Josie, for so much promising and good that had no chance, and for her own part too, in having to permit the things she'd found, and coming back to self, to normal streets, and normal lives, and dinner she'd prepared. But also she knew, however stunned and drained, her spirit would recover force, like catching breath, and leaving wasn't ending or release, but just the opposite, and obligation now.

Mary Lloyd told her Rose Morgan was going out with Louie's Tony from upstairs, and they'd been messing around in the warehouse during lunch. "And that's just stupid here. And that guy, he's as bad as Louie used to be, and I warned him, I'll tell; he just better keep away from my women or else. I won't have that in my department. And not like it used to be either: this is Harry now. And she's no kid, she oughta have more sense."

Rose had been working hard and steadily; she was withdrawn, but there'd been no problem with the other women, or with her dress, or being late, or any sign of disrespect, or of her fighting the job. One way or another, she'd gathered that Rose had made her choice and taken steps and had her private life resolved. And knowing the treatment Rose had been through, the punishment, and the weight of her responsibilities, she'd felt so proud for her and good;

and that her trust had been repaid. So it wasn't the sordidness now, or her breaking the rules, or the threat to Rose's job that troubled her, so much as whether there had been some new shock, or just the same had gotten worse, so inside Rose had turned on care. She didn't know how to bring up her private life again, except that Rose must know that there had been this talk, that she and Tony had been seen, and as far as the job went, the seriousness of this offense, and that, if it kept up anymore, or Harry heard, or other heads complained, then she'd be fired. And she wasn't telling her how to live, but that this talk was damaging to discipline, that romance made for tensions and feuds and got in the way of work, and if there was anything that Leinhardt's was determined to root out—as part of everything unbusinesslike and shoddy here—it was fraternizing between personnel.

So once or twice, she tried to speak, but Rose allowed no opening, fixed on work, and as if nothing wrong; and each time, caught in an awkward pause, about to speak, with Rose behind her blandness, dangerous and aware, she'd let it go, as if she'd agreed that it wasn't worth the ugliness and harm. Except in failing, she became part of it, and weak, and if anything happened, she must share in the blame.

Later, talking with Louie, she mentioned that Rose was on her mind; and he asked who? And when she said, he went all pained: "Didn't I tell you? I mean, before. It just ain't worth fooling around with a person like that? Two-bit general helper, doesn't give a damn one way, another, and you think treat her special and she'll turn all right. So what'd she do this time?" She tried to tell him: It's not like that. It's she's been up against so much, with her husband deserting her and three young children to support, and that she'd been trying very hard, and that since the last time she'd warned her, Rose'd been one of her best and hardest workers, and there's been nothing like before; that this was Tony now, as much as Rose, and he was taking advantage of her being worn out and lonely and hurt and angry at her life.

And, "Tony? What Tony? Iacone?" he asked. "What, she's been messing around with him? He's coming around the job?" She explained: No, but Mary Lloyd had told her; they'd been seen, and they'd been going back behind some cartons in the warehouse during lunch; that Tony had some hideaway.

He said, yeah, he'd heard some talk, and that was Tony all right, and he was a wiseguy, grabbing any he could get, but nothing you could catch him at, and besides, he's shop steward and too important at his work, and no point crowding him.

She said: The point was Rose, and talk was sure to get to Harry, and maybe Tony's job was safe, but Rose was only here now on her say, and the slightest cause and they'd get rid of her.

So tell her, he'd said. You get any more complaints or you see anything like that, then you're suspending her. You done all you can; you've stuck your neck out far enough, and I don't care if you feel sorry or what, if she can't make it, get her out. I'll tell Tony to watch himself, and Harry can't do nothing just on rumors; but this is a woman, far as I'm concerned, she's bad news all the way. Be a whole lot smarter to drop her now, instead of waiting for something else.

She meant again to speak with Rose, but always there were other things to do, and anyhow the problem seemed to solve itself. There was no more talk, and Rose kept on the same, and Harry never mentioned it, and even Mary Lloyd forgot.

But then next Tuesday, early afternoon, as she was showing Mrs. Chosiad (whose English was poor) how to make up cartons on the treadle stapler, Peggy Nolan came running:

"Anna Maye! It's Rose!"

"What? What is it?"

"Rose, she's walking off."

She stepped out and looked at the assorted line, where Rose had been weighing. The women had stopped.

"She just got up, she's over at her locker," Peggy was saying.

"All right, Peggy, you go on, take the weighing." And as she hurried after Rose: "All right, all of you," she told the other women, "get back to work; I'll handle this."

Rose was putting on a sweater, stuffing a street dress in her bag, changing crepe soles for pumps: all with jerky, fixed intent.

"Rose. Stop. What are you doing?"

"I'm getting out," she said; and took her leather coat. "Let me alone."

"Wait, what is it? Are you sick?"

"Nothing. I don't want to argue. I'm just getting out of here!" And slammed her locker door, and turned.

"You can't just leave. No, please, whatever it is, don't. Listen to me. You walk out now, there's nothing I can do."

"I don't care. What you think or they think, or this whole stinking place. I just can't, and I won't sit weighing candy and listen to their stupid talk and slurs and prying in my life. I don't need your fussing either! So go on, fire me. I don't care." She pushed on past.

"Rose, no!" She chased after her, glancing at the others. "You don't know what you're doing." She caught her at the door. "Look, I know you're upset. But you've been doing so good. Come in my office, talk it over. Get a grip."

"Get lost, willya? Whatta you know? Any of these fat-assed bitches!" And dragged open the door, and out. Stunned a moment, still she followed, into the concourse, pleading: "Rose! You're acting crazy!" But Rose never turned or slowed, and she could only watch her marching off (past men, who also turned to watch) towards the shipping door.

And somehow Harry found out right away, because not twenty minutes later he called her to his office—up front, where her uniform felt conspicuous and the secretary told her to wait, and Mr. Manville's name was still on the door. "Okay, go in." Everything was different, new decor, metal desk, and Harry with his jacket off, and sleeves turned up, and young and cold and curt. "Sit down, Anna Maye. Now what's this with a woman walking off?"

She gently eased into a chair: "Well, I can't say exactly," she apologized, all prickly and alert. "I mean, she's a very good worker. It must've been some kind of argument."

"Don't you know?"

"It happened so fast. I was on the other side of the room, and next thing I knew she was back at her locker, and I went, I tried to speak, but she was too upset; she just went right on out. And I can't think what would do that, but I know she didn't mean it. She needs this job. And she's been having personal troubles, but she's trying hard to keep them out of work. And she's got four good years."

"Morgan, right? Same I told you before. And don't give me that sob story routine. This woman's got a series of complaints, absenteeism, temper—and pretty sleazy morals, so I hear. And I've been waiting for you to take an action, but you keep playing along, and now you've got her walking off the job, in front of the whole place. And wasn't for that soft-heart, buddy-buddy attitude of yours, there'd never be a situation like this. So get this straight. That woman comes in here tomorrow, tell her she's through. Check'll be in the office. That's final. I don't want arguments. You get her card and give it to the bookkeeper, and if she don't show up we'll mail it. But it's time you figure too. This isn't a tea party. You got a department to run and I don't want any more incidents. I want some sound supervision. That means handling these women and keep your personal feelings out. Okay?"

Struggling, she nodded yes.

But later, home, well after nine, the phone ringing that startled her, and must be Louie (whom she'd missed and had no chance to tell), or Mary, suddenly was Rose, who sounded drunk, her voice shaky and speech slurred. "I'm sorry calling you at home, and late like this, but just I had to tell you how ashamed I am. I lost my head. Anything I said to you or anything, I never meant it, Anna Maye, I swear. I just been all mixed up, and I'll never let it happen again; I promise you, I won't. I want to work. I've been trying hard, you know I have, and doing good, if it weren't for this. And I've been grateful for you've done. And this was, see, I don't know, but just with Rudy and he's trying to take the kids away, and I been alone. And I was dumb, but I been going with that guy, that Tony Iacone works upstairs. I knew he was married and chasing all the time, but still I wanted back at Rudy, I dunno, and he was smooth, and looking for fun, and all I thought, why not, it's better than sitting home and feelin' sorry for myself. But just he's such a bastard! He's been bragging, like I'm some kinda joke, and he's got other girls, and top it off, he gives me this infection, all up my tubes, and then he says I'm not clean and I've been trying to give a case to him. Lunch today, we had it out, and I'm like, I dunno, all wild inside and sick at myself and then that Allen bitch starts saying stuff, and so I'll hear, about some people got no character. About how this Tony, upstairs, he's got a love nest, and any woman goes with him, she don't belong in a decent place. About how he'd propositioned her friend's daughter, she's sixteen, and offered her money . . . , and just, I couldn't take anymore, anything, and maybe that's no excuse, but see, it's over now; I'm through with him. Nothing's ever gonna mess me up like that again. I got my kids, and please, you can't just fire me over this. Fine me, you have to, okay? Suspend me, I don't care, but let me keep my job. And see, it's not just money; it's Rudy finds out he'll use it for the custody, and they will, too, twist it all around, and say like I been fired, and for bad character. I'm not fit to keep my little girls. They will!"

She had to tell her. That she felt terrible about this, but it wasn't up to her. She'd done all she could. Harry had called her in, right afterwards, and she didn't know how he'd found out, but he had said that she, Rose, was through, and that they'd send her check. "I'm sorry, Rose. He wouldn't listen. All he said was rules, and just I wish this never happened, but it has; and he was very definite. I don't know what else I can do."

And there was silence, breathing. "Please. It isn't just the job, it's my children. And I'm not asking let me off; I'm saying go on and suspend me, then. That's three, four weeks, no pay; that's hard enough. I worked for you four years, I've done good, and any trouble recently, it's not something I been looking for. And what about Tony? Bastard's getting away with murder; they don't do a thing. None of this'd happened, weren't for him. And why get tough on me? I mean, can't you go, go to Mr. Walsh? Tell him I'm sorry, and won't be nothing else, and just I need this job? It isn't just rules; it's people's lives. I mean, suspend me, that's enough; firing don't prove anything. You think I'm worth the chance. Please. I'll never ask nothing else."

And she was ready to say no, I can't, I don't owe you that, it's already gone too far, except she couldn't say that to this voice. It wasn't only Rose, but something she felt bound to in herself. "All right," she said. "I'll try. But don't expect too much. He doesn't set much store by me. It's this whole Leinhardt's business and the way they look at all of us."

Later she lay awake thinking how Harry would react. She'd tried her best. But just the job was different under Leinhardt's, and only the building was the same, and these were strangers, with strange goals and hard demands, which just seemed more against her all the time. And she was different too. Money wasn't the point; she'd have her share when Mary sold the house. And she was young enough and qualified to find another job. And more and more, Louie, Josie, and things apart from work involved her.

The next day, early, she waited outside his office. The book-keeper came in, and glanced at her; next was the switchboard girl; next Mrs. Hersome. And finally, Harry, brisk and fresh, and morning, morning; then irritation, seeing her. He stopped and turned: "What is it? You waiting for me?"

"Please, yes, Mr. Walsh. It's that woman we talked yesterday."

"Thought we settled that."

"I know, Mr. Walsh, but she called me last night. There's more we need to consider."

He looked at her, hard. "Okay, let's get it over with." He went ahead, turned on the lights, set down his briefcase, took off his over-coat and hat. "Sit down, go on." He closed the door, and sat behind his desk. "Well, come on, let's have it."

"It's not like you think," she said. "She's a decent, hard-working person, who's been with me for four years; and she's trying hard to get back on her feet, after a bad marriage, and with children to support. And yesterday was nothing deliberate. But it was one of the men here, and he's been a problem both with my women and with Mary Lloyd's, and he was bothering her, and that's why she was so upset. And just she's very sensitive, after what she's been through, and this man was insulting and mean, and later some women started taunting her, and that's when she blew up. And she's ashamed and sorry for what she did, and she says that's all over now, and all she wants is to keep this job and make good here. And please, I know her, Mr. Walsh, and know that she's sincere; and she's been doing so well otherwise. And it was serious, I agree, there has to be a strong response. But we don't have to fire her. I think a two or three week suspension would be harsh enough, especially in this case. And much more fair. She deserves to stay."

He shook his head.

"You just don't get it. We're through fooling around here. We've got a full-scale operation here, and that means weeding out the problem personnel. We're not in social work. We got a plant to run. Now I don't care this woman's motives or her problems; she's a risk. So let's just leave it there. The answer's no. Now get on back to work; I want your start-up eight sharp. Pull a woman off of Mary Lloyd, you need her."

Two days later he called her in.

"Look, it's not this Morgan thing; it's something I've been thinking for some time. I'm giving you notice, Anna Maye. I'm sorry, but we got to look ahead, and this is I think best for you as well as for us. You aren't cut out for what we need. And what I'm talking here, we're bringing in our own top people, and reequipping and expanding your whole department. And it's no reflection on you, or the hard work you've put in, or your long, good record under Manville. I've got nothing but regard for you here, personally, same as everybody does. But this is just too big a job, and it takes skills and a background in a different kind of operation. Now, you'll get severance pay, and I'll be happy to help you any way I can. You got my recommendation. And any woman with your experience and record here, you shouldn't have much trouble finding something good, and something you'll feel more comfortable, and a whole lot better off."

She was over losing her job, but having lost the factory as a meeting place with Louie, and the work there as a life to share, she and Louie were thrown back more on sharing their private lives, and on interests still more intimate and personal. And after her day without work, a day whose luxury and leisure she must learn to explore (she would think of him there, think of the others, starting up, and at different moments, what they would be doing, and she would be doing, if she were there), that he would seek her out, and call, and stop by before going home, and that he chose, and she chose too, to keep this up: all seemed more serious. Sometimes they'd go out, but mostly she would cook, and he'd stop over maybe three, four times a week, tired from the job, and full of stories about the Leinhardt's woman in her place. She was skinny, bloodless, mid-forties, he said, like some prison matron or WAC officer; she'd stopped their morning coffee break; she was always on his back and bitching about his men; she'd gotten her quotas up with two new automateds they'd brought in, but meanwhile she'd fired Mrs. Shanker, and two other old-timers had quit; try to tell her anything and she'd treat you like some meddling jerk.

Other times, he'd ask her what she'd been up to. He knew, in general, that with her savings and severance pay, she wouldn't have to find work right away, and that she wanted free time for herself, but she wouldn't have much to tell. Nor could she admit how big a part he played in her new attention to herself, in her making new clothes, in her cleaning the apartment, in rearranging, trying to make it nice, in her trips to shop; or how much she enjoyed cooking surprises for him, like the cheese lasagna, or the veal parmesan he'd showed her the week before.

Sometimes in the course of things, she'd tell him about her pleasures in the weekday world, sights seen and people met, the conversations with the grocer and his wife, the laundromat man, the girl upstairs, and Mrs. Gould (or of her awkwardness that time that the Jehovah's Witness people, the woman and her daughter, had knocked one Sunday morning and she couldn't get rid of them, and finally had to buy their magazine).

And several times, weekends, they went to see Josie again, and Josie seemed now to remember her. For herself, as Josie grew more in her mind, and as she talked with him and thought of things to do and bring, and trips to take, and became more familiar with the school, and met Miss Stromley, Josie' supervisor, more and more seemed possible, the contact surer and more full.

They took her first to the zoo; then to the aquarium (near the art museum, on the river through the park), where none of them had ever been, and Josie stared and stared, and held hands tight, while

Louie read from information cards beside each tank, and all around was bathed in underwater glow, and echoing with human sounds, as in the tanks, through glass, the beautiful (like striped fish, round and thin as plates), the comical, the shivery (like mantel ray and shark), swam in otherworldly pulse and glide, or hovered motionless, or suddenly moved off. And Josie liked the giant lobster best, but for her, the longer she watched, the uglier and stranger it got, with its antennae and eye stalks, and claws as large as boxing gloves, and scuttling suddenly, and crawly as a centipede; while what she loved were anemones, like living flowers, tendrils opening and closing up; and Louie seemed most drawn to dangerous things, piranhas ("strip the flesh off of a man, sixty seconds or less"—he tapped the glass—"those little fish"), five-foot barracuda, six-foot shark.

And as before at the zoo, here other parents led their children, or children ran unsupervised, and shouted, pushed, and chased, and Josie seemed as interested in them as in the fish, yet at the same time clung tighter, as if for pride and shyness. And if there were looks, or even when there weren't, she felt defiant tenderness, for Josie's rights the same as any other child's, to be here as she was, to babble, croon, or issue hoarse cries of delight. She'd had a tantrum on the trip before, which Louie had handled firmly, simply, while she herself had been unnerved, but next time she'd know better how to help. And somehow there could be no bond closer than in Josie, no touch more intimate than holding her, brushing her hair, or kissing (as he kissed), all naturally, without reserve.

But still, between the two of them alone, when they wanted to touch, they couldn't yet. There would be bodies' brush, or touch of hands, or his arm around her as they walked; but times he tried, the awkward goodnight kiss (she'd turned her cheek), and later, the time on her couch (she'd pulled away and gotten up, not angry, but pleading), and other times the moment seemed right, she only knew she couldn't trust to love, and they were strangers still: his with dark confusions, which she could forgive, but never fully answer with herself; and hers at once too special, needy and ashamed. Better just to keep as brothers, sisters, persons to each other, separate from sex.

Except their feelings needed more, and she would blame herself, and then blame him. He had to challenge her when she pulled away; he had to overcome her fears. But then he did. They'd come back home from the movies and were talking on the couch. Talk had stopped and then he'd reached and she had flinched and stiffened, trying not to move, but close to tears.

"Hey, what is it? What's the matter, don't you like me?"

"Please. It isn't that. I'm sorry," she'd said. "I don't want to talk about it."

"Hey, c'mon now. Hey. We're grown up people here. I mean it's serious. We got a feeling for each other, but every time I try'n touch you, you're acting like I'm someone else. I'm not going to hurt you. I want you. I want to hold you, that's all. You're a woman to me. And more we see each other, and talk, and care about each other, the lonelier it gets. You're making me lonely. You can't just close your feelings off; gotta trust them. Here. Here, honey. I'm scared too, okay? I'm scared because you're good, and fine, and you got plenty reasons to want to keep me off. I never said you don't."

And she was lost in his eyes, face and lips, her choice dissolved, and there was only need, and happening, and force of holding, force of kiss, which he was the one to stop. He pulled her head down to his shoulder, where she nestled, held and holding, grateful now for silence, grateful not to meet his eyes. The boundary had been crossed, and everything was on a different footing suddenly, and truer to themselves.

The next date they kissed, and the next; there was the sudden hug hello, or nestling close, or times in his car, and kisses quick and shy, or as their passion grew, long fevered kisses on the couch, and always he would guide and lead, as if more certain in this way than her; and always he knew when to stop. And partly she was glad for his restraint, partly scared her passion would offend. But what she felt was love, and having named it to herself, she longed to say it to him, must, whether he could say it to her or not. She knew that they were good for each other, and good for Josie too; she knew the strength and fullness of life that they could have. But she couldn't know, and couldn't question even, how much Paula's memory held him back.

Then Mary had called. This was the first they had talked since she left the factory, and when she told her, Mary grew excited: Why? How? But that's crazy.

She explained that most of the Manville regulars were gone or would be soon. That she'd find something else. She had her severance pay. She hadn't been looking yet, but she would. She'd be just fine. And meanwhile she'd been fixing up the apartment, taking a pottery course, making clothes, and going out; and there was someone she'd been seeing.

"Wait a minute; who?"

"Louie," she told her, "from the factory."

After a moment, Mary remembered: "Louie? Wait, wait, you mean that guy, he was there when I was there? Short guy? Italian? Must've been fifty or something then. Had a bad name everywhere?"

"We're very good friends. His wife died recently, he's been alone; and first we just went out as friends, but we've been seeing each other seriously for the last month or so."

"What do you mean, 'seriously'? What're you talking about now? Marriage?"

"I don't know. I'm not ready to say."

There was a silence, strained.

"You just, you seem so far away, Anna. I mean all this happening, big things, your job, and talking marriage suddenly. And someone like that, you don't even know what you're getting into. He's so much older than you, and god knows, I mean he's got family or what kind of problems he's got. It's something we have to talk about, at least."

"We are far apart. But this is something private. And when there's more to tell you, then I will. But I don't want your opinion, and I don't want to be pushed. Okay? Now what about you? How's the baby? How're the girls?"

Mary, with a sigh, had let her: All right. They all were fine. The baby had engaged, and she could feel its rear end high, and it wasn't due for three weeks, but it would probably be sooner. Then she'd asked: If she wasn't working, could she come and help, maybe? For a couple days afterwards? And she'd said yes. But what Mary had called for, really, was the house. They had some papers that they needed signed—this weekend if they could, or Howard could stop by—so they could put it with an agency.

She waited for his calls from work. Nothing but their time together, or planning, knowing he would come, had point or pleasure for her now. She grew tired of her apartment; everything familiar seemed no more than holding place. So she went out for walks, long walks, where the air was mild and the neighborhood seemed all event. Maybe she should look for work. She started reading want ads, and circled, vaguely, "counter person," "laundry," "general factory, Lady Athena Products." Sunday's paper would have more. If not in candy, then in foods, in packaging; or something nearer by.

One night, not so different from others—they'd just come back from Josie's—except for the silence that had grown between them: "Look," he said. "Listen. Why don't we get married? What do you say? I been thinking. And apart from feelings, I mean; does it make sense? For all of us? I want it right for you—I don't want you wasting your life. I got good years left, but I'm not getting younger. I got my job, my house; pension coming later. I don't know there's any hope of getting Josie back, but if we can, that's asking you to love her too. And that's a big order. I mean, no matter how you love her now. But we got something good together, something strong. It's there, we want to try. Something like we're meant to be, and not this stumbling round alone."

The choice was more than choice, larger than herself, and surer and more strange; she felt swept forward in its course.

Possession

The ceremony was in a side chapel. Howard gave her away; Mary was matron of honor, Susan a flower girl, and David (their new baby, which she'd helped care for for the first few days, but Louie hadn't seen before) was crying in Mary's arms, so Mary had to take him back. Frank was best man. Frank's baby, Sally was there, along with Ruthie in her new dress. Louie's sister, Theresa, had come. And Dominic. His third son, Victor, had refused to come; and they'd decided better of disturbing Josie. Mary Lloyd had asked to come (with Tom), and she was responsible for the presents, cards, and notes from nearly everyone at Manville's, including Mr. Manville and "Harry Walsh," and Ralph and Mrs. Dawson and Louie's men, and her own regulars, who signed group cards. Everyone was there to wish them well, with doubts and oppositions set aside. And Mary Lloyd had hugged her hard.

Afterwards, together now, alone, she and Louie had driven to his house for suitcases and a change of clothes, and then went on for the two hours to Atlantic City, where she'd been once as a child, and remembered playing under the boardwalk in cool sand. They were silent much of the way, and then were entering the city, driving through downtown traffic snarls, and out through residential blocks— salt air, and large, expensive houses, rooming houses, cottages; and eager for the first sight, she glimpsed the ocean suddenly down side streets. Their motel was luxurious and new, air-conditioned, with a pool and sundeck in the courtyard, and only one block from the beach. Their room was so large and fancy she felt out of place—with double beds, TV, a huge mirror over the dressers, full-length drapes. All this was theirs, and private, to enjoy; they had no responsibilities, or worries over money, or anything that others thought.

She was shy of using the towels, or even of trying the bed: "C'mon," he chided her, "relax. It's what we're paying for. C'mon, now, here. Here, sit down; okay, now stretch out, go on. That's it. Ever try one of these?"

"What?"

But he'd already put a quarter in, and the bed was rumbling, shaking. "What, what is it?" She jerked up. Then "Good lord!" and laughed. "What's it doing?"

"Massage," he said. "Go on." After the first surprise, as she lay back, and partly for the joke, the shaking lulled and felt voluptuous, and stopped too soon.

"Umm. That's good."

"Hey, well, where's my turn? No, go on." He put in another quarter and hurriedly lay down, and they were side by side then, on their backs, trembling with it. "Yeah, yeah, that's the stuff. That's the treatment!" She laughed; and when he reached to hold her, the shaking made it seem like a joke, but then it wasn't a joke, and the bed went still. Propped on an elbow, leaning over, gently he stroked her hair and cheek, and seemed to study her; then their deep kiss.

"I'll be a good wife to you," she said. "I will. You'll never be sorry."

"Hey," he said, "here." He held her, and kissed her again, her neck, her breast, and she held him tighter, her hand in his hair and feeling the shape and muscles of his back. All his body was moving;

he was squeezing her breast; then through her clothes, his hand was on her thigh, and under her dress, meaning more. She felt the helplessness of limits gone, and of fullness both (not as she had planned, as ceremonious, as a moment they'd approach; not her coming out of the bathroom, showered, fresh and wearing her new nightgown, and into a room all dark, where he'd be waiting, patient and grave; but like an accident, abrupt, the moment come, apart from choice, except as choice lay deeper, fixed). He was opening her dress; he kicked his shoes off, then sat up, solemn, and pulled her dress off her shoulders, off her arms, and with her helping, under her hips, and off her legs, then pulled off her shoes; she pulled up her slip, and after a moment's queasiness, pulled it over her head, and he was helping her, the bed was rocking with his weight. His shirt was off. Not his gentle, but some lurid grin, and shaggy chest and gray, as he undid and stripped off his pants, his penis stark, and he rolled to her.

The joy and freedom was lost to the suddenness and his bruising kiss, his angry struggling with her bra, and with her panties next. It was all too fevered, brusque, his knee between her legs, and then on top, and he was kneading her sides, his face was in her breasts, all blind; he was grunting "umm" and "nice" and "that's my baby, yeah"; his hand was on her mound (she tensed and forced herself: relax), and squeezing, gentle there, while her own hands moved feebly on his back. The room was too visible and the light too harsh. They were chest to chest, his cheekbone hard, and he was kissing her neck and ear (she was trying to kiss back, but found no face, no mouth); and then he raised his hips, and it wasn't his hand, but floppy, blunt, and he had it in his hand and worked it against her vulva, pulling hairs; then his knee beneath her leg, he levered, hauled, and told her, "Get your leg up, up, that's it," and spit in his hand, and started working in, too big, and pushing down, and suddenly drove in. She felt him deep in a space that she didn't know she owned, and only felt as a shock, this fullness in, this pulling back and thrusting in, too new for pleasure or for pain, He slowed, then short and quick, then circling, then plunging deep, and nothing she could grasp or join, his will apart, his face aside, his holding tight. She was drawing her knees up, wide; and then more regular, but just as she was rocking to his thrusts, and this was her as well, and just as their motion had turned motionless, and almost a lull, and the rudeness had turned to grace, he started deep again, and hard, and all his length. The bed was knocking against the wall; there were their bodies' smack and suck, his rigid grip, his grunt, and pulse, then writhe, and then the force was gone, and slackening, while her mind still rocked, and her nerves, and she was trying to keep on, to quicken where he slowed. She felt him withering and soft, and slipping from her as she moved, and then was gone. He lay heavily, and dense, on top of her, as if beyond her reach, his stomach heaving slowly, as in sleep, and she was trailing fingers on his back, and needing him to turn and speak, to offer her some tenderness, and meaning to her doubt. She heard him yawn, and felt him pushing up; he gave her a token kiss, then rolled off. She felt the cool and freedom from his weight. Then looking off: "Okay," he said, then: "You okay?" Wanly, bravely, she smiled back.

He got up. She watched him naked now, his hairy buttocks, cleft, and legs and back, as he walked into the bathroom, leaving her. Then he washed at the sink, and dried himself, then half-shut the door; she heard his stream in bowl, the flush; then coming back, he seemed just too off-handed, casual, dismissing everything, even as he settled back, and moved his arm around her, drew her close; as if for him now what had been was over, and their feelings were private, and bothersome, and never to be said or asked. He waited for her, then, holding her as idly as if they were clothed, while she grew more aware of the room, of the day, and of the outside noises; there were voices in the hall.

"Think anybody heard us?" she asked.

"Huh? Nah." He shifted and sat up. "Let's see what time we got. . . . Hey, how about we clean up, get dressed, go out and look around a little, huh? See the sights, get some dinner; how about it—Hey!" He turned his face, and sobered suddenly: "You sure you're okay?"

"I'm fine," she said, but fighting tears.

"C'mere. Here." He held her now. "C'mon. I love you, okay? We got a long, long time." He stroked her back. "We'll be okay. It's nothing to be worried now. We're fine. C'mon . . . there you go." Then he held their hands up, matching rings. "Hey, how about that, huh?"

"I love you too."

Then the kiss: his reassuring, firm, to hers too desperate and full.
He squeezed her hand.

"Let's go."

There was nothing but to trust his lead; turn to the business
of a quick shower, change, and hang up the clothes, and straighten
the bed. She liked dressing with him, intimate, as if they belonged
to each other, and readying themselves together for world. He wore
blue slacks, a white shirt open at the neck, and was putting on his
sunglasses; she wore a light sleeveless print, her sandals, and picked
up her purse, a straw hat. "All set? Got the key?" He locked the
door, as if on the memory; and holding hands, they walked down
the hall, proper, smiling, on through the lobby and past other
guests, the bellman, clerk, and out into the sudden heat, late afternoon and others' day.

They walked down the sidewalk towards the beach; she smelled
the salt air and felt the ocean breeze. Children were starting back, in
bathing suits, and one with a raft. There were two girls, wet, on skates,
and deeply tan; and farther on, an older woman, her flesh burned
pink, who carried a beach bag and chair; there were teenaged boys
with a radio; a man with a dog that strained on its leash; the ocean
meeting the sky. The boardwalk, then, as wide as a street, with people sitting on park benches, or leaning on the railing. Other people
were strolling, or starting down or coming up the stairs from the
beach. The beach was below, with fifty yards or so to the surf, and it
was crowded still: people lying, sitting, beach umbrellas, chairs, children running, lovers shamelessly embracing, families gathered, radios
and blankets, baskets full of food and drink, and swimmers in the surf.
The beach front curved right to thin line at the horizon (Ocean City,
he informed her), and left, for two miles or more, to the city skyline
and the amusement piers. It was teeming, even more than here, with
people its whole length. There were combers breaking in, and out
beyond the beach: the vastness of the sky and sea, too much for her
eye, except to drift and gaze, to fix on the sailboats, graceful, part way
out, or on a motorboat with a skier. "Hey, let's go . . . c'mon," he urged,
impatient for the crowds, the curiosities, and the main attractions

stretching far ahead. All along the boardwalk were low, awninged concessions, hot dog and hamburger stands, frozen custard, golf, and children's rides; and then there were the first grand hotels with high-toned shops, and restaurants, and the traffic grew busier, both ways, with rolling chairs (double- and triple-seaters, pushed by porters), and bicycles, and people of all ages, kinds, including one girl just up from the beach, who walked ahead of them in nothing but a bikini, clogs, with hair down to her shoulder blades (he kept watching as she vanished into the crowd). Sailors in strange uniforms. Convention Hall, immense; more hotels; the "Million Dollar Pier," with a Ferris wheel, merry-go-round, and children clamoring. He was silent, vague, as if the blur of sights, and crowds, and the walking in itself, took the place of thought, or any purpose in each other.

Then later he'd begun to drink. First he had a beer, at an open stand, while she bought souvenirs (postcards for Mary Lloyd and the others, sea shells for Josie and the girls, salt water taffy); next he had whiskeys at dinner: "C'mon," he'd said, "let's celebrate," and ordered her a Dubonnet, which she nursed gingerly, for his sake. She had flounder, watching as he slid oysters from their shells (which she'd refused to try), and swallowed them whole, then gave her a mocking leer. She looked at the other couples, younger mostly, smartly dressed, and one that must be honeymooners too, nestled into a corner, with eyes for nothing but each other.

She'd said something about Josie; how seeing the children's rides, and the parents, she couldn't help but think of her, and how much she'd love being here. He gave her a look, and a rueful nod; he told her: yeah, they used to bring the boys down, when they were small, Frank was six or something and Victor was still in diapers; it was during the war and they were living in this apartment in South Philly; they'd come down for the day; they'd had an old bum Ford, and they'd save up ration stamps for gas; his mother'd come down too; they'd spend a whole day on the beach; had real good times; but things were different after that. Family life was different. A couple of times, he'd come down with some guys; and once, with Manville's oldest son, Jack—for a confectioners' meeting down here. But they did nothing with the kids; no trips or nothing, later on.

She'd brought the wedding up; about Theresa, how much she had liked her, really, and found her different from how she'd expected; and Victor, not to let it bother him (she understood); about how nice Frank had been; and what had he thought of Mary and baby.

He had listened and replied, but idly, as if his mind were on something else. Then, oysters done, he'd winked at her over the rim of his glass, and set his glass down. "Ain't seen nothing yet. We'll catch us one of those rickshaw deals and ride down to the big piers. Then we got the night time fun. Nightclubs, big name acts, floor show, singers, comic acts; wait'll you see. We're going to have us a really great time."

"I don't know if I'm up to all that," she'd apologized.

"Hey, come on. What do you, you want to go back and sit in the room all night? I mean, hey, we've got the 'Fun Capital of the East Coast' here. Let's make a night of it."

"We don't have that much money."

"We got the travelers' checks. C'mon. Don't worry about it. We're not here to pinch pennies. Loosen up a little, willya? If we get tired; we'll go back, then. Anytime you say. Just catch a cab. But don't go quitting on me yet."

"It isn't that."

"C'mon."

The first part, after a ride in rolling chair, where she felt foolish and exposed, was a stretch of honky-tonk and carnival amusements, with twilight settling in, and the neon garish everywhere. There were movie-house marquees, a billboard lit up over the pier; a fortune teller, shooting gallery, sideshows; then a pin ball arcade—"Let's try in here," he said. They sat for pictures in a vending booth; he'd won her rhinestone sunglasses after try after try at pitch ball and tossing rings. Even though he drank more beers, and his hilarity built up with no real need for her, she found herself caught up, enjoying his strange mockery; enjoying, too, herself, at such a distance from herself, like she was looking in a fun house mirror, or trying on a silly hat.

But then it wasn't glad, or innocent; and he was trying to desert himself. His joking turned to belligerence, profaning what they were or meant; the drink took over his senses. She felt lost with him, and powerless, as if he'd changed to someone else; yet someone she must follow still, and recognize, and try to understand, and through her own hurt, fathom his. In the nightclub, he'd grown worse, and it didn't matter why, but only that he was drunk, and that he kept on drinking more ("Naw, I'm fine; willya. Don't start nagging me. Christ. Lemme alone"). He snorted at the comedian's lewd jokes ("Guy's funny, right?"); he leered at girls nearby, and at the waitress with her halter and tight slacks; and when the band began, all black, with the lead singer grinding his hips and wildly stroking his guitar, and the beat so loud it shook through her, he stared at the dancers, their backs and bottoms jammed up close, and the young girls shaking their breasts, the faces sweaty with fixed grins, and he was jiggling his own foot, swinging his shoulders, bobbing his head: "How about it? Wanna dance? . . . yahhhn," he sneered, and waved her off.

"I want to go back," she shouted. "Please! I'm not enjoying this! . . . I'm tired! I want to go back!"

"Okay here?" The waitress shouted, bending close.

"Jay'n Bee, rocks, huh; straight."

"No. Louie—We're leaving!"

"Jay'n Bee—I'm fine, okay? We'll go, a little while!"

Then band had stopped, but only to start up again.

She shook her head. "We're going now. Not later: now." She gathered up her purse and hat. "Louie. Louie! I'm talking to you. Look at me, please." She took his arm. "Right now. I mean it. I'm not going back alone, and I'm not going to sit here watching you like this."

"Got my drink comin'!"

"She'll take it back. You've had enough."

For a moment there was a threat, but empty now of will, and mixed with conscience and regard. He shrugged then, and nodded sourly, and glanced, and pulled away: "Okay, okay! It's what you want. That's how you're gonna be. There's no point stayin' here." He pushed on table, getting up. "You're gonna go, let's go!"

She got up; but then the waitress came: "Hey, wait a minute. Where you goin'? Who's payin' for this?"

"We don't want it. Thank you."

"Someone's gotta pay for this!"

He was fumbling with his money, paying the tip. "We're gonna go, we'll go." He downed half in one swallow; and stood, and blinked, then drained the rest. "Let's go . . . go on, willya. I'm okay, just go ahead."

Angrily she made her way through tables, bodies, noise, and looks; she glanced back, went up the steps, and waited for him to keep close; then they were outside, with the openness, the ocean darkness, the breeze, the simpler lights, and the normal, milling crowds. He was standing, looking around, as if still trying to decide. "This way. Come on, I'm not arguing. Come on; will you, Louie?" She led him off of the pier ("S'early yet, hey . . . over here . . ."), and off of the boardwalk, up a main street, and then to a taxi stand. She was angry having this on her, having to demand, to push, and to find the way back herself. She gave the cabbie the address from her key. And as they rode, Louie slid down in the seat, with his head laid back, his eyes closed, and smiled dimly; then he turned to her: "Hey, I'm a mess, huh? Celebratin' . . . don't mind me . . . s'nothing . . . s'nothing, okay?" She was sitting stiff, withdrawn; she felt him squeeze her hand, which she pulled free, and then her thigh; and turning, threatening now, she seized his hand and pushed it away.

Back in the room, he opened Frank's champagne, with a pop! and poured it, frothing, spilling, into water glasses, one for her ("C'mon, willya . . . shoulda got some ice!"); he opened his shirt, turned on the TV. Shoes off, then, and pants, he lay back to watch, the champagne bottle next to him by the lamp; he kept on drinking steadily, with neither of them saying more. Then he was snoring, fast asleep. She sat dressed in a chair. She watched, unseeing, the end of a show, and a movie was starting next. Then she gathered up his shoes, the pants. Turned off the TV. Took the bottle and his glass, and found the cork by the door. She lightly covered him, and turned off the lamp, his side. Barefoot she went into the bathroom, changed into her nightgown, and brushed and brushed her hair, washed, cleaned her teeth, flushed, turned off the light. She opened the covers of the other bed, eased inside, and turned off the light. He was snoring: schnaw! She watched his shape; then looked at the room, at the mirror, at the neon glow through the blinds, at the light beneath the door; heard the air-conditioning blowing, heard a door closing, heard the city still awake. Feeling the unfamiliar pillow, the starchy sheets, and her body sore where he had been, her muscles' strain, she fought off images of harm, of wrong, of ugliness and fault, to the surer, truer moments of their vows, to the love and lives that lent them strength, to the tender courage in his voice and eyes, to all they'd come to know and grasp, and all they'd pledged to mean and prove. She twisted as she thought, and lay in the dark, like a talisman, or like a fact surviving from a dream, her wedding ring.

They settled in his house. Her things were moved, and she accepted first, like a visitor or guest, not only the patterns she found fixed, but also the shape for a woman in his life. The house was unchanged, but cleaned now, his laundry cleaned and pressed, the towels and bedclothes fresh. There was the urgency of dawn, and while he showered, fixing his breakfast, coffee, eggs, and packing lunch; then still in her robe, seeing him off, and the letdown once he'd gone. Then she'd make breakfast for herself, get dressed, clean up, do household chores, and take a bus trip maybe to the mall (to spare him errands after work), and later she would cook (long-simmered stews, pastas, roasts and complex recipes) and get ready for his return. But she wanted more than simply managing, to feel the house as hers, as theirs together now. She wanted the freedom to choose and sew and put up curtains of her own, at least, and to take on the house that way, take on life; to think of things he hadn't thought of, such as new slipcovers for the chair and couch, or of buying a different chair and different lamps (instead of gaudy porcelain), or repainting the kitchen and the hall. These were all things she could do alone and without spending much money; yet she felt that he opposed any changes, and wanted things as his, as his and Paula's from before. Then he'd come in tired from work, 6:30 or 7:00, take his beer, and during dinner tell her about his day, and after dinner, while she did the dishes, disappear to watch TV or sit out smoking on the back step. Their routine was close and fond, kept them at a certain distance. Weekends, he'd help with the house and fixing things; he'd take her for a big shopping, or he'd work on the car, or sleep, or drink his beer and watch TV; and even their visits to Josie now seemed routine, as if just going were enough. When she tried to offer an opening, remarking that Josie really liked today, or repeating some special things Josie had said or done, or how they really seemed like family now; she only met with silence, or with his, "Yeah" (dully), or "Look, I don't know, I just can't talk about it now," and his tone would cut her off.

But then her feelings left her no choice. Love was her right. She started with the yard, which he'd let go. She worked whole days in the heat and sun, took out the mower from the garage, mowed in front and sides and part of the back, pulled up weeds; then she turned to the flower beds along the back wall, all weeds and hardened dirt, with some green plants, chrysanthemums she guessed, and daisies, petunias; and here and there were marigolds, a rose bush blooming pink, and near the rainspout two tomato plants, one sickly, with little tomatoes starting, the other withered on its stake. She knew then, like something found, that she wanted a garden, and always had; she wanted the weeds cleared out and the living plants to thrive; she wanted the beds dug up and mulched, and filled with new plants and seeds. She'd need to learn what kinds of plants, and how to plant and plan, what gardening supplies to buy (she would ask at the neighbor's down the street, where their whole front yard was planted with flow- ers, beautiful).

Then he came home. "Hey, what you been doin'? Who cut the grass? You're kidding. Hey, I would've done that. I mean, that's a big job. You're out there with the mower; what, out of the garage?" She told him it had needed doing; she didn't mind; she'd had the time and liked working outside; she had never had a yard before, and she wanted it nice. She wanted to dig up the garden, and replant; to cut back the bushes and hedge and rake out the back corner. If they repainted the picnic table and cleaned up the grill, they could sit out there and eat.

He shook his head; okay, but let him do the heavy work, he'd get to it. On the weekends from then on, listlessly at first, he'd help; but as they worked together, her in the garden, him at clipping the hedge or pruning, or cleaning out the garage, or scraping and retouching the siding, he seemed to feel the purpose as his own, and for their life.

Some days, working with him, or working alone, as she was hanging the wash, or gardening, or up on the ladder cleaning windows, she felt proudly assured and vivid in her place.

There was one lady, Mrs. Grillo (Belinda), who stopped to watch from the walk one day, smiling and obvious, as she was watering out front. They began to talk . . . yeah, she'd known the other . . . Paula . . . used to say hello . . . so you're the new Missus, yeah. (Mrs. Grillo's English was poor, so she had to guess at her meanings or pretend to understand; they were both frustrated when she failed, but there was always good will).

Mrs. Grillo asked about Josie: the little girl, how was she? She used to see her out sometimes.

She told her about school and how he'd had to put her there towards the end (Mrs. Grillo nodded and frowned—yeah, yeah, that's a terrible thing, yeah); and after Paula died, how they would visit Josie, and she had gotten to love her, and they were still hoping to take her back.

They talked about gardening. Mrs. Grillo would bring cuttings, nice, real nice, she'd see. You plant them right, just so, you get a whole big vine; she'd show her how. She just lived four doors down. Their ages and backgrounds were too unlike for Mrs. Grillo to be a friend; but as a neighbor, who recognized her now as a neighbor, she made her feel that she belonged.

Later, inside, when he balked—Hey, what you want curtains for? What's wrong with ones we got? or: Why paint? Hell, it's good, what's wrong with it? What's wrong with beige? Whatta you want to change everything for?—she stood up firmly: Because it's not the same. I have my own ideas, and I'm here every day alone, and just I want to make things for myself, feel it's my doing, and this is our life, not like you had with her. That was another marriage. This is ours. I'm not here to just fill in. I love you my own way, and I'm not grudging you her memory. But you grudge me; that's how it feels. We have to talk and plan and think about the future now. (She imagined Paula more and more, like a dream, from pictures on his dresser, and in the album from the drawer; imagined her approving, tendering, the way she might if they'd met, and not with jealously, but with sorrow, pride, telling her: here, take care; I trust in you. You're what I would have wanted him to do. You have to stand up more. You have to lead him for his good. He isn't strong.) And when she went ahead and acted on her own in the small things first—the curtains, rearranging furniture, setting up her sewing machine in Josie's room, and later painting the kitchen a fresh, soft yellow she picked out herself, he still would fight, but she stood up to that, and then he'd quit ("Go on, do it, anything you want; I don't care. Have it your own way") and later, he would come to see, and like the difference, and even take a certain pride in it ("No, you know, it's nice like this. It's okay. You got a real nice touch. It's brighter, clean; it's got a whole new feel").

She felt he grew to trust her more, reacting less each time as if her love were a threat. But still, concerning Josie, he seemed lost, and at the same time stubbornly withdrawn, as if the need and hurt were his alone. But she loved Josie too. And the more they seemed together otherwise, the more this last refusal weighed, and at the heart of everything. Where he faltered, she must press: "I want her here. I want her here with us, Louie; we have to talk. We can't just leave her there, like somehow later we can settle this. There is no later anymore. We've got a home to offer her, now what else is there? What else are we waiting for?"

"Not that. More to it than that."

"Well, what then? We have to discuss this, at least. You can't just shut me out. This means too much."

"It's the money, okay?"

"What money?"

"Look, with Leinhardt's pulling out and Manville's closing, I don't even know if I got a job. I'm still in debt. I don't know where I'll find new work. Or if I got a pension. Or even we can keep this house, okay? There's no security. It takes some steady money coming in. You couldn't work, you're here with her."

"You did all right before."

"It's not before; it's now, and two, three months from now, and years, okay? I'm not what I used to be. I'm fifty-seven. I'm tired. I can't see we got any kinda income like that, or anything to count on. We take her out of there, it's gotta be for good. And then the boys. They don't want this over them. And something happens, then they're the ones to step in. You see what I'm saying?"

"Don't you want her?"

"Christ, I want her, but there's no way. Even if I get a job, or find some program that can help; or say we sell the house. It's still no good. I got eight, ten years where I can work, and whatta we do then? You got to think like that. Look at what's against you, not just what you want. And you, I don't want this coming down on you. It's not just loving her; it's day by day, the whole responsibility, with no room for yourself. I don't know, it's better for her like it is; better for us. We're just kidding ourselves to think any different."

Her eyes filled, and she blinked, wiping tears with her fingers; swallowed. "I can't believe you think like that. She belongs here. We're her family. And yes, there's risks and things we can't know answers to, but we'll manage; we'll have to. You've seen her future there; you said so yourself. We love her; we can see her through her teen and into adult years, and see she has the skills where she can look after herself, and maybe work. Maybe that's not possible, but you don't know that, or how much can be. All you know is there's nothing else otherwise. Not even the chance. Listen, I'm young; I'm strong; I know I can be a good mother to her. And just I want this, Louie. I want it with all my heart."

He looked at her, too long, as if he were measuring her love and still remained torn, helpless to decide.

"Say something. Say yes. You want it too. We can call Miss Stromley and ask her where we start."

Still he looked; and then went dull.

"Okay," he said.

She breathed and swallowed.

"You mean it? We can?"

He nodded. She wanted to embrace, to lose herself in him; but he sat slumped and too upset. His only smile was strained.

The money problem, meanwhile, solved itself. Mary called, first to tell her that Howard's father had died; and then again, to tell her that they'd sold the butcher business, and that they had a buyer for the house; her share would be $18,000; they were moving in three weeks.

They had found a laundromat for sale, out in Bryn Mawr, out Lancaster Pike; and farther out, in Devon, they'd found a three-bedroom ranch house; it had a quarter-acre yard and trees. She and Louie should come over, maybe this weekend, so they could talk. The laundromat was a going business; good location; and something that Howard really felt he could make go. Maybe she, Anna Maye, should think of coming in. They still needed capital, for new improvements and machines (a dry-cleaning machine, especially), and they would rather keep it in the family than look for loans. Maybe she and Louie could drive out for a look. Also, Mary was breaking up the house and told her she should come, rent a trailer maybe, and look through the basement, and through the other things they had to leave; she could take back anything she wanted; the rest they'd sell or call Good Will, or just throw out.

Everything was ready. He should have picked Josie up at two, and they'd be back by four. She'd wanted him to go alone, to sign the papers, settle the arrangements, while she had this time in private too, with all her thoughts on welcoming, to clean the house, to put on a special dress, cook the roast, bake a cake.

She'd put away her sewing table. She'd bought new sheets for Josie's bed, new curtains for her window, a yellow spread, sewn bright new pillow covers, washed and ironed old clothes from the closet and hung them on hangers or folded them in drawers, along with the new clothes they had bought the week before; she'd put stuffed bears on the bed, and in the new shelves he'd helped to build, she set out the blocks, games, and books, the plastic doll house that Susan and Ruthie had outgrown. She'd painted the dresser white. Later she and Josie would choose pictures for the walls, and maybe a bulletin board (for Josie's drawings and cut-outs).

What would she and Josie be like alone?

She had tried to imagine, with nothing more to go by than their visits, things Louie had told her, and the things Miss Stromley had instructed her about. There was a fixed routine, all written down. Up at seven, shower, brush her teeth, make the bed, then breakfast time (Louie would be gone for work), then time for medicines, then classroom drill in speech, then structured play or exercise ("She needs as much physical exercise as you can give her, out for walks, or running games outside, or visits to a playground," Miss Stromley had said), then help to clean the house ("Give her specific tasks"), help make lunch, eat, take an hour's nap, time for medicines again, then free play or watch TV or a trip outside to shop; later dinner, Louie's coming home, bed by eight, the bedtime regimen.

Later there would be school, the same school as before. A bus would pick Josie up at eight and bring her back at noon. She must take her in the Wednesday after next for tests, and to meet her new teachers. If there was a parents' group, she wanted to belong, share concerns, and learn from their experiences; maybe she would make new friends, and friends for Josie too.

She knew there would be scars, Josie testing her, the acting out, self-abuse, everything Miss Stromley had warned about; and that she would have "a lot to make up for." She knew not to be put off or to look for too much all at once, but just to be firm, patient, and ready to confront problem feelings and behavior. She also knew that Louie would criticize her when she was lax, and blame her when she was stern, and if she had to punish Josie, that he would hurry to protect her. Yet she must stand up for her right. She knew she'd make mistakes, and that she had a great deal to learn; but she also knew that she had to trust herself and simply look from day to day.

When Louie saw how good, how workable and whole they were together, then he would open out and join in the happiness, and mean his consent.

He'd already found a new job with less trouble than he'd expected. He worked at Minter's across town now, under Mike Gardella, whom he'd known from his South Philadelphia days. He complained about the low pay, the stupid work (when he could do Gardella's job), the kids he had to work with (screw-offs, no accounts, he said, with Mike expecting him to give them pointers and to make up for their mistakes). He complained about Mike himself, who asked him for ideas and then took credit for himself and didn't want to get upstaged. But at least the work was in chocolate; and he was better off, and said as much, than other Manville heads when the factory closed—the Leinhardt's crew had all gone back to their main plant; Mary Lloyd stopped working; Ralph Sheets drove for a paper company; and Dave Case, the last he had heard, had only found some part-time jobs and was talking about moving south.

He'd rolled his Manville pension funds into the Minter's plan. Together with her money, his income now, and her ability to work again when he retired (she would still be in her forties), the house was safe. The debts were cleared up. They could manage.

Also, besides the money, he seemed grateful and relieved to keep in contact with the men and the world. The closing of Manville's had shaken him more than she had guessed; and now he was back working he seemed more settled, bluff, and like himself.

(But still, as she wandered through the house, she felt his panic about Josie; she worried, too, about the comments of his sons; and still felt something dangerous and raw in him, which maybe love could never satisfy or heal.)

She took out the cake and let it cool. Then readied the roast with seasonings (bay leaf, salt, pepper, onions sliced, oregano); peeled and washed potatoes, set them in; and slid in the pan and reset the dial. Next, for the cake, made icing: beat sugar, water and butter, and a touch of vanilla, until it thickened, tasted it, and then sat down to spread it on the bottom layer, join the layers, spread more the sides and top, and finish off with swirls (just so, professional). Pleased with herself, she washed up, humming along with the radio; she cleaned the counters, put on the table cloth. She gazed outside and wanted flowers suddenly, so she found her scissors and went out to the brightness and warmth of the day, and overhead, to the faint, tearing sound of jets, which, squinting and shading her eyes, she sought for in the clear sky, but never saw. She turned to the flower beds along the back wall, in shadow now, and cut nasturtiums for yellow, phlox for blue, daisies for white, and baby's breath, and set them aside on the grass. She weeded for a while (careful of her shoes and dress), glancing now and then at the street. Later, she got up stiffly and went in, and fixed the flowers in a vase, drank iced tea; then she went out again and sat at the picnic table in the shade, deciding to wait here as well as anywhere, and to enjoy the breeze and fragrant air, the birds, the garden's colors and luxuriance, to listen all around to the world's business (horn's bleat and counter horn, passing cars, and even next door's basketball). She looked at the house, admiring where they'd painted and repaired, and at the well-kept yard. She waited, feeling as glad and as content, as if already they'd arrived, and they were all together here.

Yet still her whole being was tense, so when they did appear, and the car turned in, as she had known it would, their arrival shocked her. All in a flutter, she jumped up, waved, and started toward them; then slowed down, shy, beaming, and on the verge of tears.

But as she neared, instead of a wave or smile or greetings in return, she saw something was wrong. She saw before she heard through the car windows that Louie was pleading, arguing or both. She saw his haggard glance her way. Josie was wailing, clenched. She hurried to help, around the hood, and to Josie's door, and opened it. "Now, come on, cut that out," he was saying. "Here, honey, here. We're home. Here's Anna Maye."

"Josie, here," she said. "It's me."

Josie stared at her like she never knew her, twisting back, rocking, tossing her head, and making her throaty moan. Edging in beside her, she slid her arm around thin shoulders, found her hand, and drew her close, feeling her struggling within her own strength, and holding her firmly to her breast and to her own beating heart. Meanwhile he sat apart, one hand still on the steering wheel, his eyes wide with distress and hurt.

"Christ, I don't know. We just turned in—she's tired. It's been too big a day."

The shortest way, according to the map, was to get off at the Roosevelt Boulevard bridge, to follow through Germantown to Route 13 and 71, then over the Tacony Palmyra right on through Mapleshade to

Moorestown; or to get off at Vine and go over the Ben Franklin, through Camden, where 30 changed to 38 and led straight in. But Howard refused to drive through city streets; he wanted fast roads all the way, which meant an extra fifteen miles, and probably would take longer. They stayed on the expressway, driving way around the city south—windows down, girls shrill in back, her, map in her lap, knees pulled up, crowded between Howard and Davy's car seat (Davy asleep, but splotched and suffering from the heat)—drove on past dreary factory-scapes, billboards, a ghetto development with the upper stories flush against the roadway, laundry hanging out, refineries, to the bluish arch of the bridge ahead; then over a rise, to cars backed up before the lanes that fed into the tollbooths.

"Good Christ."

"We're okay," Howard said. He slowed, and pulled to a stop, and a creep, and a stop, behind the same new Pontiac, with a white-haired couple inside, air-conditioning, and a schnauzer dog that jumped around in back. They waited for ten minutes, the motor idling, the heat stifling, the girls complaining. She got out the thermos jug with lemonade and told the girls to share. She offered him, but he refused.

"That's all," she warned them, putting the jug away. Davy was stirring. "Shhh!"

Only four cars were left, then one; he tossed in coins, and they were through—"Okay!"—gaining speed, overtaking and then passing the Pontiac, and speeding high on the six-lane span. He took the right lane, by the edge. "Hey, lookit," he said. "See the boats? See, in the river?" Below there were ocean-going freighters, docked with cranes, and out beyond them, a view of the Jersey flats and dirty haze.

"Where?" Ruthie cried. "Let me see! I can't see!"

"Be quiet! Sit down!"

Davy was already struggling, his face screwed up, the first gasps, then his full cry.

"Will you just sit still! Both of you!" She slapped at them. She found Davy's juice, which he took greedily, his hands on the bottle, blinking up. "That's it, that's it. . . ." Coming down, they approached the junction with the New Jersey expressways.

"Which is it? C'mon, willya? They're both 76!"

But the sign had passed overhead before she could read it, and traffic had forced him to go right.

"I'm sorry. I've got my hands full!" she said.

"Just tell me, willya? You're supposed to tell me this stuff! This right or not?"

She studied the map. "It's 76 and 42, south; look, there's a sign. It's what you want. But watch out for a branch; it's 45; it'll go off right. And you keep to the left; get left. It's coming right up. You better get over."

"Is this New Jersey now? Ruthie asked. "Is this New Jersey, Mommy?"

"I told her, Mommy!—Look at the license plate!"

"Get down!—Down!"

He'd gotten left; and where the road divided, he kept on left, up hill; then they turned off at the next exit, for 295; followed slow around, and sped into the merge. This would take them east and north, all the way; now they could relax. No trucks, no tolls. Moorestown came after Cherry Hill. Davy had dropped off again.

"It's such a goddamned trip," she said.

"It's not so bad. We'll be there."

"Not for you."

"C'mon," he said. "You wanta see her too."

They had kept putting off this visit—their first since before they'd moved, when Anna Maye and Louie had come up and looked through the cellar. Now here it was after Labor Day. Anna's life had grown farther than ever from her sympathy and grasp, but this time Anna had called pointedly to ask. Josie's birthday was coming up. They'd have a cook out and a party; it would mean so much for Josie to meet her cousins; she'd told her all about them.

Just Anna's asking had disarmed her: open, plaintive, and direct, where all this time she'd never asked. So she'd said, sure, and meant it, somehow proudly, apart from any differences. No trouble, no. They hadn't seen her in so long.

But afterwards she felt put out and somehow caught in her promise. When she told Howard ("so I said yes"), he'd seemed surprised, then pleased, as if congratulating her: "Good. No, fine; that's something we should." She'd made a sour face. "C'mon, what? Don't you want to go?"

"Not particularly."

"Why not?"

"Because it's a pain. You're supposed to work Saturday. The girls are starting school. It's not that easy for us. It's a long drive down there with Davy. And once we get there, what? You don't talk to Louie. It's awkward enough, but now this child. Why's she have to drag us into it?"

He shrugged. "C'mon. She wouldn't ask us down there, if it weren't okay. You know, it's working out; we oughta be glad for them. It's sort of paying our respects. It's not asking for our pity or anything."

"Oh, I don't know. I don't. I mean, I told her yes. I know all the reasons. But it's always her big sacrifice, and now it's this retarded girl. If we say no, then we're just selfish, all that. I'm sick of it. We sacrifice too; we have healthy, normal children; we have our own hopes. I don't see why we get second place; I mean, the minute she calls."

"Aw, cut it out, willya? Don't start up."

"She doesn't respect me."

"Sure, she respects you. What do you think asking us down there means? It's a pretty touchy thing for him too, you know, for both of them; ever think of that? They're trusting us. C'mon now. Give it a chance."

She snorted, looked away.

"Jesus, you two. Why can't you appreciate each other a little?"

He had carefully prepared the girls.

"She's your cousin now, that's right."

"Is she funny looking?"

"I don't think so, not really. She may look a little different; she's probably smaller than other girls her age, but not a whole lot."

"Oh, Howard—We don't know, honey," she'd said. "We've never really met her. She's your Uncle Louie's little girl. She wasn't at the wedding."

"Retarded, see, it's just a special way you're born. You don't grow as fast as other boys and girls. You have trouble learning things. And even things like you and Ruthie learned when you were little, like talking right, or reading books, or playing different games. She can't do some things, you can. But that's not her fault."

"Like being crippled?"

"Sort of. Good, Ruthie. Not really crippled; but just she's not as fortunate as you. So you should never make fun of her, for how she looks, or talks, or things she'd can't do as good as you can. Okay? She's very nice. She likes lots of the same things you do. And this'll be her birthday, Saturday. She needs you to be patient with her, and try to understand, even though she's much older than you are."

"How old?" asked Susan.

"She'll be fourteen, I think—Right? And see, her real Mommy died. Now Aunt Anna is her Mommy, and she loves her very much, and hopes you'll love her too."

"You're confusing them."

"What grade's she in?"

"Don't know if they have grades where she goes—Do they? See, it's a special school, and just for children like Josie. In a regular school, they couldn't help her as much."

"Don't worry, Susan," she said. "Maybe you'll have to get used to her a little. But you won't have any trouble."

"Do we have to get her presents?"

"Hey, yeah'll. It's her birthday, right?"

"What kind of presents?"

"Well, things you'd like. Or you could make her something."

Later she had taken them to shop; and they had asked her, this? or this, Mommy? She didn't know. She told them, yes, the paint set; yes, the ball and jacks. Clothes were safest, but she didn't know her size. She looked at kitchen sets, the toy sewing machine, embroidery kits, and then, more seriously, at the dolls, the kind that you could dress, undress, wash and set their hair; at the smaller ones, like Ruthie's, and then at the largest and most costly one, much nicer than she'd ever bought for them, with a wardrobe all of its own, and a case that served for a trunk. "It's just a very, very special present," she'd told them. "This is from all of us to Josie, okay?"

Now in the lull of driving, she was thinking of their own lives (she glanced back at the girls): that Davy would be easier with both the girls in school; that their house was like a first break, first hold; and that the laundromat was part of it, a partnership and effort that she and Howard shared. She kept the books. Later, she would take a course in accounting. She had designed the remodeling, persuaded Howard to get the dry-cleaning machines, and then, through Bob, she had helped to persuade the bank. She felt real satisfaction to walk in and know that the laundromat was hers, and that what they made of it was up to her nerve, business sense, and skill. Having property and a business made them somebodies. They were in a new development, with families their own age and starting new; these couples weren't stay-at-homes, not second or third generation squatters, old people, or a fixed neighborhood. They were people with ambition, brains, and on their way. The girls had playmates their own ages, a yard to play, the neighbor's yard. They'd go off; and the other mothers would watch them. The husbands were salesmen and executives, white collar; some, small business people like themselves. One had a pizza shop; another a bar, and he practiced golf outside on his lawn. Another owned a garage, and he had been a race car driver; he worked on a low-slung sports car, muscled, with his shirt off, in his backyard. With the older families, the wives worked too, good jobs, helping in a dress shop, or secretarial, or a nurse. And then all around them as the Main Line, with native well-to-do's and the rich. New cars; smart clothes; well-cared-for faces and bodies.

There was that sense of casualness and wealth in everything, in the schools, in the stores, in the park-like beauty of lush greenery, in stately old Victorian houses, in the sudden woods, with twisting roads. They'd found some friends: the Rileys, two doors down, with a baby and a pre-schooler (the mother had been an art teacher, and the father worked for the phone company); they had had some dinners back and forth, with the kids. The Rileys' friends were the Langs, who took them all as guests to a private swimming club; then there were Bob and Jean, of course. She enjoyed having a social life and meant to have an even busier one once Davy was old enough for a sitter. She enjoyed matching lives with equals; enjoyed her own attractiveness, even after Davy, in a swimsuit or a party dress; enjoyed meeting new men. She saw their future here, in business, in property, in educated friends; in the girls growing up and dating boys from families of wealth; in their chance for college, maybe. She felt satisfied in what she'd brought them to, and that the doing had been hers.

They exited 295, slowed, and followed a cluttered route 38 west, to a right on Mt. Laurel, and into Moorestown center (store-fronts, traffic lights and local traffic). She felt edgy, curious, and wished it would be farther, longer still, while at the same time she worried whether they were late. Davy was awake and playing with her fingers; she was sick of their fussing, of all of them being cramped in the car. "Is it soon?" "Is it here, Mommy?" "I'm hot!" "I wanta pee!"

"We're almost there; just hold it okay! Just a little farther."

Anna Maye had said, take 547 east one mile from the center; Plum Street was a right hand turn off of 547; they'd see a water tower, then a Mormon temple, and they should turn just after that. She wondered what the house would be like, picturing something ill-kept, embarrassing, and small, like these along here, one after another. They saw the water tower, passed the temple, but saw no street marked Plum. Finally they turned around and stopped in a gas station to ask. Third left.

This was nicer than she'd thought. Older houses, trees, real yard, one with a swimming pool. Her heart was beating fast; she peered. They drove some blocks in, wound around, found Lenape, another right. "I do," she thought; "I wish her all the best."

For a moment she thought that was it, the three story on the next corner; and her heart caught, envious. Except that wasn't it; no, of course not. They prowled ahead. "It's somewhere around here."

"What number?"

"It's on Aubrey. It's 58 or something."

People looked back at them. A girl on a bike. There were shrines to the virgin in front yards. A man mowed the grass; an old man was gardening. Arbors, hedges, flowers. A woman hanging wash. A man on a scaffold, painting his house.

Then Aubrey, yes; there; that must be it. Neat, plain, close to the street, in the shade. She glimpsed a larger yard in back, a separate garage, Louie's car. Howard pulled over, and rolled on farther, towards the back.

"There! There they are! I see them!" Susan shouted. "There's Aunt Anna!"

There they were. All in one glance she saw the house, the yard and garden, the swing set, the plastic pool; saw waving beside a bar-becue and starting towards them: Anna Maye, looking slimmer in a blue dress and eager in her welcoming. Saw stumbling after her, the girl, with a stocky body, pageboy hair, her eyes pulled down and her bloated face, and her even wider grin. Saw Louie, hatless, at the grill; he was watching, wry, and taking one last swig of beer.

"There they are!" Susan shrilled.

She shook her head, and shook her head. Then she snorted, smiling. "I see," she said softly.